A House Divided
Terran Armor Corps Book 4

Richard Fox

Copyright © 2018 Author Name

All rights reserved.

ISBN: 1720536058
ISBN-13: 978-1720536055

CHAPTER 1

Corporal Jerry Marris struggled down a sand dune, one hand gripping his gauss rifle, the other gripping PFC Valencia by the carry handle across the back of her shoulders. He dragged his squad mate down the slope, his eyes locked over his shoulder as he struggled to keep her from sliding away, a difficult task even in Ranger power armor and the too-high gravity of Thesius II. Valencia left a trail of congealing blood in the sand.

Distant explosions sounded after them and gauss bullets and laser bolts snapped over sand dunes around them. Jerry checked the compass heading on the inside of his skull-shaped visor. He had a good idea which direction would get him back to Terran lines, and which way led to the Kesaht, but the mounds of sand around them had a bad habit of disorienting him.

"Talk to me, Val," Jerry said.

"I'm cold," she said, pain lacing her words.

"Rook rook!" echoed over the battlefield. Jerry looked to the top of the surrounding dunes but didn't see any of the alien Rakka.

"Your armor's not functioning right." Jerry hauled her up a dune slope, positioning her so her head was angled higher than her heart. Her left foot was a mangle of broken armor and bloody flesh. A bullet strike to her sternum had cracked the armor plate but hadn't penetrated.

"Get this off…need to breathe." Valencia pawed at her skull visor, but Jerry pushed her hands away and took a spool off her belt.

"Air's bad," Jerry said. "Just hold tight while I get a tourniquet on you."

"You said my leg was fine." She struggled to sit up, but her elbows sank in the sand.

"It will be." He drew a length of wire from the spool and fed it into an eyehole just below her left knee. As blood oozed from the chewed-up remnants of her foot, Jerry ignored the white bone fragments mingled with the beige armor. Pulling the tip of the wire through the exit hole below her knee, he wrapped the wire over itself, then put his thumb against a button on the spool.

"Ready in three…" He pressed the button and the wire tightened against itself, the auto-tourniquet squeezing against her leg and strangling her femoral artery.

Valencia gasped in pain and her left leg reared up. Jerry caught her just below the knee and stopped her from bashing the abused limb into the ground.

"Son of a bitch!" she cried.

"Hurts me too," Jerry said.

"Rakka." Valencia slapped a palm against the sand.

"Gonna get you out of here," Jerry said.

"Rook rook!" sounded again and ice ran down Jerry's spine. He turned around and found the enemy charging over dunes and right for them, their red eyes bright with murder, their hodgepodge armor rattling against their bodies as sunlight glinted off their crude blades and serrated bayonets at the ends of their laser rifles. He snapped up his weapon and opened fire.

Gauss bullets snapped out and smashed into the Rakka, the rounds hitting with enough force to punch through a Rakka and kill the alien behind it. But the bloodshed only seemed to make them charge faster.

Jerry put himself between Valencia and the enemy.

"Saint Kallen," he prayed as he dropped an empty magazine and slapped in a fresh one, "witness this." He shot a Rakka with a severed human hand still in Ranger armor dangling from a necklace. The screaming aliens closed in as he unloaded another magazine.

As Jerry swung his rifle butt into a Rakka's hairy face,

crushing it with the blow, an axe chopped into his shoulder. Although it deflected off his pauldron, the blow still stung and he lost his grip on his rifle.

A Rakka stabbed a bayonet at Valencia, but Jerry flung himself toward her and grabbed the blade. As he held it firm, the edge cutting into the thin padding over his palms, he locked eyes with the Rakka and saw his skull-shaped visor reflected in the alien's eyes.

The Rakka grunted at him like an angry ape, then backed off, leaving the weapon in Jerry's grasp. The rest of the mob pulled away from the two Rangers.

"The Saint heard you," Valencia slurred.

A shadow passed over Jerry and the whirl of a rotary cannon rose in the air.

A black suit of armor towered over Jerry, a Templar cross emblazoned over the chest and shoulder. The armor held a Mauser rifle in both hands, the wide-bore weapon almost as large as Jerry. The rotary cannon, spinning so fast the barrels were a blur, spat fire and tore through the Rakka.

The aliens broke and fled, some managing to scramble over the dunes before the rotary cannon swept through their ranks, killing dozens within seconds.

As the armor stepped off the dune, its massive foot crushing a dead alien, the rotary cannon snapped back, and an empty ammo can spat off its back and fell smoking into the sand next to Valencia.

The armor's helm turned to the Rangers.

"Get her out of here," Roland said, his voice booming through speakers.

"I will never leave a Ranger…" Jerry said, shaking blood from his hand and grabbing Valencia by the carry handle with the other, "to fall into—"

"I know your creed," Roland said. "Head east."

The breech on his Mauser snapped open and Roland loaded a magazine the size of Jerry's helmet. He strode west, crushing dead aliens with each step.

"No!" Jerry yelled, reaching for the armor. "There's too many! A full-scale counterattack. They tore up our platoon. Sanheel and—"

"I am armor." Roland beat a fist against his chest and bounded over a dune in two steps.

"I lost too much blood," Valencia said. "Swear that was the Black Knight."

"You ain't dreaming." Jerry hauled Valencia around the slope.

****

Roland charged up a three-story-tall dune where bodies of Rangers and Rakka lay partially buried in the slope.

The noise of his feet slamming into the sand caught the attention of a Rakka on the other side and the alien stuck its head over the slope just as Roland's helm crested. The armor swatted the foot soldier, launching it into the air, an arc of blood trailing it.

Beyond the dune was a wide bowl in the desert, inside which Rakka milled around their Sanheel officers. The tall centaur-like leaders of the Kesaht assault clustered around a field captain with wide silver thread woven through his hair to mark his rank.

Roland kicked through the top of the dune and opened fire with his Mauser. The massive rifle boomed and kicked back with recoil strong enough to kill an unarmored soldier if they'd been foolish—or strong—enough to wield it. The fist-sized shell bounced off the energy shield protecting a Sanheel lieutenant and tore through a pair of Rakka nearby.

The Sanheel captain pointed at Roland, roared a challenge, and jabbed the butt end of a haft against the ground. A wide spear tip snapped out of the haft and the captain charged toward Roland, the weapon aimed at the armor soldier and glinting in the sunlight.

The rest of the centaurs brandished their own spears and galloped after the captain, forming a wedge of alien bulk. Rakka scrambled to get out of the way, but a few were too slow and were trampled into paste.

Roland came down the slope, still firing his Mauser, but each shot was just as ineffective as the first. The Sanheel captain charged faster, spittle flying off its tusks.

Roland flung the rifle behind him, embedding the barrel in the sand. He pulled a sword hilt off the side of his leg and flicked a button on the Templar cross worked into the hand guard. A seven-foot blade snapped out in segments, and an omnium lattice spread within the weapon, locking it rigid.

The armor took up a fighting stance and held the sword level with his helm, resting it on his left arm, the tip pointed at the oncoming Sanheel. The double-barrel gauss cannons on his right forearm powered up.

"Come on." Roland twisted his front foot in the sand and felt the vibration of the charging Sanheel through his womb.

An energy field formed around the captain's spear tip and the alien pulled his elbow up to deliver a strike aimed right for Roland's chest.

Roland fired a single round from his forearm cannon and struck the Sanheel's spear on the haft. The bullet slapped the weapon to one side and left the captain's guard wide open. Roland lunged forward like a fencer and stabbed his sword through the captain's shield and into his sternum. Momentum carried the alien forward, impaling it up to the hilt and stopping like it hit a brick wall.

Roland's optics locked with the stunned captain's face, then he wrenched the blade to one side and dragged the dying Sanheel into the way of a lieutenant's spear thrust. The spear pierced the captain's back and the lieutenant's jaw went slack in shock. Roland ripped his blade free in a geyser of blood and spun it over his head, striking through the lieutenant's neck and sending the head flying.

A Sanheel charged past Roland and managed a glancing blow against Roland's side. Sparks flew from the impact and left a silver gash across the matte-black paint of his suit. The rest of the aliens overshot Roland and wheeled around, leaving their backs to the dunes from where Roland had emerged.

The alien that managed a hit grabbed his spear at the end and swung the tip in a wide arc aimed at Roland's neck servos. Roland blocked the strike with the flat of his blade and hooked the spear head with his edge. He yanked back, pulling the Sanheel forward. Roland lowered his shoulder and lunged forward, catching the alien in the chest, crushing its ribcage and snapping the bones.

Another Sanheel stabbed at Roland's arm and got the spear wedged in his elbow servos. Roland kicked the attacker's foreleg and shattered it at the knee. The Sanheel pitched forward, crying out in pain. Roland kicked it in the flank just as it hit the ground and sent it barreling into two more Sanheel, knocking them all down in a tangle of limbs and spears.

A Mauser boomed and a Sanheel's shield flared just as its head exploded. Two more Mausers opened fire, felling the alien officers with each shot. Roland slashed across an alien's chest, leaving a deep gash that severed a rank sash and sent a gout of blood down the alien's front.

The Sanheel whirled around, confused by Roland's continued assault and being fired upon by weapons that defeated their shields.

As an alien reared up and beat at Roland's shoulders with its front hooves, Roland ducked to one knee and cut across the Sanheel's underbelly. Its legs gave out and Roland stomped a boot against its skull, splattering its head across the bare, rocky ground. Mausers fired another volley and he spun around. All the Sanheel lay dead and dying.

Three suits of armor stood atop a dune, smoke rising from the red-hot barrels of their rifles.

Roland turned to face the thousands of Rakka that had just witnessed the fight and raised his bloody sword overhead.

"I'll have you next!" Roland pointed the sword at a wide-eyed foot soldier and Sanheel blood snapped across the plain.

The Rakka hooted in fear, turned, and ran.

Roland charged forward, bellowing a war cry at the highest volume his speakers could manage. He slowed as the Rakka kept running, frantically climbing the dunes at the far end of the basin and vanishing into the deep desert.

He slowed to a stop and slapped the flat of his blade against his leg, knocking blood free.

"Your plan was stupid," Cha'ril said from behind him.

"If it's stupid but it works, it isn't stupid." He turned around and Aignar tossed the Mauser from the sand dune to him. Roland caught it by the grip and reset the power output on the rifle to HIGH.

"How did you know they'd charge instead of shooting you?" Aignar asked.

Roland touched the Templar cross on his chest and slapped a hand against his black armor.

"They know me," Roland said. "Sanheel are ambitious, prideful. If I plug them a few times with my underpowered rifle, it looks like I'm helpless. If they kill the Black Knight in hand-to-hand combat, they're sure to be promoted. Once they were committed to a close-in fight, it was like shooting fish in a barrel for you three, right?"

"Target acquisition was simplified, yes," said Cha'ril, the lance's Dotari member.

"We should finish them." Aignar gestured toward the

last of the Rakka as they disappeared over the dunes. The basin was littered with Kesaht vehicles and supplies.

"No need," Lieutenant Gideon said. "Flyboys finally decided to send close air support to this sector now that the enemy's broken contact. Kesaht know we won't bomb them when they're right on top of us."

"A little space is all we needed." Roland looked up as a flight of six Condor bombers streaked overhead. Canisters loosed from the bombers and came apart over the retreating Kesaht. Hundreds of submunitions rained down on the aliens, exploding into metal flechettes with a ripple of pops.

"Not bad, Roland," Aignar said. "Right, sir?" he asked Gideon.

Gideon didn't even look at Roland as he watched another flight of bombers cross over the first attack run.

"Prep for transport," Gideon said. "We're needed in another sector." He locked his Mauser over his back, across the spine from his rail cannon vanes, and pointed to the west where a Dragonfly aircraft flew over the dune wall. The ship was little more than a cockpit attached to massive engines at the fore of the craft and a long keel ending in an aft made up of another engine.

The Dragonfly hovered over the four armor and robotic arms came out of the centerline and gripped each soldier just under the shoulders. The transport hefted them into the air and flew off, engines straining.

Servo arms in the Dragonfly went to work as they cut over the desert. Roland's ammo was reloaded, batteries swapped, and the gash on his side repaired. The amniosis inside his womb flushed cool as the oxygen-rich fluid was recycled.

"He's still mad at you," Aignar said on a channel open to him, Roland, and Cha'ril.

Roland checked the data fed into his vision cortex by the plugs in the base of his skull connecting him to his armor. Gideon was in a private channel with a higher command element, one that didn't show on Gideon's status.

"I can't imagine why," Roland said.

"I'm sure it has something to do with you fighting alongside the Ibarras on Balmaseda," Cha'ril said. "You were with Gideon's old lance mates, the ones that defected to the Ibarras and left him behind."

"Yes, I'm sure that's it," Roland dead panned.

"Then why did you—"

"Irony, Cha'ril. Is there a Dotari word for *facetious*?" Roland asked.

"Checking," she said. "No. We would never joke about something like this."

"What's a little light treason between friends?" Aignar asked.

"I fought on Balmaseda against the Kesaht," Roland said. "It wasn't against Earth and I did it to save lives."

"We get that," Aignar said. "Don't we, Cha'ril?"

"The reasoning is sound," she said. "Though I think Lieutenant Gideon will never see it that way. Humans can be irrational."

"Well, it's not like Roland was slaved to pheromones and beating people nearly to death with sticks," Aignar said. "Or spitting phlegm all over people. Did I tell you about that, Roland?"

"You have shared that story eight times," Cha'ril said.

"I leave you two alone for a few weeks while I'm in an Ibarran prison cell and look at all the trouble you get into," Roland said.

The Dragonfly passed over Terran lines. Rangers in the desert below raised their rifles and cheered as the armor flew overhead.

"We're coming up on the ship," Aignar said.

"Patch me your video," Roland said. "I'm facing the wrong way."

When the screen came up on Roland's vision, he saw a gash of blackened sand and rock stretched across the desert, ending where a strike carrier lay cradled by dunes. The ship's forward hangars were angled to the sky, the bridge and dorsal rail cannon batteries battered but largely intact. The upper hull was white with wide green stripes—not Terran Union Navy colors, but those of the Ibarra Nation.

"Amazing that the *Narvik* survived the crash somewhat intact," Cha'ril said. "Even more impressive that some of the Ibarran crew survived."

"You'd think they'd be a bit happier to see us and the Rangers," Aignar said. "The Kesaht would have killed them all had we not arrived in system with the *Argonne*."

"Being taken prisoner is rarely a plus," Roland said. "Don't think it matters by who or why."

"Man'fred Vo told me there are prisons being built on Mars," Cha'ril said. "Near the Ulysses Tholis, not far from Olympus."

"How does your almost-husband know about that?" Aignar asked.

"Mars flight command put the area off-limits to Dotari pilots," she said. "Naturally, that made all the pilots in Man'fred Vo's squadron curious and they 'accidentally' skirted that restricted space and got a few pictures. Lots of life-support equipment and a few air defense batteries. Has to be a prison. You humans are terrible at keeping secrets."

"Maybe Dotari are nosy," Aignar said.

"A prison on Mars makes sense," Roland said. "The planet is a giant military base. And if you break out, where would you go? Without a suit, you'd die in a minute in Mars' atmosphere. They build a prison in Siberia, an escapee could still get away…until the bears or tigers catch up with them."

The Dragonfly banked to one side and Roland got a look at the crash site for himself. A cluster of Terran Mules and a field hospital were set up nearby. He zoomed in on a circle made up of several strands of barbed wire and saw Ibarran sailors inside.

"We have our next mission," Gideon said on the lance's channel. "Pathfinders had to wave off a rescue mission to the south. Enemy presence was too heavy. We're to clear it out and keep the area safe for the extraction."

"Who? Is it a downed pilot from the *Ardennes?*" Cha'ril asked.

Man'fred Vo flew a fighter off the ship and Roland felt the emotion in her voice as she realized her joined husband was possibly in danger.

"Not a pilot," Gideon said. "Armor. Simon's Lancers are off-line."

Roland looked over at Gideon in the harness next to him.

Simon's Lancers were all Templar and had joined with Roland at the pre-battle prayers aboard the *Ardennes*. For every Lancer to be off-line was highly unusual and a touch of dread appeared in Roland's heart.

A satellite map of the surrounding area flashed across

Roland's HUD and a pulsing red icon appeared to the south. A blue arrow in place of their Dragonfly vectored toward the icon in time with the ship's movement.

"What were they doing that far out from the battle lines?" Aignar asked.

"Ask when we catch up to them," Gideon said. "The area's hot with Kesaht presence. The pilot wants to do a fastball special."

"What?" Aignar asked. "No. No, I have a bad feeling about this."

"The gravity of Thesius is higher than any simulations we've done," Cha'ril said. "The risk factors for that kind of an attack are significant."

"Not like you to be so cautious, Cha'ril," Roland said. "We've done insertions from ballistic torpedoes. What's a little high-grav toss in comparison?"

"There are acceptable risks and then there are suicidal tendencies," the Dotari said.

"Pilot has the ballistics loaded up," Gideon said as the Dragonfly accelerated. "You all stick your landings or we'll rehearse this maneuver until you sprout wings and learn to fly."

"We have the aerodynamics of a brick." Aignar cycled gauss rounds into his forearm cannons and put one hand on the Mauser on his back. "I'll just point that out."

Dunes blurred beneath the transport and a pair of Eagle fighters flew level with the Dragonfly.

"Oh good, an audience," Aignar said.

The Eagles wagged their wings and raised their noses to the sky, then they shot away, afterburners blazing.

"Release in three…" Gideon said as the Dragonfly sped up, rattling as a gust of desert wind blew across the ship.

"That's a good shaking, right?" Aignar asked.

"Two." Gideon pulled his legs and arms toward his chest.

"*Sancti spiritus adsit,*" Roland intoned as a laser blast snapped past the ship.

The Dragonfly nosed up and the clamps around the armors' waists released.

Roland went flying, carried through the air by the Dragonfly's momentum at the moment it let them loose. A semi-opaque column of light on his HUD marked the target location, and he scanned the dune sea for Kesaht and any place he could land safely.

He lost altitude quickly in Thesius' strong gravity and his ballistic projection ended against the middle of a sand wall.

Rakka laser blasts shot past his helm as he flew over a patrol. Ignoring a single hit to the back of an arm, he deployed the thrusters in his lower legs. The thrusters were meant for zero-gravity environments, but Roland needed just a little boost.

The rockets flared and his projection went fuzzy. He unsnapped the Mauser off his back just as his thrusters overheated and cut out. His projection reformed, showing he'd land slightly higher against the sand wall.

Roland kicked his feet forward and came down a sold four feet short of the dune crest, bursting through in an explosion of sand and rolling down the opposite slope. He came to an ugly stop as his feet slid across bare rock.

His helm snapped up next to his rifle pointed at the sky. A suit of armor lay a dozen yards away, the breastplate perforated with smoking laser strikes and an arm ripped away. Ixio clustered around the armor. The lithe aliens with wide, almond-shaped black eyes held power tools and were frozen in shock at Roland's sudden appearance.

Roland thrust his gauss cannon arm at the aliens and opened fire. The hypervelocity shells didn't kill the Ixio so much as the impacts made them pop like balloons. Rage blossomed in his heart as he strode toward the downed armor and saw two other suits lying in the sand. Ixio scavengers raced toward a Kesaht transport.

"Sanheel and foot soldiers coming from the east," Gideon radioed, his voice laced with static.

"Also the south," Cha'ril said, the thump of gauss

cannons carrying with her transmission.

    Roland stood over the fallen Lancer and brought his rotary cannon up onto his shoulder. He cut down the fleeing Ixio with short bursts and the transport lurched off the ground before a half dozen of the aliens could reach safety.

    There, just beyond where the transport had lifted off, was the fourth Lancer. The armor's breastplate had been cut away and the womb removed.

    "They've got a prisoner." Roland reloaded his gauss cannons and took aim on the transport. "I'm taking the shot."

    "He won't survive the crash!" Cha'ril shouted.

    "Take the shot," Gideon said.

    Roland led his target as the shuttle accelerated and fired one round.

    The Kesaht ship wobbled, smoke pouring from the port engines, and banked hard. It corkscrewed to the ground and careened off a dune top before crashing. It spun around and tilted up on the undamaged wing, which crumbled, and the transport flipped onto its back. Flames exploded out of the cargo bay.

    "Not like this," Roland said and ran to the crash, his massive feet thumping against the ground. He charged into the smoke and flames as a section of the transport's hull went flying through the air. Aignar was there, tearing through the wreckage.

Ignoring the heat warning from his HUD, Roland gripped the metal with both hands and ripped the hull open. He found a black oval with a red Templar cross in the wreck and clamped his hands against the sides. He wrenched the womb out, carried it away from the crash, and set it down. A small probe extended from his forearm housing and into ports on the womb.

"Come on, talk to me," Roland said.

Readings splashed across his HUD and an EKG showed an active heartbeat.

"—my lance!" rang in Roland's ears from the other armor. "Leave me and save my lance!"

"This is Roland of the Iron Dragoons. We have the area secure." He looked over at the first suit he'd seen. Gideon was there, one arm on the fallen armor's shoulder. The lieutenant shook his head.

At the second suit, Cha'ril touched armor wet with spilled amniosis. She sent readings to Roland: the fluid was thick with blood—too much to believe the soldier within had survived.

Roland looked over the scorched womb.

"Chief Tarkos?" Roland asked. "Give me a check."

"My lance! We were ambushed and—"

"You are an inch away from redlining," Roland said.

"Too much strain from battle damage and whatever the Ixio did to remove you from your suit. Focus small. Pull back."

"Is Simon online?" Tarkos asked.

"Say a prayer with me," Roland said as he found Aignar at the last suit. The breastplate was mangled and a pool of amniosis bled into the parched earth.

"Which?" Tarkos' voice sounded far away and Roland realized he was losing the soldier.

"Saint Kallen, come to their aid," Roland said.

"No. No, not that one…please."

"You know the rites. You must be the one to give it to them." Roland went to one knee and drew his sword. Releasing the blade, he drove the point into the ground.

"Come to meet them, angel of our Lord," Tarkos said, his voice stronger.

"Receive their souls and present them to God," Roland said.

"May Kallen, who called, take them to her side. Give them eternal rest, O Lord, may their light shine through us the living forever…which, Roland? Which are gone?"

"All of them, brother, but not you. You will avenge them, you understand?" Roland asked.

"It was an ambush." Tarkos' heart slowed down.

"I'm going to put you under." Roland keyed emergency protocols and the womb flooded Tarkos with tranquilizers. His life signs stabilized as the drugs sent him into a near-coma.

"Look alive!" Gideon shouted.

A target alert flashed on Roland's HUD. He looked to the sky and saw a burning comet bearing down on them.

"Last Kesaht battleship went kamikaze," Gideon said. "On course to the Ibarra ship."

"Bastards know how to die hard," Aignar said.

"Drop anchor and ready rails," Gideon said.

Roland hurried a few feet away from Tarkos' womb and raised a foot. A diamond-tipped drill bit emerged from his heel and he slammed his foot into the rock. The anchor bore into the ground, sending vibrations through his armor and jiggling him in his womb.

"That's a *Daeva*-class ship," Cha'ril said. "Our rails don't have the mass to—"

"Better to do something useful right away than figure out the perfect solution two minutes too late," Gideon said.

Roland's anchor bit firm. He raised twin rail gun vanes off his back and lowered them toward the oncoming ship. The Kesaht vessel was alight with fire and trailing a long line of smoke. Electricity crackled along the metal vanes as a magnetic field formed. He snapped a long cobalt-encased tungsten dart and set it in the rail gun chamber.

"Simultaneous strike or sequential?" Aignar asked.

Roland waited for Gideon's answer, but the lieutenant hesitated. Roland turned his helm to look at the other armor.

"*Daeva* ships have a single flight deck," Roland said. "A mass strike will send a blast wave that will—"

"Cha'ril?" Gideon asked.

"I concur. Assuming they fought with their hull pressurized."

"We've been in their ships," Gideon said.

A targeting reticule appeared on the battleship amidships. When a timer appeared on Roland's HUD, he shunted power to the rail gun.

In the sky, Eagle fighters appeared and launched missiles toward the battleship.

"Idiots," Aignar said. "Like a sparrow fart in a hurricane."

"Abort strike?" Roland asked. "The blast wave from—"

"Fire on the mark," Gideon said. "Too many lives at stake on the ground. Even if they're Ibarran."

Roland's hands clenched into fists as the timer ran to zero.

Four rail cannons fired, splitting the air with sonic booms as the shells shot out, leaving burning contrails in their wake. The shells closed so fast one could have blinked and missed the sprint. The rounds hit the Kesaht battleship and the vessel's belly exploded outward. The ship bucked like it had been kicked and then lolled to one side, angling down and diving toward the planet. Roland watched as it slammed into the sand and sent out a shockwave that blew a sudden storm of sand and superhot air over the Iron Dragoons.

"Status," Gideon sent.

"Green across the board." Roland pulled his anchor up and went back to Tarkos' womb. He reconnected to it and found Tarkos awake and alert.

"What the hell was that?" Tarkos asked. "My womb almost dumped me out. Some sort of massive system disruption."

"Rail fire…and a Kesaht battleship crashing nearby."

"Must have been bad for you to fire rails in atmo…"

"That ship might have smashed the crash site and killed thousands," Roland said. "You're still in one piece."

"The Saint was with us," Tarkos said.

Roland set a hand on the cross carved into the womb and looked back at the three dead armor soldiers.

"She was," Roland said, "and what a price we paid."

"Extraction en route," Gideon said. "Fleet figured out where the *Narvik* went before it crashed. We need to break orbit."

A map of Thesius' third moon appeared on Roland's HUD.

Chapter 2

The *Scipio* zoomed across the barren and crater-pitted surface of Thesius-gamma. Roland stared down from the corvette's hell hole—an open iris in the bottom of the ship's cargo bay—as the moon passed by.

"Landing zone coming up in thirty seconds," Lieutenant Commander Tagawa, the ship's captain, sent over the IR.

"Set for insertion." Roland loaded gauss rounds into his forearm cannons.

"LZ clear on the scope…calling ice. Green ring in five. Good hunting…"

Roland bent his knee servos slightly. Green light lit up around the hell hole and Roland hopped out of the ship. With no atmosphere, his descent to the surface was smooth. He pinged the area with his sensors and an area of disturbed soil came up on his HUD.

His feet skidded across the surface as he landed, kicking up a torrent of dust in his wake. He waited until a cloud of the gray-brown dust billowed around him, then leaped toward the area his sensors picked up. Thermal imaging cut through the dust as he bounded out of the cloud. Low-gravity moons weren't meant for walking or running, so he jumped low and long, using thrusters on his shoulders to keep him close to the surface and not provide an easy target for whoever else might be on Thesius-gamma.

The rest of his lance landed in the distance, forming a loose semicircle around the center of a crater as wide as Phoenix.

"Why can't every landing be like that?" Aignar sent over the lance network.

"You prefer an easy glide from a corvette over being spat out of a high-velocity torpedo?" Cha'ril asked.

"The only fun thing about Tactical Insertion Torpedoes is the acronym," Aignar said.

"Focus," Gideon growled.

Roland landed next to a wide patch of bare rock and sent a picture to his lance.

"Looks like a grav engine liftoff," Roland said. "Residual heat indicates it was recent, maybe hours old."

"Fleet sent us snipe hunting," Aignar said. "How nice of them."

"Ibarrans use the same grav engines we do," Cha'ril said. "Why set down here? This place is empty."

"Tracks," Gideon said as an image of treads in the dust snapped up to one side of Roland's HUD. Parallel to the tracks were footprints—not prints of overshoes or a vac suit, but simple impressions in the dust, like normal footwear.

"Someone forgot their boots?" Aignar asked. "I doubt those armor treads and prints were laid down when this place had atmosphere. Which was likely never."

"Or someone who doesn't need a vac suit," Roland said. "Someone like Stacey Ibarra."

The leader of the Ibarra Nation was…Roland wasn't exactly sure how to describe her. Her mind resided inside a metal body, transferred there after her flesh and blood received a mortal injury.

"Ibarra was here?" Aignar asked. "The Rangers didn't find her on their strike carrier that crashed on the surface."

Roland skidded to a stop next to a circular mound that came level with his chest and leaned over, leading with his gauss cannons. A swath of metal had a light coating of dust and a jagged hole cut through it, a hole wide enough for armor to fit through. Inside was darkness.

"Sir?" Roland asked Gideon. "I'm guessing your tracks lead here."

"Correct," the lieutenant said, stopping at the

opposite side of the mound.

"This is strange," Cha'ril said. "There's no wind on this planet. For dust to accumulate over this structure…it must have taken millions of years."

"Artifacts," Gideon said. "Fits the Ibarrans' M.O. Isn't that right, Roland?"

"It never came up," Roland said, ignoring the barb.

"Qa'Resh artifacts?" Cha'ril asked with some hesitation. The last time she'd encountered the ancient and extinct civilization's remnants, the architecture and strange environment had proven almost too much for her Dotari mind to process. She'd nearly redlined.

"You stay here and maintain a comms relay to the *Scipio*," Gideon said to her. "Rest, follow me."

Gideon strode through the dust and dropped into the hole. Roland went next, falling slowly in the weak gravity to a wide hallway with bare, slightly curved walls. The walls were pristine, showing no sign of wear and tear, even though they were possibly older than the entire human race. Roland activated his lamps, flooding the area with light. Gravity normalized to almost Earth standard, though Roland couldn't detect the source of the field.

He followed behind Gideon, orienting his weapons to the right, opposite the direction Gideon covered. They passed by a circular arch that led to a small room with no discernable way out.

"Portals," Aignar said. "Why did it have to be portals?"

"They're off-line." Roland brushed fingertips through the arch with no effect.

"Good. Better than having Ibarran armor jump out and cut my armor in half. Again," Aignar said as he spun around and walked backwards, covering their rear.

An alert chimed in Roland's ears. He froze, but Aignar and Gideon kept moving. Roland accessed the alert menu.

"Sir, got a distress signal. Thirty-seven kilohertz," Roland said. "Simple code. SOS."

"That's not a freq we use." Gideon stopped. "But SOS…"

"It's an Ibarran freq," Roland said. "I'm in the same womb that I was picked up in back on Balmaseda. Some of the settings are still in use. I didn't realize it until the alert went off."

As Gideon turned his helm to Roland, the lieutenant's gauss cannons slowly did too, but stopped short of aiming right at him.

"There's an Ibarran armor distress signal in here?" Gideon asked. "Can you get a bearing?"

"To the northeast." Roland pointed at a branch

31

farther down the hallway. "Distance is coming back irregular. The walls must be attenuating the signal."

"Any other Ibarran surprises in your armor?" Aignar asked.

"The maintenance teams must not have dumped the emergency protocols," Roland said. "That's not standard procedure anyway. If they—"

"Full-system purge once we get back on the *Scipio*," Gideon said. "Let's move."

Roland felt his cheeks flush with embarrassment inside his womb. It was hard enough to shake the stigma of having fought beside the Ibarrans to save their colony on Balmaseda, though no one seemed to hold that same act against the Rangers who manned the defenses beside Ibarra legionnaires during the Kesaht attack. His armor suddenly detecting Ibarrans nearby carried an air of suspicion with it, no matter how valid Roland's explanation.

They turned the corner and the hallway opened into a wider space with a curved dome on the far side. A set of doors had been torn away and lay strewn across the ground. Roland looked down at a scuff on the floor, then back at the near side walls. Bullet holes stitched across the wall, each surrounded by a spiderweb of cracks.

"The caliber matches gauss shells." Aignar tapped the side of his forearm cannon. "There was a firefight."

"Against what?" Roland asked. "It's not like armor—ours or theirs—to miss."

"The Qa'Resh left a security system?" Aignar asked.

"Not likely," Gideon said. "Sending a sensor pod ahead." He reached behind his back and pulled a small metal ball off the back of his ammunition housing. The ball pulsed in his hand and he tossed it into the breached doorway.

Roland felt vibrations through the floor and he readied his cannons.

What came charging out the door bore a faint resemblance to armor—twelve feet tall and bipedal, with long arms that ended in irregular hands like the end of a tree branch. Its shell looked like it was made of thick cables wound tightly over a wire diagram of a squat, wide-shouldered creature. The head was a simple dome with open metal jaws.

If there'd been an atmosphere, Roland was sure he would have heard it screaming.

He fired off both barrels and struck the attacker in the chest, his salvo hitting simultaneously with Gideon's and Aignar's. Cables split and air hissed out of the wounds, but the thing kept coming.

It sprang forward on both hands and pounced at Gideon. The lieutenant swung an uppercut into the attacker that struck just beneath the chin, arcing its head up. Gideon fired a single round from his forearm cannon and blew the dome apart. Viscera splattered across his armor, steaming and popping in the vacuum.

Three more emerged from the other room, snapping and swiping at each other as they all charged toward Aignar.

"Ah…great." Aignar backpedaled, firing his gauss cannons and bringing his rotary weapon up and into action. The gauss shells broke through the enemy's outer shell but didn't slow them down. Though the gauss cannon churned through an entire magazine, the bullets bounced off the enemy with no effect.

Roland hit one of the attackers in the hip, causing it to stumble. As his cannons reloaded, he ran forward and snagged it by the ankle before it could leap at Aignar. The enemy's arms snapped backwards, rearticulating as it pulled back. Grasping claws clamped down on Roland's arm and its head snapped around in a complete one-eighty.

It scrambled up Roland's arm as he swung a cross into the side of the dome. The blow seemed to stun the attacker and it fell to one side. It rolled over, still holding on to his arm, the blades on its fingertips scouring Roland's paint. It snapped back into action and scrambled up the underside of his arm. Its mouth bit into the ammunition line feeding into his forearm cannons and ripped it open.

"Oh no you don't." Roland kicked his feet up and

used the artificial gravity to slam into the attacker and pin it against the ground. Talons popped out of its feet and it braced the new weapons against Roland's chest. Its feet ripped across his breastplate, leaving deep gouges in the armor.

Alerts blared across Roland's HUD and his ears. Another attack like that would kill him.

He brought his other arm around and delivered a weak punch to the dome. Instead of pulling back for another strike, his fist recessed into the forearm housing and a spike plunged through the thing's head. It went still, black blood sizzling as it emerged from the edges of the puncture.

Roland got back up and found Gideon wrestling with the new type of armor, one already dead at his feet. Roland checked that he had two rounds in the chamber, but the melee was so fast and furious, he risked hitting the lieutenant.

One of the attackers sailed across the room and into a wall.

"Sir!" Roland detached his sword and tossed it to Gideon. The weapon unsnapped as it flew and Gideon caught it in the middle of the blade. He stabbed it into his attacker's chest and it backed off him. Gideon grasped the blade by the handle, yanked it out, and slashed the enemy armor across the throat. Its head popped off and bounced against the ceiling.

Roland fired on the enemy that hit the wall, ripping its mouth off and hitting it in the throat. Two more shots from Aignar blew its head off.

Aignar picked his left arm off the ground and looked at where his arm ended at the elbow.

"What the hell are these?" Aignar asked.

"Toth?" Gideon asked Roland.

"No. These aren't like the Toth I fought on Balmaseda," Roland said.

Gideon wiped a hand through a black streak and pulled a sticky clump off his shoulder. A laser on the side of his helmet swept over the sample.

"Brain matter," the lieutenant said. "Reads as Rakka."

"Kesaht want their own armor." Aignar kicked a corpse on the floor. "But there's no way a Rakka can fit in this…"

"They plugged a Rakka brain into the suit," Roland said as he looked down at the bloody stump that was once a Kesaht armor's head.

"Sounds like something the Toth would do." Gideon flicked the viscera off his hand and tossed the sword back to Roland.

"No weapons, just savagery," Aignar said. "I think these are prototypes, early generation."

"We need to get these back to Earth," Gideon said.

"Let our engineers find a weakness."

"Bullets to the dome work well enough," Aignar said. "For now."

"The distress signal…" Roland hurried to the doorway, realizing that his gauss cannons were empty. He held his sword at the ready, hilt at his hip and blade angled away from his centerline.

Inside was a crystalline dais. Bullet strikes and claw marks marred the surface. There was no sign of any power in the room. Roland went to the dais, and on the other side, propped up in a sitting position, was a mangled suit of armor. The head and limbs lay in a pile against the far wall. Crude glyphs had been carved into the breastplate, but beneath all the damage was a Templar cross.

"It was a trap," Aignar said. "The Kesaht must have heard the same distress call, left those uglies to kill anyone who showed up."

"And the Kesaht didn't care about recovering their armor," Gideon said.

"Who is it?" Aignar asked.

"Check for life signs," Gideon said.

Roland reached for the armor, but Gideon pulled him back.

"Aignar. You do it." Gideon guided Roland away and pointed at the door. Roland stepped away, seething. Again,

Gideon didn't trust him.

Probes extended from Aignar's forearms and plugged into the fallen armor at the base of the neck.

"Got a pulse and brain activity," Aignar said. "Womb sent her into an induced coma to stop a redline...nine hours ago. She should pull through, but we need to get her out of here."

"Her?" Roland asked.

"Biometrics data says her name is Morrigan."

As Roland's sword tip dipped to the floor, Gideon's hands balled into fists and gauss shells cycled into his cannons.

"No! Don't—" Roland stepped away from the door and raised his sword.

Gideon's cannon arm snapped toward Roland.

"Don't what?" Gideon asked as Roland stopped. "Don't kill this traitor right here and now?" His cannons swung toward Morrigan's armor.

"Sir," Roland lowered his sword, "I know she was in your lance before...before what happened. I know there's—"

"You know nothing!" Gideon snapped his cannon arm up at the elbow. "You have no idea how long I've waited for this, Roland. For justice. And a summary execution is not justice, is it?"

"No." Roland shook his helm.

"Aignar, unplug," Gideon said. "I'm taking Morrigan back to Mars in chains."

Chapter 3

Roland paced along a catwalk over the *Scipio*'s cargo bay. Below, armor technicians worked around the beaten-up torso of Morrigan's armor while a medical team and ship's armsmen waited nearby.

An extraction from damaged armor was a dangerous procedure, but Chief Henrique and his mechanics had been maintaining armor since before the Ember War ended. There was no better crew in the fleet to safely remove Morrigan…but Roland was ill at ease.

Leaning his hands against the railing, he said a silent prayer, which was interrupted by the clomp of clumsy metal feet against the catwalk.

"Aignar," Roland said.

"I can't sneak up on anyone, can I?" Aignar said, his voice tinny as it came from a speaker embedded in his throat.

Working prosthetic knuckles against his jaw, Aignar snapped it back into place. He'd lost his arms below the elbows and legs below the knees to a Vishrakath grenade years ago. The same grenade took much of his face as well. A genetic disorder prevented him from grafting cloned organs to his body, and outside his armor, he seemed less human than when he donned his suit.

"She didn't say anything to you?" Roland asked him.

"She was down for the count." Aignar shook his head. "Lucky her suit took her off-line when it did. Losing limbs is a bitch of a neural spike." He bent his left arm, the same one that had been ripped off his armor on the moon. "You lose it outside your armor, it's an altogether different experience. You don't redline, but you'll probably bleed to death. Or die of shock."

Roland looked at Aignar's metal fist and bumped it with his.

"I'm trying to make you feel bad," Aignar said. "Is it working?"

"No," Roland said, motioning to the work being done on Morrigan. "I'm just trying to…to not…"

"You know her," Aignar said.

"I do. She trained me while I was a guest of the Ibarras. Vouched for me when I volunteered to—never mind. Where is Cha'ril?"

"You're a filthy traitor. It's the noose or the firing squad—pick one." Aignar nudged Roland with his shoulder.

"There's no way to sugarcoat this, is there? I care about Morrigan, which makes me an Ibarran sympathizer, but if I turn my nose up at her, what does that say about me?" Roland brushed his fingertips over the Templar patch on his right shoulder.

"Did you really think Gideon was going to kill her?" Aignar asked.

"He hates her." Roland stood and crossed his arms across his chest. "Hates Nicodemus. Hates all the Ibarrans. We are armor. We are fury. We are not…not ones for forgiveness or restraint."

"There was a moment," Aignar said. "A moment I thought he was about to do it."

"At least we were both wrong," Roland said.

"How did I know I would find Roland up here?" Cha'ril asked as she came around a corner.

"He's obviously planning to help his Ibarran confederate escape Terran custody," Aignar said.

Roland slowly turned to look at Aignar. "You're not helping. One hundred percent not helping."

"I'm bitter you got to go kill Kesaht with the Ibarrans while I had to officiate the Dotari equivalent of a shotgun wedding," Aignar said. "Did I tell you I got spat on?"

"He will not stop squawking about that," Cha'ril said.

"Twice." Aignar ran the back of his prosthetic hands down his chest. "Two giant loogies square in the chest."

"It was a compliment," Cha'ril said.

"They're almost done," Roland said, leaning over the handrail as Henrique and his techs stepped away from Morrigan's armor. A robot arm lifted the breastplate open and amniosis fluid gushed out of the womb and onto the deck, sloshing against absorbent booms circling the work area.

The womb cracked open on one side and lifted up slowly. Inside, a red-haired woman wearing a skinsuit lay curled in a fetal position.

"Wake up…please," Roland said.

A medic climbed up onto the workstation and reached a scanner toward Morrigan. Her arm snatched up and grabbed the medic by the wrist, who yelped in fear.

Armsmen rushed the womb, shock batons and gauss rifles ready.

Morrigan blinked fluid away from her eyes and let the medic go. She rolled over and looked from side to side at the Terran navy personnel around her. Her midsection heaved and she vomited amniosis into the bottom of the womb.

"I hate that part," Aignar said.

Armsmen slapped cuffs onto her wrists and dragged

her away from the armor.

"She's not ugly. By human standards," Cha'ril said.

"I fought by her side," Roland said. "Her looks had nothing to do with it. You've been with human armor for a while, Cha'ril. Can you understand my concern for her?"

"I would have killed as many Ibarrans as necessary to rescue you," Cha'ril said.

"She's developed such a loving attitude since she got married," Aignar said.

"Joined," she said, wagging a finger in the air.

"Since her pheromones caused a riot on the *Ardennes*."

"A few minor injuries amongst suitors was hardly a riot," she said.

Gideon and Commander Tagawa walked into the cargo bay. The armsmen parted and Morrigan locked eyes with Gideon. She leaned to one side and spat on the deck.

Tagawa marched forward and gave commands to the armsmen that Roland couldn't make out. They strapped Morrigan down to a backboard and took her away, followed by the medics.

"Gideon and the Ibarran have a history?" Cha'ril asked.

"And not a pleasant one," Roland said.

Gideon touched his forearm screen. "Lance," the

lieutenant's voice sounded in their earpieces. "Get down here and do post-action maintenance. I want all armor fully mission capable before we make Crucible jump. Which is four hours from now."

"I'm collocated with the others," Cha'ril said into a mic on her screen. "Moving."

"So much for eating and sleeping." Aignar beat his fists against the handrail.

Roland watched as Morrigan was carried around a corner. Looking back at Gideon, he found his lieutenant staring daggers at him.

****

Roland twisted a wrench against a bolt and cursed as the tool refused to budge. Stepping back from where his armor's right arm sat on top of a workbench, he wiped sweat from his brow, shook his arms out, and tried again.

"I'm always wobbly when I come out of my armor," Aignar said. He had a toolbox pressed between his metal palms, which he brought next to Roland, his gait unsteady.

"It takes hours before our nervous system can fully switch over from armor to—careful!" Roland bent forward as the toolbox slipped from Aignar's grip. One corner landed on

Aignar's foot and the toolbox clattered open, spilling metal instruments across the deck.

"Sorry," Aignar said as he reached down to pick up a rotary sander. His metal finger popped open and closed slowly around the tool, but it slipped away when he picked it up.

"I've got it." Roland tossed the scattered items back into the toolbox.

"Chief Henrique is giving me the look," Aignar said. "He's cursing me out in Portuguese. I know it."

"Let him. We're picking up the slack while he and his pit crew get the suits turned around," Roland said. "Where's Cha'ril?"

"Sick bay." Aignar looked down at his hands and lifted his fingers up and down one at a time. "Something about nausea."

"That's been happening a lot lately." Roland reached under the workbench and grabbed a head bolt socket. "Every time she leaves her suit. Think it's a Dotari problem?"

"Ask her about it," Aignar said as he lifted up the ripped, loose end of the ammo belt and examined the tooth marks from the Kesaht armor. "See how quick she bites your face off."

Roland snapped a bolt on to a power drill and whirled the head from side to side.

"She's been weird since she got married. Or joined? Almost married, whatever the Dotari call it?" He removed the nut bracing the ammo belt to the armor and handed it to Aignar.

"Yeah, there's that and the phage that's killing off all the Dotari on their home world," Aignar said. "Her parents are there. The Dotari military's quarantined the whole system. Who knows how the Dotari are dealing with that. Remember when we came back to Earth and the Xaros had wiped out the whole system?"

"I was a kid." Roland removed another bolt. "Mom and Dad were in the service and were too busy to get emotional about things like that. I was prepped to live on one of Saturn's moons, to never see any of my friends or family for years and years…I guess learning that they were all gone wasn't much of a hurdle for me."

"I was a teen," Aignar said. "I got roped into a labor battalion that got Phoenix livable. Having work to focus on helped deal with what happened to Earth, the ongoing war with the Xaros. You'd think with all the crap the Kesaht and the Ibarras are giving us, she'd—oh hi, Cha'ril!"

The Dotari brushed past Aignar and looked over Roland's cannon arm.

"What are you doing? You skipped at least four steps from the manual." Cha'ril snatched the power tool from

Roland.

"We've got to get the belt replaced in the next two hours," Roland said. "This is a four-hour task by the book, so we don't do the—"

Cha'ril whacked the drill against the ammo belt and two gauss shells tumbled out and rolled across the deck.

"Oh," Roland said, his face turning red.

"We're getting the look again," Aignar said. "Chief Henrique hasn't come over yet, but I think we're on borrowed time."

"Move." Cha'ril elbowed Roland out of the way and picked up a screwdriver from the toolbox. "Aignar, we need to do this like we're back at Knox. Would you read from the manual?"

"We're not that bad." Roland dropped the two shells into a drawer in the workbench.

Cha'ril raised a finger in front of her face, her beak clicking rapidly.

"Step four," Aignar said with a sigh, reading from his forearm screen.

It took another half hour to remove the ammo belt before Cha'ril called for a break. Roland ran his hands against a gash on the metal where the Kesaht armor had bitten through the ammo belt.

Cha'ril sat on the toolbox, humming a tune as she

drank from a water bottle.

"Cha'ril," Aignar's brow furrowed, "what song is that? I think I know it."

"I've been researching human music. I don't know the name, but the artist is Michael Jackson," she said. "He was a prominent singer last century, correct?"

"Who?" Roland asked.

"Philistine," Aignar said. "How can you not know the King of Pop?"

"Because I'm not an old man like you?"

Aignar swiped at Roland, who ducked out of the way.

"I was unaware that human beings could undergo such a metamorphosis during their adult life," Cha'ril said.

"We do what?" Roland asked.

"Your music royalty's facial structure changed a great deal from childhood," she said. "This seemed aberrant as I studied the careers of many other artists. Toward the end of his life, he resembled a Bukhasha clan lord. Can you explain this?"

Roland shrugged and looked at Aignar, who raised an eyebrow and said, "Michael Jackson…did not look like most humans, yes."

"The Karigole are born neuter and develop their final gender during childhood. Did Emperor Jackson undergo a parallel change?" Cha'ril asked.

Roland's forearm screen beeped with a text message.

"Jackson," Aignar said, snapping a finger up next to his face. "He...he had money. Lots of money. And he spent it on doctors that...you know what? Humans can undergo a metamorphosis. But we have to ingest a special flower...from the triffid plant. It only blossoms once a century in...Sidonia. Yeah, that's it. Right, Roland?" He nudged Roland on the shoulder.

Roland shot to his feet and looked over the workstation to a door across the bay guarded by two armsmen.

"Sorry, what?" Roland asked, glancing down at his screen, then back to the door.

"You have someplace else to be?" Cha'ril asked.

"Morrigan—the prisoner—wants to see me." Roland tapped his screen.

"Let him go," Aignar said. "He'll be useless while he's pining."

Cha'ril's beak clicked and she motioned him away with a wrench.

"Be right back." Roland wiped his hands against a rag and hurried away.

"Aignar," Cha'ril said, "explain 'disco fever' to me."

Roland dodged a drone cart carrying gauss shells and stepped off the *Scipio*'s cargo bay. He recognized one armsman from pre-battle prayers—she was the ship's junior navigator. The other had an engineer's badge on his chest.

A ship the size of the *Scipio* didn't warrant a proper brig or internal security element, but crew could be reassigned and a storage locker could be repurposed should the need arise. The navigator-turned-naval-police smiled and tapped her knuckles to her heart as Roland approached.

"Can I see the prisoner?" Roland asked.

"We're not supposed to—" the engineer started.

"She gave her word," the navigator snapped. "If we can't trust the Black Knight, then who can we trust?"

Roland's face flushed at the name. Video of his fight against the Kesaht on Balmaseda had leaked onto the nets and gone viral. While he could walk unrecognized out of his armor in the middle of a busy Phoenix street, the crew of the *Scipio* knew who he was.

"You're not going to help her escape, are you?" the navigator asked with a smile.

"By my honor and my armor," Roland said.

"Fine," the engineer said, glancing from side to side. "Sir, can I get your autograph on something later on? For my son back on Earth."

"Chief of the Boat will have you scrubbing the head for months if he finds out you asked for an autograph." The navigator keyed in a code to the door. "I won't mention that if you don't mention this."

The door cracked open and Roland slipped inside.

Morrigan sat behind an energy field, her ankles and wrists cuffed and chained to a ring in the middle of the floor normally used to secure cargo. She had her back to the wall, and her unkempt red hair dangled over her lowered head. An unopen field ration pack and bottle of water lay next to her.

"Morrigan?" Roland approached the force field.

Her face snapped up and she brushed hair away from her eyes. "By the Saint I thought my eyes tricked me when I saw you," she said, her Irish accent thick with fatigue.

"I don't know how long I can stay here." He glanced back at the shut door. "Are you hurt? You almost redlined when we found you."

"Groggy." She stretched a leg out. "Your medics hit me with enough stims to burn through the sedatives my armor forced through my bloodstream. You've not asked about Nicodemus or Lady Ibarra. They must have escaped."

"Wait—Nicodemus was with you?" Roland cast a nervous glance at the door. "He just left you behind?"

"Nicodemus is a lance commander and a fine soldier for the Saint," she said. "You know that. The Kesaht were waiting for us with their bastardized versions of us. Hit us soon as we got the chamber open. I took the brunt of the attack, but Nicodemus got a fair bit of hurt to him as well…He was right to leave me behind."

"Stacey Ibarra was there," Roland said and Morrigan looked away. "I saw her footprints in the moon dust. Don't feign ignorance."

"Aye, Lady Ibarra was with us," she said stiffly.

"She must have ordered Nicodemus to abandon you. He'd never—"

"We are armor, Roland." Morrigan touched the Templar cross on her shoulder, the same one Roland wore. "We fight for a purpose. And Lady Ibarra is more important than any one of us. You and I, and Nicodemus, know that."

"What was so valuable that she'd just leave you behind for the Kesaht to…do you know what they do to prisoners?"

"I do. I know damn well what would happen if they took a true-born human like me." She tapped the plugs in the base of her skull. "They'd take me to see their Toth overlord. Thank the Saint your pit crew followed proper protocol to get me out of my womb. If they'd gone and cut it open like the Kesaht would've, my womb would've put me down for good."

Roland took a step back.

"That's…Ibarra would rather kill you than let you be taken prisoner."

"Prisoner by the Kesaht," she said. "They have ways

of getting information that no training or iron can stop. Better I died than they get everything in my mind. Being held prisoner by Earth…not as bad."

She picked up the ration pack.

"Kesaht wouldn't have given me chili mac, that's for sure," she said. "So I hear you're famous. The Black Knight, heh. 'None shall pass' should've been my line back on the moon."

"Honestly, I'm surprised they let me back into my armor," Roland said. "Don't think the Terran Armor Corps will ever give you the same chance to fight that Ibarra gave me."

"Lady Ibarra's wiser than President Garret or General Laran," she said.

"What was Ibarra here for?" he asked. "And how did the Kesaht manage to ambush you?"

"Lady Ibarra does what she will. We're sworn to serve and protect her," Morrigan said.

Roland knew she was evading the first question but decided to let it pass. He'd found her in a Qa'Resh site. There was a short list of reasons for why the Ibarrans would search it.

"As for the Kesaht…I don't know how they did it, but they were waiting for us in system," she said. "Tracking our fleet through the Crucible network shouldn't have been possible. We had a few ships with us, not enough to be detected. The distress call from the *Narvik* reached us right as the Kesaht armor attacked. Things got a bit rushed after that."

"Maybe the crew of the *Narvik* knows more." Roland shrugged.

"What? Some survived?" Morrigan went pale.

"She crashed on Thesius—bad—but our Pathfinders managed to rescue a couple dozen from the wreckage. Then we had to fight off the Kesaht who were in system waiting for—"

"You have Ibarran prisoners?" She got to her feet and began pacing across her cell. "Where are they now? Does New Bastion know about them?"

"I think they're going to a POW camp on Mars. What does New Bastion have to do with this?"

"That the devil will break your Terran bones, you've no idea, do you? The crew of the *Narvik* are proccies. Fresh proccies," she said.

"There are a lot of procedurals on Earth," Roland said. "It's almost impossible to tell them from true born."

"The Omega Provision of the Hale Treaty, you blithering dunce," Morrigan said. "Did they tell you nothing about that? Ibarran proccies were all born after Garret and Hale betrayed humanity to the rest of the galaxy. Our proccies are a violation of the treaty. Doesn't matter if the Ibarra Nation's part of it or not. By the treaty, and the Omega Provision, your Ibarran prisoners must be destroyed."

Roland shook his head.

"No. That can't be right." He took a step back. "It's a lie the Ibarras told you."

"What you believe doesn't change what's true." She ran her hands through her long red hair.

"Earth can't just…kill them all," Roland said. "They're soldiers. We don't punish anyone for fighting on the wrong side—that's not who we are."

"They'll be killed for *what* they are. Nothing else," Morrigan said. "And Earth will do it to keep New Bastion happy. I pray I'm wrong about this."

Roland raised his palms toward her. "Is that what you wanted to see me for? To find out if the other Ibarrans are in danger?"

"What are you talking about? I didn't ask to see you. I didn't even know you—"

The cell door slammed open. Gideon stood in the entrance, Tagawa just behind him.

"Chief Shaw," Gideon said to Roland, "you're not authorized to be here."

"Not anymore, is that it, sir?" Roland asked.

Gideon stepped to one side and held up a hand,

signaling Roland to leave.

Morrigan touched her knuckles to her heart as Roland looked over his shoulder to her. He left with a nod as Gideon closed the door behind him.

"You look well, Isiah," she said. "Still sport your old Toth scars, I see. The lieutenant bars suit you."

Gideon stepped up to the force field. "Nicodemus is alive?" he asked.

"Far as I know. If the Kesaht had taken him, there would've been a trail of their dead behind him. Did you find one?"

"Then he lives."

"You tricked young Roland into sneaking in here. Why? Think he's going to admit he's loyal to the Ibarras? The boy's a Templar. His loyalty is to a higher purpose, not a badge or a chain of command. Why the cloak-and-dagger nonsense? That's not like you, Gideon. You're the kind that confronts his enemies head-on."

"You're right about me…you're right now, and you were right when you shot me out of the *Warsaw* onto Ceres when you chose to turn traitor," he said. "I would have never sided with the Ibarras or your religious nonsense."

Morrigan stepped toward the field and was caught short by her chains.

"Saint Kallen is true," she said. "You think we

survived the Ember War through luck? It was Providence, Gideon. When the martyrs stood against the Xaros on their world ship, it was faith in—"

"Spare me," Gideon said.

"Pearls before swine. It's *always* been that way with you," she said, taking a seat on a cargo container.

Gideon looked at her bare ring finger.

"I took it off after Bassani died," she said. "It hurt too much to keep it around."

"I helped him pick it out," Gideon said. "Bassani could face down a battalion of Vishrakath tanks by himself, but proposing to you scared him to death."

"He was such a spaz about it." Morrigan's fingertips brushed over her left hand. "He took me to Deco's—that trendy place in Phoenix—spent a month's pay on wine he didn't drink and Lord knows how much on food he was too nervous to eat. But when he finally worked up the courage…it was easy to say yes."

"How'd he die?"

Morrigan's face darkened.

"Not well. His suit took damage when we fought the Naroosha for…something Lady Ibarra needed. He redlined and passed a few days later," she said.

"He went with you because he loved you," Gideon said. "Not for your saint."

"All that mattered to me was that we stayed together. He's buried on Navarre with our heroes. Maybe someday you can go see him." She looked up at him, her face an emotionless mask. "Pay your respects."

"I have no respect for traitors." He turned and knocked on the cell door.

"You did well training Roland," she said. "He fights with your fury."

The armsmen opened the door and Gideon stepped through. With a last look at his former lance mate, he slammed it shut.

****

Gideon stood just outside the cell, his shoulders heaving with each breath.

"I think we got it," Tagawa said. "The cameras got Roland's entire conversation with her. Should be all the evidence the brass needs."

"How much longer do I have to share a ship with this traitor," he asked, pointing at the cell door, then to the cargo bay where Roland worked on his armor, "and that traitor?"

"Once we're to Mars. Admiral Lettow said he'll pull the trigger then," she said.

"Roland's not to see or speak with her again," Gideon

said. "Understood?"

"Are you telling me how to run my ship?"

Gideon stared her down.

"Admiral Lettow wants enough evidence for a charge. Once we get that, I'm to keep the prisoner quarantined, so don't think you need to get into a dick-measuring contest with me." She put her hands on her hips.

"It's your ship, Skipper," Gideon said. "How long until Mars?"

"We'll make the jump in a few hours. Just keep playing your part."

Chapter 4

President Garret strode through the bunker beneath Camelback Mountain, his shoulders slightly hunched forward and a scowl across his face. He'd been an admiral during the Ember War and his management style as a flag officer was well-known to the Terran Union's military.

As with any senior leader in human history, the boss's mood had a major impact on how aides approached that leader. And right now, Camelback Mountain knew that Garrett was not to be bothered with anything other than the sudden appearance of a Xaros armada.

Bodyguards and aides struggled to keep up with Garret as he marched down the low hallways.

Officers and NCOs that caught a glimpse of Garret shouted, "Make a hole!" to keep the president's path clear.

Garret stormed into a conference room where flag officers from across the Terran Union's armed forces waited, already on their feet and at attention.

"Sit." Garret plopped down in a leather chair on a raised platform set up in a horseshoe around a massive holo table and felt a small pill container rattle in his coat pocket. He touched a hand to his chest and then to the pocket, ensuring that his medication was still there.

His body ached for his next dose, and he could feel tremors working their way through his limbs. But Garret wouldn't find relief in front of his admirals and generals, not when faith in his leadership was so crucial right now.

"All right." Garret situated himself in his chair and motioned to General Emery, his chairman of the Joint Chiefs of Staff. "Let's hear it."

"Sir," Emery said as he clicked a button on a small remote in his hand and the lights dimmed. A holo field of the galaxy appeared, then zoomed in on a small swath of green.

We've colonies on almost two thousand worlds and it's barely anything in the grand scheme of the galaxy, Garret thought.

"The Kesaht assault on Koensuu was defeated by a joint Dotari-Terran task force," Emery said. "Kesaht losses were total. Our casualties were minimal, but the colony sustained significant damage to outlying infrastructure."

"How did our joint task force get from Yalta Prime to Koensuu?" Garret asked. "I thought the jump-gate network was broken to Koensuu."

"The *Breitenfeld*," Emery clicked his remote and the holo shifted to the infamous strike carrier surrounded by Dotari ships near a Crucible jump gate. "She returned from deep space with the last of the Dotari Golden Fleet and Admiral Valdar…requested the Dotari loan him a battlegroup to relieve Koensuu. Valdar used his Keystone gate to make an offset jump into the system and caught the Kesaht with their pants down."

"Del Aroz," said the president, spinning his chair around to face one of the few men in the room not in uniform. Garret's head of Information Services smiled from ear to ear. "Full-on media blitz. The *Breitenfeld* returns to save the day. I want interviews, combat footage, a movie like *Last Stand on Takeni*, but with less cringe. The Dotari returning the favor for us saving their bacon. Again."

"The script's already in treatment. This should be viral enough to get the Black Knight out of the public zeitgeist," Del Aroz said.

"You mean to squash the video I ordered you to suppress weeks ago?" Garret gripped his armrests tight enough to turn his knuckles white.

"That's been a problem…" Del Aroz shifted in his seat. "We think Ibarran hackers have been sabotaging the algorithms to—"

Garret turned back to the holo tank, ending the

conversation with his chief propagandist.

General Emery switched the holo tank back to the view of human-occupied space and a half-dozen star systems blinked amber.

"Kesaht attacks continue in the outer systems," Emery said. "Raids on low-population colonies followed by deeper jumps into the Crucible network. We finally realized the true purpose of these raids." A wire diagram showing linked Crucibles appeared and several went off-line, leaving a single star system cut off.

"They pruned back the Crucible network and isolated Syracuse," Emery said. "It will take weeks to repair the Crucibles, and the Kesaht have Syracuse blockaded. The planet's orbital defenses are holding, but we won't be able to do an offset jump to send reinforcements for…"

"Sixteen days," Keeper said from Garret's right. The woman looked like a well-built person in her early fifties with a lined face. That she was a former Strike Marine named Torni, her consciousness transferred into the last Xaros drone in the galaxy, was classified above everyone's pay grade but Garret's.

"So that's the Kesaht's new strategy," Garret said. "Isolate a planet and wear it down before we can help. Can Syracuse last that long?"

"Not by the projections we're running from the last

data transmission from the colony," Emery said. "The colony has a population of just under fifteen million, the biggest target the Kesaht have gone after to date."

Garret swung his chair to Del Arroz.

"Sir?" Keeper asked. "There's more to this."

Garret raised his hands in confusion.

"The *Breitenfeld* managed to get into the Crucible network before the Kesaht cut off Syracuse. Admiral Valdar and the Dotari are on their way to the system now," Keeper said.

"Lead with that next time," Garret said. "They have a chance?"

"Valdar's outnumbered nearly five to one by the Kesaht fleet," Emery said. "But it is the *Breitenfeld*, the ship of miracles."

"We can't depend on miracles. Get the Crucibles repaired and ready a relief expedition to Syracuse. Then I want evacuation plans drawn up for every phase-four colony that's outside offset jump range from any fleet anchorage," the president said.

Murmurs went through the flag officers as the implications of that retreat worked through their minds.

"If we pull back, we're open to a mass driver attack," Keeper said.

"Then ramp up the macro-cannon build at our strong

points," Garret said. "We don't have the ships to guard every single colony and we can't leave our people out there for the Kesaht to pick off like low-hanging fruit. Speaking of the Kesaht, where are we on finding their home world? Or a colony? Something we can blow up and plant a flag on."

"The Kesaht will not be taken prisoner," Keeper said. "Their ship's computer cores slag as soon as the captain dies and we've recovered nothing from them. I haven't detected them moving through the Crucible network, so they must be traveling in small packs. A massive fleet will send a graviton ripple through the network. They're smart enough not to leave a trace back to wherever they're coming from."

"So you've got nothing?"

"There's been a development. Colonel Gaeta?" Keeper looked to a hard-eyed woman in Pathfinder blue.

"Mr. President," Gaeta said as she waved a hand through the holo field and it zoomed in on a star. The designation came up as a series of letters and numbers, marked as Vishrakath territory. "The Vish had an outpost on the star. I say 'had' because the Kesaht raided the place three days ago. We picked up the distress signal through one of our implants we left in a connected Crucible back before we gave up this sector as part of the Hale Treaty."

"I know what the Hale Treaty is," Garret grumbled. "I signed the damned thing."

"The Vish were slow to respond," Gaeta said. "Mostly because they sent three full battle swarms to react to the raid. I managed to get a Pathfinder team in and out before the Vish arrived."

The holo changed to Vishrakath domes surrounded by dead ant-like aliens on a world with bright orange skies.

"Looks like a Kesaht raid," Gaeta said. "At least thirty percent of the outpost's personnel were unaccounted for. My team went to clone the system's central computer and they found this."

The holo changed to a Vishrakath computer—loops of tightly wound, glowing cables stacked on top of each other like grapes on the vine. Deep inside the cluster was a length of cable that glowed with a slightly brighter hue.

"Fascinating," Garret deadpanned.

"This isn't Vishrakath tech, sir," Gaeta said. "It's…something else. One of my Pathfinders recognized it as being—"

"Cut to the chase," Garret said as sweat broke out across his forehead. He waved an aide over to him.

"We were able to access the device and determined it's a data shunt. We pulled the records on it and reprogramed the device to send us a copy of everything it sends in the future. The Vishrakath were tracking some unusual graviton readings across the Crucible network." Gaeta swiped through the field again and the holo changed to a map of the galaxy. Crucible gates lit up across the stars seemingly at random.

"And?" Garret rubbed a temple.

"The detections correspond to known Ibarra Nation sightings," Gaeta said. "The last was on Thesius, where we captured an Ibarran crew after they were ambushed by the Kesaht."

"The Kesaht tracked the Ibarrans?" A chill went down Garret's spine.

"The Vishrakath found a way to do it," Gaeta said. "Then the Kesaht decided to piggyback off their system…and now we're doing it too. Just how the Kesaht knew that this outpost had the tracking technology remains an intelligence gap."

"Don't suppose they found the Ibarran capital of Navarre?" Garret asked.

"Negative, sir. The tracks are incomplete. We think the system can't pick up the Ibarrans when they use their own version of the Keystone gates," Gaeta said.

"I want to know about every single new reading that comes through," Garret said. "The Ibarrans are still a threat to the Terran Union, am I clear?" he asked the conference room, receiving scattered responses of "Yes, sir" and nods.

He turned away to the aide kneeling beside his chair and whispered, "I want Gaeta in my office after this. Classify every document from the mission to that Vish world Obsidian-3 right now, understood?"

The aide nodded furiously, then passed a data slate to the president.

Garret's lips pressed into a thin line. "How long ago did Ambassador Ibanez arrive?" he asked.

"Five minutes, sir. She's heading straight for the Scottsdale House…just as you ordered."

Garret tossed the slate at the aide's chest and scooted his seat closer to the table.

"General, you've got fifteen minutes to get me up to speed on the rest of the war against the Kesaht," Garret said. "Skip to the slide with our manning and warship construction and please tell me there's some bureaucrat somewhere that needs his face bitten off. Please."

He tapped the bottle of pills in his coat pocket and reassured himself that relief was close.

****

Ambassador Ibanez examined a burnt, torn flag in a glass case on the wall of Garret's office. She knew the story of the 8th Fleet, how it was lost with all hands in deep space fighting against the Xaros armada that later besieged the solar system. The flag was one of the few artifacts that survived from the *Midway* when the Xaros used the ship as a Trojan horse to attack the Crucible over Ceres.

Just why Garret insisted on keeping the garish memento in his office was lost to her. The picture of Admiral Makarov—the 8th Fleet's first, last, and only commander—next to the flag gave her chills.

Garret burst into the office and went straight for his desk.

"Are we at war with the rest of the galaxy or not?" He opened a drawer of the wooden desk, a re-creation of the Resolute Desk used by presidents of the United States, and pulled out a glass bottle of whiskey and two shot glasses.

"Not…" Ibanez said, "not *yet*."

"And how 'yet' are we?" Garret poured shots and slid one toward her, then he took out a pill bottle, popped two in his mouth, and washed them down with the liquor. He leaned back in his chair and let out a slow sigh.

"That depends on you, and Congress." She tossed back her shot and poured herself another one. "The Vishrakath and Naroosha want our blood, which isn't unusual."

"But we removed the Ibarran colony on Balmaseda just as they demanded," Garret said, taking a swig straight from the bottle.

"You are technically correct." She sat on an antique upholstered couch and crossed her legs. "But our military also fought side by side with the Ibarrans as soon as the Kesaht showed up. If there hadn't been some bloodshed between us and the Ibarrans before the aliens showed up…we'd be in a slightly worse position than we are now."

"New Bastion's not convinced the Ibarrans are our enemy too?"

"'The enemy of my enemy makes that first enemy my friend' is pretzel logic—reasoning that's hard to get across to alien ambassadors." She sipped her whiskey. "The prevailing theory among the ambassadors is that we'd ally with the Ibarrans in a heartbeat."

"They're not wrong." Garret picked up a baseball from his desk and worked his hands against the leather. "And we've formally declared war against the Kesaht…but not the Ibarrans."

"The bill to declare war on Stacey and her tube babies is still in committee," Garret said. "The public won't have it. Not after the last almost-fight and that damn video with the Black Knight floating around." He rolled his eyes, then asked, "New Bastion knows which side's been attacking our colonies and murdering our people, don't they?"

"Most of the ambassadors are reasonable enough to see that," she said. "But not all. The war with the Kesaht might have been enough to smooth over the current crisis as the Kesaht have been raiding more worlds, not just human ones. New Bastion's OK with us doing all the fighting and dying to get rid of the Kesaht. But there's a wrinkle."

Garret huffed and set his bottle on the desk.

"The Ibarran prisoners from the *Narvik*," Ibanez said. "They're…not compliant with the Hale Treaty, are they?"

"Not a one."

"Then by the treaty, they must be destroyed." Ibanez held up a hand as Garret's face went red. "Choir. I'm the choir. The Vishrakath are screaming about the treaty and somehow they know about the *Narvik* proccies. Which begs the question of who told them. Sure wasn't the Dotari and it sure wasn't us."

Garret opened a drawer and took out a pill blister.

"You've had enough. I think." Ibanez glanced from the pills to Garret.

He tossed them back into the desk and slammed it shut.

"What does New Bastion want from us?" he asked.

Ibanez looked away and her voice lowered almost to a whisper. "For the Terran Union to comply with the treaty we signed in good faith."

"That's a diplomatic way of saying we should execute them all." Garret swiped the whiskey up and took a drink. "If we do that, we're violating the Naissance Act that protects everyone in the Union against discrimination for the circumstances of their birth."

"The Ibarrans aren't Union citizens. And if you're worried about the Naissance Act, what about the military you've got stuffed in a bolt hole on Mars? The prison in Ulysses Tholis?"

"They're compromised—proccies the Ibarrans altered just before they took off. Sleeper agents. All of them." He set the bottle back on the desk.

"They don't know what they are. The Ibarrans have to activate them first."

"Then we're painted into a pretty tight corner, aren't we?" Garret asked, his eyes wobbling from the alcohol and pills. "If we execute the Ibarran prisoners, the public will lose their goddamn minds. I don't know what Stacey Ibarra will do, but I can guarantee she won't take it well. If we don't kill them off, then what? What will New Bastion do?"

"Expel us and declare war in the same session. If we try not to slip on this ice, we'll fall right through it."

Garret kicked the alcohol off his desk and it shattered against the wall. Ibanez clasped her hands on her lap and kept her head down.

"Stall," Garret said. "You get back to New Bastion and buy me at least a week."

"I can do that," she said. "You tell me what the week's for and maybe I can manage a few more days."

"If we comply with the Hale Treaty, will New Bastion join the fight against the Kesaht?"

"Several races have promised to join us, but not while our compliance is in question."

"So we end a few dozen Ibarran lives or lose millions of proper humans. That about sum up my options?"

Ibanez stood and brushed her hair away from her face. "That's a fair view on this situation. Yes, Mr. President."

"Then I'd call that a bargain." He jabbed at an intercom button, missed, and managed to press it on the second try. "Sheila, get General Laran in here."

He sat back and kept his eyes on Ibanez as he rotated his seat a few inches from side to side.

"I need to work up a distraction," Garret said, "and you don't need the details. Get out."

****

The weather on Navarre was unusually calm. Sunlight broke through the near-constant cloud cover and shone across a rain-slick parade square atop a massive building. Skyscrapers surrounded the square, the faint slopes of their sides closing into pyramids at their apex.

On the parade field, ranks of legionnaires in their black armor stood in formation as they loaded onto troop transports at the far end of the square. They passed by several armor, all arrayed in a loose, even line just beyond the ramps of the transports. The armor knelt in prayer, swords gripped in their hands.

Stacey Ibarra watched the soldiers from a balcony, her metal body gleaming in the sunlight, Ibarran officers standing behind her: General Hurson, with his armor plugs and red sash over his chest; Field Marshal Davoust, his bald pate gleaming almost as much as Stacey's body; Admiral Makarov, who looked almost too young for her rank; and a final officer with a neat goatee.

"Thank you for attending," General Diaz said. "The legionnaires consider it a blessing from Saint Kallen to see you before they deploy off world for the first time."

"Of course they do," Stacey said as a sprinkle of rain fell on her shoulders and hardened to ice almost instantly. Her doll-like face was almost unreadable as she raised a hand into the air.

"*Ferrum corde!*" rose from thousands of throats and echoed off the skyscrapers. Iron Heart.

"Marshal Davoust," Stacey said, "what of the *Narvik?*"

"Our agents in Terran space have gone underground due to security concerns," Davoust said with a thick French accent. "But we have enough scattered reports to confirm that there were survivors. All rescued by the Terrans."

Stacey turned her head to Hurson.

"Morrigan lives, my lady," said the commander of the Ibarran armor.

"Does the common man know of the prisoners?" Stacey asked.

"That they have our prisoners has been kept secret," Davoust said.

"And why do you think that is?" Stacey ran a hand against a railing, leaving a thin patina of ice.

"Garret will have them all killed to placate New Bastion," Admiral Makarov said. "There will be no public outcry if no one knows anything."

"He wouldn't," General Hurson said. "They're prisoners of war at worst. To just execute them would be a violation of the laws of warfare."

"All those honorable notions went away after the Ember War," Diaz said. "You're judging Garret by our old standards."

"Standards *Admiral* Garret once held," Hurson said. "He's not so far gone that he forgets who he used to be…or how the Union remembers him."

"You're letting your faith in him cloud your judgment," Makarov said.

"Faith is always a factor." Hurson turned his chest slightly and light glinted off a Crusader cross badge on his sash.

"And if our people have already been executed?" Ibarra asked.

"War," Diaz said. "If the Terran Union kills any of us for being procedurals, they'll kill all of us."

"War," Makarov said.

"War," said Davoust.

"My armor is with the Lady," Hurson said.

"It will be war," Stacey said. "The galaxy is full of enemies that see us as abominations to be killed on sight for nothing but what we are. There will be no quarter. No mercy…and it's a war we're not ready to win yet."

"The shipyards and procedural crèches are operating at full capacity," Davoust said. "Expansion on all fronts as we—"

"I know. I know." Ibarra waved a hand at the marshal. "So long as Navarre and the first-phase worlds remain hidden, we might win a war of attrition. But it will take decades before we could take on all of New Bastion."

"The Kesaht will come for us if they can find us," Makarov said. "Doesn't matter what action New Bastion takes."

"We will not abandon our people," Stacey said. "No one in the nation is disposable. Makarov?"

"My lady?" The admiral stepped forward.

"I want the crew of the *Narvik,* and Morrigan, returned to me. I don't care how it's done or what it costs."

Makarov opened her mouth, took in a quick breath, then paused. "As you command, my lady. I'll need access to our assets in the solar system," she said.

"Every resource." Stacey looked at Davoust, who nodded once.

"They're being held on Mars," Hurson said. "My old home."

"In Olympus?" Makarov asked.

"No." Hurson shook his head. "The Templar still there would never allow Garret to murder our people. Our oaths are to protect the innocent, and no one is guilty by the circumstances of their birth."

"Faith again," Makarov said.

"Faith," Stacey said, "the righteous shall live by faith. It takes no faith to know the Templar. To know their hearts, one must simply *see* them. I was there when armor sacrificed everything to win the Ember War. I need no faith to believe in the Templar."

"Excuse me, my lady," Makarov said. "I must see to

my task."

As Makarov turned and left, Stacey continued to watch the legionnaires as they marched off to war.

Chapter 5

Roland gripped a handrail as the all-encompassing white static of a jump gate faded away. He shook his head quickly to clear out the cobwebs that came with every trip through a Crucible. The observation deck windows were full of stars.

"That's never fun." Aignar adjusted his prosthetic jaw from side to side and nudged the speaker embedded in the front of his throat. "Cha'ril, does wormhole travel make the Dotari dizzy like humans?"

Cha'ril had her eyes closed and her chin pressed against her chest. The skin around her beak flushed red, then drained away to an unnatural yellow.

"She OK?" Roland asked Aignar, who shrugged.

The Dotari armor retched, then opened her beak and gave off dry trill.

"It's nothing." She gave a dismissive wave of her hand.

"Sounds like you had a hairball," Aignar said.

"Do I inquire when you have indigestion? Or when Roland inebriated himself when we were in Australia and…What did you say, 'prayed to the porcelain god'? No. Not every one of my bodily functions is your business. In fact, none are your concern," she said.

"Excuse me," Aignar said.

Roland glanced at the screen on his forearm.

"We're back in the solar system…no alerts. Why hasn't Gideon called us to the simulation center yet? Got a good couple days before the *Scipio* can make the sprint to Mars," he said.

"Look." Cha'ril pointed to the observation window.

The red planet swung into view, and a thin ring made up of the remnants of Phobos glinted in the sunlight. Basalt-colored spikes of a Crucible gate swept across the port edge of the window.

"When did Mars get its own Crucible?" Roland asked.

"The foundry on Mercury built it while you were…indisposed," Aignar said. "It was supposed to be assembled on Pluto, but the Kesaht War threw a wrench into those plans. The Armor Corps is here on Mars. Some colony needs us and its best they don't have to wait for a sprinter to bring a squadron or two over from here to the Ceres Crucible over Earth."

"I'm surprised Phoenix didn't order the entire Corps back to Earth," Roland said.

"Eggs. Baskets." Aignar knocked metal knuckles against the handrail.

"There's the *Ardennes*." Cha'ril pointed to the carrier as it accelerated past the *Scipio*. "I can see Man'fred Vo soon."

"You think Gideon will let you go see your almost-husband?" Aignar asked. "Mars has the best live-fire training facilities anywhere…other than the two-way shooting range of a fight with the Kesaht. You know how he is about drills and proficiency ratings."

"I'm allowed a full day-night cycle pass with my joined once a month if we're close to each other. Our mutual-defense treaty is explicit about this…and it's been too long since I've seen Man'fred Vo," Cha'ril said.

"The *Ardennes* has our casualties." Roland tapped his Templar cross. "I have duties on Mars. The dead must be interred properly." He gave Aignar a look. The other armor soldier had been a Templar initiate along with Roland but had backed away from the faith after the encounter with Ibarran armor on Oricon.

"More range time for me," Aignar said. "I wonder if there's a quantum link between this new Crucible and the one over Ceres. I could get a real-time call to my son on Earth. The time dilation makes for garbage conversations."

"Busy busy," Roland said as he gave them a wave and left the observation deck.

"I'm worried about him," Cha'ril said. "He's different. The Ibarras affected him too deeply."

"He's a full Templar now," said Aignar as the first knuckle of his left index finger popped up and down of its own accord. He clamped his other hand over the offending digit. "That changes a man. And it was the Ibarran armor that gave him the final nod to take the vows and stand his vigil. You think he'd be normal after that?"

"Change is constant. Change is normal. But *what* has changed isn't normal. I'm surprised Gideon hasn't transferred him to another lance. Do you think the lieutenant still trusts him?"

"No." Aignar's brow furrowed. "I doubt Gideon has any confidence in Roland either."

"Then why is Roland still with us?"

"Because the brass don't trust him either, is my guess. Back when I was a Ranger, there was a soldier the First Sergeant was sure was…foraging supplies from other units and redistributing them around to those who'd pay for it."

"You mean stealing."

"There's stealing and then there's stealing. The First Sergeant didn't transfer that kid to the supply section to make his suspected extracurricular activities easier. He kept him under the nose of someone he trusted until they caught the kid in the act," Aignar said.

"Roland remaining in our lance isn't Gideon's decision?"

"How would a Templar lance react to Roland?" Aignar asked.

"They'd take him in like a brother. While we…"

"Will keep our eye on him."

"I don't like human politics, human games. Roland fights with fury and is a fine soldier. That should be all that matters," Cha'ril said, pressing a hand to her stomach.

"It is to me…but not to Gideon or those way above our pay grade. I've been in uniform long enough to know what I can change, and I don't lose sleep over the grand plans of those detached from my reality."

"So you don't care what happens to Roland?"

"Of course I care. But if I oversleep, I don't try to turn all the clocks back an hour to fix it."

"Some things are beyond our control." She clicked her beak. "No matter our feelings."

****

Roland knelt with his sword planted tip-down in

Martian soil. Templar knelt around him in even rows; the assembled were divided into two halves facing inward with a wide strip between them.

He wore his white tabard embroidered with a Crusader cross on the chest over matte-black coveralls, the under uniform representing the womb in the heart of each armor suit. The Templar chanted softly as Chaplain Krohe, followed by Colonel Martel and Major Tongea, swept a smoking censer from side to side. One after the other, each of the three led a mag-lev platform bearing a broken suit of armor.

The smell of burning copal and frankincense wafted over him, and part of Roland knew that scent would forever remind him of death and mourning.

Roland resisted the urge to look up as the platforms slowly passed. He knew what damage the Lancers' suits sustained. Knew the names of the fallen. A fourth went by, bare of armor but carrying *momento mori* of a Templar lost to the battlefield: a fencing epee and several antique books with frayed spines.

That Rocha of the Conquistadors had perished when her landing pod was destroyed by Kesaht fighters was not in question. Her armor had burnt up in reentry, the fragments dispersed across Thesius' wilds.

Would they let Morrigan attend? Roland wondered. *The*

Ibarras were accommodating enough when they learned I was Templar. He banished the thought and concentrated on the funeral chant.

The armor and *momento mori* went into a tomb, and the three men that led the Templar order emerged a few minutes later.

Chaplain Krohe raised a hand and gave a blessing as the massive red-rock doors to the tomb shut with a boom.

The room went silent—dead silent—until Krohe tapped the censer three times against the door.

The ceremony was over, and Roland stood and sheathed his sword as the Templar broke into small groups, speaking amongst themselves. Dozens of lances must have been present; more Templar were here than he'd seen when he stood his vigil months ago on Phoenix. For so many to be on Mars while battles raged against the Kesaht perplexed Roland. Armor's place was the battlefield, and Templar did not fulfill their vows to protect humanity on a world at peace.

Seeing the other Templar in their lances and squadrons sent a tinge of loneliness through Roland. He'd set himself apart from his lance when he took on the cross, and the Iron Dragoons had operated apart from most other armor after his return to the Terran fold.

"Roland," said a voice from behind him.

Tongea clasped the young Templar by the forearm in

the traditional salute. "Good to see you again, brother." The Maori's facial tattoos wrinkled as the man smiled.

"Circumstances could be better," Roland said.

"Always." Tongea nodded toward a side door leading to a maintenance tunnel. "The post-funeral feast is about to begin. Krohe made that potato casserole with all the cheese and corn flakes on top."

"That...does not sound appetizing."

"They're incredible. I'm just letting you know there won't be any left if you come with me to see Saint Kallen," Tongea said.

"The Saint…" Roland felt color drain from his face. The venerated woman lay buried deep beneath Mount Olympus, the location unknown to but a few in the Templar. Visits to her damaged armor and *momento mori* had been restricted since the incidents with the Ibarra Nation, under orders of General Laran, the Armor Corps commander.

"You performed the rites for the fallen," Tongea said. "Chaplain Krohe, Colonel Martel and I agree you earned an audience. Been some time since you've seen her."

As Tongea led Roland toward the side door, Templar got out of the way, nodding to the older fighter and Roland as they passed.

"Not since I first arrived on Mars," Roland said.

"Different times." Tongea shouldered the door open

to a small four-person transport on tracks leading into a dark tunnel.

Roland climbed into the transport, careful with the ceremonial sword hanging on his belt. Tongea sat next to him and keyed in a code. The transport accelerated forward with a hum of electric motors.

"How is Gideon?" Tongea asked.

Roland shifted in his seat. "He's…formal, sir."

"Of all the Templar that went with the Ibarras…you had to fight beside those two." Tongea shook his head. "Gideon's not the forgiving type."

"Still a professional. Still a brave lance commander."

"You saw the Ibarran armor during their ceremony. Perhaps you saw a woman with *Ta Moko*." Tongea waved his fingers over his tattooed face, then brushed his chin several times.

"It…it was dark during the ceremony and my focus was on Stacey Ibarra. I don't remember seeing someone like that. Sorry."

"Kaia is fighter. I doubt the Kesaht could kill her if they tried," Tongea said.

"Kaia?"

"My sister," Tongea sighed. "Stationed on the *Warsaw* when it left Terran service."

"I didn't know."

"Why would you? I don't share that bit of information with many. The Templar are under enough scrutiny," Tongea said as the transport cut down a branch of the main tunnel.

"If the order's suspect since the Ibarran exit, why let me take the oaths and become a full Templar? I would have understood if my vigil had waited until things—"

"When do Templar care for politics? For timing?"

"Never."

"We hold to the rod of iron through all temptation and chaos. To waver is to fail." Tongea frowned and tapped the control panel.

"I'm sorry, sir. Perhaps I shouldn't be in the Saint's presence just yet."

"Doesn't matter…seems we're not going to the crypt. Someone changed our route."

The transport cut up a ramp and into a warehouse where massive cargo containers were stacked against the far walls. An armored personnel carrier blocked the tracks, and military police armed with gauss carbines flanked the vehicle. They snapped their weapons to their shoulders and a group moved to flank Tongea and Roland as the cart came to a sudden stop.

There was a slam of metal as a hatch cut off the ramp.

"Chief Warrant Officer Roland Shaw." An MP with

lieutenant bars and a pistol in one hand approached. "You are under arrest."

"What is this?" Tongea snapped to his feet and marched toward the lieutenant.

"Stand down, sir." The MP gripped his pistol with both hands and angled the muzzle at the ground between him and Tongea. "We have a warrant."

"What charge?" Tongea stopped, one hand on his sword's pommel.

"Treason." The lieutenant waved a hand to the five police flanking the cart.

"Drop the weapon!" an MP shouted at Roland.

"No!" Tongea held up a hand. "Olympus is Armor. You have no jurisdiction—"

"General Laran signed the warrant, sir," the lieutenant said.

"She what?" Tongea's face fell.

"Templar," Roland said as he rose slowly and unfastened his sword belt with an easy, deliberate motion, "my faith remains."

He set the blade aside and stepped away from the cart, hands up and level with his face.

Two MPs rushed him and wrenched Roland's arms behind his back. They slapped cuffs on him and a hood went over his head.

"We were told this would be a signal-one arrest," the lieutenant said, relaxing slightly but keeping his eyes on Roland. "Armed and dangerous suspect."

"Why didn't you come for him during the funeral? Frog-march him in front of everyone?" Tongea asked.

The passenger side door of the APC opened and a navy commander stepped out.

"I wanted to," Commander Kutcher said, "but none of the MPs would do it. Care to explain that one, lieutenant?"

"Respect." The MP glanced at Tongea's Crusader cross, then holstered his pistol as Roland was led into the back of the APC. "And it would be my men fighting armor if the Templar were a bunch of treasonous fanatics like you told us."

Tongea stared daggers at the commander.

"Just that one." Kutcher winked and jerked a thumb back to the APC.

"Where are you taking him?" Tongea asked.

"He's got an appointment with a judge, then an all-expense paid trip to a special hole we dug. Real destination spot; you want to come see?" Kutcher asked.

"He's an officer and innocent until proven guilty, no matter the charge," Tongea said.

"I expected more...chutzpah from you armor types," Kutcher smirked. "You don't live up to the hype outside the suits. Clothes really do make the man." He poked two fingers at the cross on Tongea's chest.

The Maori snatched the digits before they could touch him and broke them with a quick twist. Kutcher stifled a cry and backed away, clutching his misshapen fingers.

"You saw that!" the naval officer said to the lieutenant.

"Saw what?" The MP traced a circle in the air and his men hurried into the APC.

"He assaulted me!"

"You fell. You better get back in the truck before you slip on this wet floor again." The MP grabbed Kutcher by the shoulder and manhandled him back to the front passenger seat. The MP slammed the door shut, then turned to Tongea and tapped his fist to his chest. The Templar salute.

Tongea watched as the MPs left with Roland, heading down a logistics tunnel. He touched his forearm screen and opened a channel.

Chapter 6

Roland sat on a bench, still hooded, his ankles chained together and cuffs on his hands. The engine noise around him told him he was on a Mule. He kept a count going in his head, sure that he was still on Mars as the Mule hadn't done a burn to break into orbit since he'd been placed onboard.

He heard footsteps against the metal, then his hood came off. Kutcher brandished his broken fingers, held straight by splints, at Roland.

"Not appreciated," Kutcher said. "That savage of yours will pay for this."

"You got off lucky," Roland said. "Maori have a habit of decapitating their enemies, then shrinking the heads to use as door knockers."

Kutcher rolled his eyes and sat next to Roland.

"Don't think you've got me—or anyone—fooled. We're in an undeclared war with the Ibarras. You don't switch jerseys and expect us to believe you're back in our fold. You know who you are? The Black Knight," Kutcher sneered. "Vids of you fighting on that bridge against the Kesaht have gone viral—despite all our efforts to restrict that little stunt. You want to tell me who your Ibarra handlers are? What they want you to do to undermine the Terran Union?"

"I am Templar," Roland said. "The Ibarras have nothing to do with who I am or why I fight."

"I know what you did on Oricon, saving all those kids from the Kesaht. That's why I'm going to make this offer—this one-time offer." He brandished a finger from his unbroken hand. "Cooperate. Admit the Ibarras sent you back as part of a fifth column. Turn back their influence on the Union and it'll go easy for you."

Roland locked eyes with the intelligence officer, then turned to the hood on the bench beside him.

"Thank you." Kutcher swept up the hood and shoved it into his pocket. "You made all this so much easier."

"The Ibarras don't care about Earth," Roland said. "They want to be left alone."

"Is this an act or are you really that ignorant?" Kutcher glanced at his forearm screen and buckled himself into the seat next to Roland. "Ibarran sleeper agents sparked the war between the Union and the Kesaht. I was *there*. Stacey Ibarra and her abomination sent a shockwave through our military, but we've got that damage under control. As you're about to find out."

The Mule's vector engines rotated and flared as the transport descended. It landed roughly, then a shadow passed over the Martian landscape just beyond the portholes.

"Now you get the hood," Kutcher said.

"There's no one with me." Roland sat up and accepted the cowl. "And I am loyal to the Templar. To Earth."

"That's exactly what a spy would say," Kutcher said. "Dome's almost pressurized. Ready to check in to the last place you'll ever call home?"

Chapter 7

The restraints fell off Roland's wrists and ankles. His eyes stung as light hit his face and his hood was removed. He rubbed his wrists and found himself in a coffin-like enclosure, bright lights humming.

"Prisoner," a voice said through speakers, "turn around and step out of the enclosure."

Roland spun in place and faced a crowd of Terran Union soldiers, sailors, and Marines sitting at long tables with trays of food in front of them.

"Step. Out."

Roland stepped out of the box and crossbars snapped across the opening as soon as he was clear. The box descended into the floor with a hydraulic hiss.

A dome spread out overhead, and Roland saw pink Martian skies and gossamer clouds above. Bare rock walls of an ancient crater formed the perimeter. Three structures were built into the walls, manned by guards wearing power armor. Small drones flitted through the air while a few larger ones hovered over the tables well out of reach. Prefabricated housing units surrounded the dining area.

"So much for my theory." A red-haired young woman with a Strike Marine emblem on her utilities walked over to him. "Unless armor found some way to stick the armor plugs in proccies."

Roland touched the neural interface at the base of his skull and realized that all the servicemen and women who saw his arrival got an eyeful of his cybernetics.

"Still true born," Roland said. "Far as I know."

"Sir, I'm Lance Corporal Adams, Terran Strike Marines." She shook his hand.

"Roland. Armor. This is my first prison…it's not what I expected."

"They told you it was a prison? At least they're honest with you." She pointed to an empty spot at a distant table. "Chow? The commander will want to see you soon. A runner's going for him now."

"Fair enough." Roland followed Adams down the rows of tables. The other prisoners were a motley assortment of various ranks from across the Terran Union military. Roland glanced at the Military Occupation Specialty badges on their utilities: logisticians, computer specialists, flight crew, medics. He couldn't pick out any pattern to clue him in on why they were there with him. Perhaps a crew of a single ship…but there were unit badges from across several fleets.

A junior sailor hurried over to a food combiner in the center of the dining area and pulled a tray from a drawer. He set it down at the empty spot and clicked his heels together as Roland sat down. Prisoners crowded around the table, elbowing each other for a better look at the armor soldier.

"Anything else, sir?" the sailor asked. "The bug juice is OK most days."

"Water?" Roland stuck a fork in a pile of macaroni and cheese, then set his utensil down. "I appreciate the attention…but what are you all doing here? You don't strike me as traitors."

Adams snickered. The woman carried herself stiffly, with the same sort of faraway look Roland had seen on warriors who'd been in too many battles over too many years.

"All the same story," she said, sitting across from him. "Out-of-the-blue transfer orders to Mars. Doesn't matter where we were or the assignment. I was in a Strike Marine team that just came off a mission to rescue a bunch of Dotari in deep space, then we were hunting down Ibarran agents on clandestine status when some pogue takes me off the line. Lieutenant Hoffman and Gunney King were *pissed*, but it didn't matter. I got a one-way ticket to Mars and had all my kit confiscated soon as I got here."

"I was on the *Ulundi*," the sailor said as he set three different cups of water on Roland's tray. Roland glanced at his name tape: Boucher. "Finished our shakedown cruise, just got watch certified and bam. Get on the transport shuttle. Do not pass go. Do not collect two hundred dollars."

"The guards didn't say why you're all here?" Roland asked.

"Guards don't talk to us. At all," Adams said. "We get called out at random for holo conferences with intel types. They keep throwing word salad at us, trying to gauge some kind of reaction. It's all weird and frustrating."

"If we don't go to the sessions, they cut back on chow," Boucher said. "Play their games or its bread and water. Not like we have much else to look forward to in here. No net access. No slates to pass the time."

"Card games and one channel in our boxes." Adams pointed at the prefab structures, which looked like they could sleep four individuals uncomfortably. "No news either."

"This must be him." A big hand patted Roland's shoulder and a commander pushed Roland down as the armor tried to rise to greet the officer. "Strickland. Formerly of the *Ardennes*. I'm the ranking officer in here."

The commander looked at Roland's name tape and

his eyebrows shot up.

"I know that name." Strickland wagged a finger at him. "You were listed as a POW after the fight on Oricon. How'd you get free of the Ibarras?"

"They let me fight to save one of their colonies...linked up with Terran Armor there. You haven't heard of me otherwise?" He rolled his eyes. "The Black Knight?"

"Nope," Strickland said. "We don't get any news in here. We're in a strange spot. We've been 'assigned' to this duty station and put under commo blackout. So we're about to pick your brain to find out everything that's happened out there. Don't suppose they let slip why they brought you in now? Haven't had a new arrival for months."

"Treason." Roland cast his gaze down. "Had a brief stop in front of a judge before I got here. They asked me to confirm my identity...then asked if I was the armor they had on video fighting in Ibarra color. That was all the judge needed for an indictment."

"Why were you fighting for the Ibarras?" Adams asked as she sat up, pushing away from the table...and Roland.

"Templar fight for humanity. *Who* we fight beside is of less concern."

"And they stuck you down here?" Strickland rubbed

his chin.

"There were all those other irregular flights the past few days." Adams pointed up at the dome. "It goes opaque when a bird lands or departs. Not sure if it's to keep us from seeing out or the pilots from seeing in."

"There's a landing every day at 9:00 a.m. standard," Strickland said. "Brings in supplies and guards. Last few days, the activity level's been high. Snooper drone activity over the other cell block for the first time." He pointed to the north end of the crater.

"Could be the Ibarra survivors from the *Narvik*." Roland looked along the tall, razor-wire-topped solid-metal fence separating the cell blocks and followed it to the east, where the air was absent of drones. "Is that another cell block? Anyone over there?"

"Not that we can tell," Strickland said. "Three cell blocks. One guard shack for each. Only time we've heard from them is when they caught us tossing messages over the wall for the new arrivals."

"'Do that again and you'll be punished,'" Boucher said. "If there are Ibarrans over there, they haven't responded to our notes. Doubt they even found them. The drones watch everything."

Roland looked up and saw optics on the bottom of a drone flash in the light. One camera lens was pointed right at him.

"This is…a little odd for me," Roland said. "I was a prisoner of the Ibarrans. I knew what my duties were then. Now…"

"None of us are traitors," Strickland said, waving a hand over the crowd. "I was right next to Admiral Lettow while he was arguing with the Ibarran admiral on Oricon. I saw firsthand how they turned our own people against us…somehow. Damn mess with the Kesaht. Then Kutcher got all squirrelly—"

"That's the guy that arrested me," Roland said.

"All right." Strickland pulled a green hardback notebook from a pocket and clicked open a pen. "Let's start connecting dots…"

****

President Garrett walked down a narrow corridor beneath Camelback Mountain as the hum of computers and machinery worked through shut doors. Not many frequented this part of the Union's military headquarters, which was the point.

Staff flocked behind the president as he went to an unmarked door that opened for him. A pair of plainclothes protection officers tried to follow him, but he waved them off. Inside was a poorly lit room and a wall of glass between Garret and an empty section.

An intelligence officer and a mousy scientist stood next to a box on a pedestal.

"She's waiting for you," the scientist said.

"Recording suite ready?" Garret took off his jacket and tossed it to the scientist.

"Yes, Mr. President," the spy said.

"Dial her in." The glass slid open and Garret went into the empty section and put his hands on his hips.

Stacey Ibarra appeared, her silver body sitting on a simple stool. She remained statuesque, then her face turned suddenly toward Garret, like a puppeteer had moved her strings.

"President," Stacey said, lowering her chin slightly.

"Where's Marc Ibarra? What have you done with him?" Garret asked.

"I tolerated Grandfather keeping a back channel with you, but using our quantum-linked hotline to share information that could harm the Nation…no. He's in a cell and kept entertained. I even let him have a friend for a bit." Stacey cocked her head to one side and Garret felt she would have smiled if her shell could have managed the expression.

"You want to keep up with pleasantries or get down to brass tacks?"

"We lead every human soul in this galaxy," Stacey said. "Let's assume our time is valuable."

"New Bastion is out of control," Garret said. "You and your procedurals upset what little balance we had with the other factions. They smell blood—an excuse to break from the Hale Treaty—and Earth and our colonies will suffer first."

"Excuses don't forgive desire, Mr. President. The Dotari and the Ruhaald haven't broken with Earth. The Vishrakath will strike once they're strong enough. This was always their plan, and the treaty gave them the time to build their capability. Ambassador Wexil had the original Bastion behind him...most of the races are still with him, even after his coup toward the end of the war. You think the Kesaht coming onto the scene just as the Vishrakath decided they couldn't tolerate the Ibarra Nation was a coincidence?"

"You have proof there's a connection?"

"I have a working theory. Nothing that would sway New Bastion."

"Then your theories don't change my situation—or yours." Garret ran a hand through his hair. "Your 'nation'...can't go on."

"I want my people back," Stacey said. "The *Narvik* survivors."

"Don't you care about your sleeper agents? We got all

of them. Took a while to dig through the code you put into the crèches, but we found it."

Stacey's head bobbled slightly.

"I can't let the *Narvik* go," Garret said. "I signed the treaty. You know what that means."

Stacey held up her arms, then opened them to her sides. "Your hands aren't tied. Don't hide behind the Omega Provision."

"It's war with the galaxy or we terminate a few dozen proccies." Garret leveled a finger at Stacey. "You can replace them in days—don't act like they're that precious. Your grandfather murdered hundreds when he blew up tainted proccies on the *Hiawatha*. This has happened before."

"I know exactly what those poor souls were capable of." Stacey stood and poked a finger against her chest with a *tink* of metal. "It was wrong then. It's wrong now. They are human beings, not constructs. They are my children and I will have them back."

"And then? I might as well rip up the treaty in front of everyone on New Bastion if I do that. You ready to fight the rest of the galaxy to protect Earth from that decision?"

"The Ibarra Nation is marked for death with or without Earth at our side. We're stronger together. If you keep trying not to slip on the ice, you'll fall through it."

Garret crossed his arms. "There may be a third path,"

he said. "The Ibarra Nation at New Bastion. You agree to the Hale Treaty. Cease procedural production. We can argue that you were a political entity before the treaty was signed and you're not bound to—"

"Don't insult me with parliamentary tricks," she said. "You didn't try to tinker with the Xaros during the Ember War. The Vishrakath and the Kesaht have the same goal—destroying us. They're just a bit wordier and more patient about it."

"Earth isn't ready for a fight on this scale," Garret said, tossing his arms up. "We don't even know the Kesaht's full strength and we're struggling to hold what we've got. We follow the treaty for a few dozen—"

"You mean murder Ibarran citizens."

"And I'll have the breathing room to deal with the Kesaht, who are the immediate threat. We'll run interference for you on New Bastion. Your navy's done a few raids for technology. You're not assaulting planets like the Kesaht or taking prisoners."

"No." Stacey stood up, and the dress making up her shell didn't sway as it should have to Garret's mind.

"Stacey. Listen to me. I can't throw the Terran Union into an all-out war with a faction I've publicly called traitors—"

"*I* am the only one loyal to Earth!" Stacey screamed.

"The only one loyal to all our future! Do you know what I've done? What was done to me? What I sacrificed to beat the Xaros? You are nothing, Garret!"

She pressed her hands to the side of her head and turned away from him. "I did it for us all," she said, her voice quavering. "Not for me. Never for me. I'd take it all back if I could." Stacey fell to her knees, rocking back and forth.

"Are you…" Garret reached for her, but stopped short. This was a hologram of her, nothing more.

"You don't know but it's my fault. My fault, my fault, my—"

Stacey vanished.

Garret stood in the silent chamber for a moment, then motioned for the glass door to open.

"Keeper and Laran," he said.

The two entered the room a moment later.

"You have her?" Garret asked.

"We've enough of a trace," Keeper said. "The next time she uses a Crucible, we'll know."

"She's insane," Garret said. "And if she's in this condition, then the entire Ibarra Nation is a threat to Earth…and the galaxy. I'll have the *Narvik* personnel eliminated soon. That should bring the rest of the galaxy around to our side against the Kesaht. Objections?"

"No, sir," Laran said.

Keeper didn't answer.

"Then your silence is consent," Garret said. "Laran, prepare a strike force. I want Stacey Ibarra dead. Her grandfather Marc is a dyed-in-the-wool son of a bitch, but he can be reasoned with."

"There's no guarantee he'd take over if we eliminate her," Laran said. "But I'm happy to find out."

"Get to it," Garret said.

Chapter 8

Roland stood in the box that first brought him to the common area of the prison. The walls of the tight confines vibrated slightly as it moved, reminding him of his armor's womb, and he wondered if he'd ever don the suit again. The modification to his neural system from the plugs was permanent, and the thought of spending the rest of his life in a cell with a tactile reminder of what he once was darkened his spirits more than anything.

I am armor, he thought. *I am fury. I will not fail.*

The box shuddered to a stop and there was a rush of air as the back panel came off. He turned around and saw a small room with a single table, two chairs, and an army officer with captain's bars.

"Chief Shaw." The captain walked over, hand out for

a shake, thumb cocked to the sky. "I'm Captain Finkledge, your JAG attorney."

Roland raised his shackled wrists as high as he could, but the captain drew his hand back before they could shake.

"Restraints in the courtroom?" Finkledge asked. "Clearly prejudicial. Especially this early in the discovery phase."

"This is court?" Roland shuffled toward the desk where the captain pulled a chair aside for him.

"It'll be done through holo," Finkledge waved a hand around his head. "Supreme Court ruled the current level of technology allows for the defendant to face their accuser without any loss of fidelity—though this is the first actual time it'll be used. Grounds for an appeal, at any rate."

"I'm not guilty of treason," Roland said. "I don't know why General Laran or anyone else—"

"That's what the trial's for," Finkledge said, smoothing out his well-tailored uniform.

Roland noted that his ribbons lacked any combat deployments or commendations for action in the field.

"Now I've examined the prosecution's evidence." The captain frowned. "And it will be very difficult for me to argue a defense that'll ensure you a positive outcome."

"Speak plainly…sir."

"Yes, you armor are the taciturn type." He sat on the

table and slapped a palm against the wood. "You're on video fighting for the Ibarras, a video I swear everyone in the solar system's seen. Perhaps the Ibarras forced you to fight? Threatened to hurt you?" Finkledge rolled his hand forward, encouraging Roland to go along with the suggestion.

"I volunteered. The Kesaht were attacking a colony. I couldn't sit idle."

"OK, do not say the V word. In fact, I'd rather you not even take the stand. So why don't we—"

"Do I strike you as a coward?"

"No! You armor are something else. But this isn't the time to be brave. This is a battle of wits, procedure, evidence. I'll stymie the prosecution with motions for so long that the war with the Kesaht will end and this...Ibarra kerfuffle will blow over. The judges will want this over with and maybe you can get off with time served and an other-than-honorable discharge."

"I will testify."

"Did you...do those plugs mess with your hearing?" Finkledge squinted at Roland. "Your best shot for—"

"You heard me."

The lawyer smacked his lips.

"And here I was planning to live on Mars for years. Ride out my service contract providing you the best defense possible and slide into one of the new firms popping up back on Earth. I might be home by Christmas at this rate." Finkledge removed a slate from his jacket and tapped out a message.

"There are law firms on Earth?"

"Two things always survive: cockroaches and lawyers…and we're about to start." He tucked the slate back into his coat. "I've been rehearsing this for days. My big moment—and yours. Of course."

Air shimmered around the table and a courtroom materialized: a long bench with three judges and a longer table beside theirs parallel to the bench but with a half-dozen military lawyers. Roland twisted around, and seated behind a rail was Gideon, Colonel Martel, and several men and women he'd never seen before. Judging by their uniformly bland clothes and stone faces, he guessed they were intelligence officers.

The holos shimmered as the room re-created another location around Roland and his lawyer. A grid shone beneath curved and irregular surfaces. The walls were pristine, but the holos of the people in the other room flickered with errors.

Martel beat a fist to his heart when he locked eyes with Roland. Gideon refused to look at his lance mate.

The middle judge rapped his gavel.

"Counsel, is there any change to the defendant's plea?"

Finkledge stood and took a deep breath, as if he were about to recite a soliloquy from Shakespeare for a captive audience.

"Your honors, my client has been removed from the front line, where he bravely—"

The judge whacked the gavel. The sound came through a speaker in the roof, at odds with what Roland "saw" via the holo field.

"Binary question," the judge said. "Change to the plea. Yes or no?"

"No change." The lawyer pulled his chair out with a squeak of wood against the floor and sat down, dejected.

"Prosecution?" asked the judge on the left.

A naval officer, her hair in a tight bun, stood up. "Does the defense object to entering the video of the defendant in the guise of the 'Black Knight' as evidence? Chief Shaw has already confirmed under oath that it is him."

Roland shook his head.

"No, your honor," Finkledge said.

"Then the state has a second video," she said and stepped out from behind the table.

Roland glanced at his lawyer, who frowned and bobbed his head from side to side.

The naval officer, Moore by her name tag, held a remote up to a wall and clicked it. Lights dimmed and a wide screen on the wall flickered to life. Camera footage of the *Scipio*'s makeshift brig came up, taken by a camera in the ceiling.

"So that's why…" Roland's hands gripped into fists.

Finkledge shushed him.

Roland watched as his entire conversation with the Ibarran armor soldier played out for the court, cutting off just before Gideon interrupted.

"Does the defense have any objection to this being entered as evidence?" the prosecutor asked.

"I…ugh…" Finkledge cleared his throat. "A moment with my client." He hit a button on the desk and the holo court vanished. "You might have mentioned this?"

"I didn't know," Roland said.

"We can make a motion to have it dismissed as you didn't consent to the recording…but you're on active duty and a reasonable expectation of privacy isn't really that *reasonable*." Finkledge tugged at his bottom lip.

The courtroom rematerialized.

"Counsel," the middle judge said as he scraped his gavel against his raised bench. "This is a binary decision."

"Then…I object." Finkledge stood ramrod straight. "That the prosecution can enter—"

"I know what you're getting at. File a rejoinder as to the admissibility." The judge leveled his gavel at the prosecutor. "Next witness."

Roland's lawyer sat down, visibly pale.

"Your honor," Moore said, motioning to the gallery, "the state calls First Lieutenant Isiah Gideon, Terran Armor Corps."

Gideon made his way to the witness stand and swore an oath on a hardback Bible.

"Lieutenant," Moore said, "please state your relationship to the defendant."

"I am Chief Shaw's lance commander."

"And how long have you known the defendant?"

"Since his initial training and selection at Ft. Knox." Gideon kept his gaze on the prosecutor, never looking at Roland. "He was assigned to my lance to respond to the Vishrakath incident on Barada. Following that—"

"The court can examine the official deployment records later," Moore said. "During the time he was under your direct supervision, did he ever express views contrary to his oath of service to the Terran Union?"

"While he was under my direct supervision...once," Gideon said. The prosecutors' table broke out into murmurs. "During operations on Thesius, he was overly concerned with the fate of Ibarran personnel while we were engaged in active combat with the Kesaht."

"And this struck you as disloyal?"

"The Ibarrans are a renegade element. Full of mutineers and traitors. Any sympathy for the enemy is tantamount to treason. That he fought beside them—in armor!—on Balmaseda is proof enough that Shaw chose to ally himself with—"

"Objection." Finkledge raised a hand meekly. "Speculation on the part of the witness."

"Sustained," a judge said. "Witness will keep his testimony limited to his direct observations."

The side of Gideon's face bearing Toth-claw scars twitched.

"Lieutenant," Moore said, "were you there when Chief Shaw was captured by the Ibarrans?"

"You mean when he defected?"

The judge rapped his gavel and leaned over the bench to a stenographer robot. "Strike that from the record," the judge said.

"Yes or no, lieutenant?" Moore asked.

"No."

"Did the defendant voluntarily go to speak with the Ibarran prisoner, one Alannah Morrigan?"

"That he did."

"Is there anything else you'd care to add that would shed light on the charges?"

Gideon slowly turned his gaze to Roland. The

lieutenant locked eyes with his lance mate and his mouth worked from side to side slowly. Gideon's mouth pulled into a sneer, then went neutral.

"I have nothing else to add."

"Your witness," Moore said and returned to her table.

Roland grabbed his lawyer by the elbow before he could stand up and shook his head quickly.

"But his testimony is—"

"Correct," Roland said. Finkledge tried to pull his arm free, but Roland's grip was like iron.

"Fine," the lawyer hissed and Roland released him. "No questions, your honor."

"Then the prosecution will enter the following recording into evidence," Moore said. "This is out of order from what was submitted earlier but is apropos to the last witness's testimony."

"OK," Finkledge said, leaning close to his client, "what *didn't* you do on camera?"

"Armor camera footage from Chief Jonas Aignar," Moore said as she opened a case and removed a data core the size of her fist. "This was recovered from the soldier's damaged suit on Oricon Prime. This should clear up any issue as to the nature of the defendant's entry into Ibarran service."

Finkledge wiped sweat from his brow.

"Relax," Roland said. "It's embarrassing for me…but

helpful."

"Something exculpatory? Maybe I can catch a break," Finkledge said.

Moore plugged the data core into a reader on the stenographer's table and a static-filled holo screen appeared between the judges and the defendant's and prosecutors' tables.

The curved walls of the Qa'Resh station appeared along with Roland's armor. Aignar's point of view was from behind and to the side of Roland's, and the two faced off against a smaller figure in the middle of a dais surrounded by rings of light. The figure, which Roland knew to be Stacey Ibarra, wasn't the pure metal shell that housed the Ibarran leader's mind, but was indistinct, like it was made out of smoke.

Roland's brow furrowed as the holo screen advanced a few seconds, then froze completely.

"There seems to be a playback issue." Moore tapped a control panel, then froze. The judges were stock-still, mouths stuck open. Roland twisted in his seat and saw Gideon half out of the courtroom, one foot locked in the air.

"What's wrong?" Roland asked.

"Great…lag." Finkledge tapped a red button on the edge of his desk. The holo field cracked, pixelating those around Roland before flickering on and off.

The holo courtroom fizzled away and the ceiling lights snapped on and off before finally going dark, plunging them into an abyss.

"That's…odd," the lawyer said.

A hidden door at the back of the room burst open and overly bright flashlights attached to the ends of gauss rifles flooded the holo suite.

"Prisoner! Hands up and freeze!" a guard yelled.

"Don't shoot me!" Finkledge ducked under the table and covered his head with his arms.

Roland complied with the instructions and didn't resist as his hands were jerked behind his back and cuffed. A pair of Rangers in skull masks led Roland out of the room.

"I'll get to work on that brief!" Finkledge called out as the door slammed shut.

Chapter 9

In a maintenance tunnel beneath Mars, a Ranger with broad shoulders stood at an intersection where a drone cart zipped by him on mag-lev tracks. The Ranger looked up and down the tunnel, glanced around the corner, and found he was alone. He leaned against the rough-hewn tunnel wall and lifted his visor.

Medvedev put a vape stick to his lips, inhaled deep, and tilted his face up to a grate near the ceiling. He blew out a fog into the metal slits.

The grate came loose with a shimmy and tumbled out. Medvedev shot forward and caught it before it could clatter against the ground.

"Sloppy," he said as a woman in a dust-clad bodysuit wiggled out of the hole.

"You know how tight it is in there?" Masha dropped

next to him and ran a hand through short, sweat-soaked hair. "And just how nimble do you think my little tootsies are?"

"Eighty-four seconds until the next cart." Medvedev reached up and set the grate back into place, then handed a shrink-wrapped bag to Masha. She ripped the plastic open and unfurled a set of work overalls.

The Ibarran spy tossed Medvedev a small black box and stepped into the overalls.

"Did you get it?" the legionnaire asked.

"I'm insulted. All I had to do was activate the implants Lady Ibarra left in the Terran armor's data core just as it connected to the network and run a mapping program before the cyber defenses could detect the intrusion—then hash scramble every trace I was in their system. The Earth pukes have updated their coding. Most of our backdoors are nailed shut." She took a small mirror out of a pocket and fussed with her hair.

"Where are our people from the *Narvik*?"

"Ulysses Tholis…I managed a scrape before the firewalls came back up. It's not just the *Narvik*. It's all our sleeper agents. The Black Knight's being held there too." She nibbled her bottom lip and gave the taciturn soldier puppy-dog eyes.

"No." Medvedev walked down the tunnel, catching Masha flat-footed. "We're not here for him."

Masha hurried after him, skipping alongside him like an overexcited toddler.

"But he's *our* hero. So what if he's not in the mission specifics? Lady Ibarra would welcome him back with open arms…I bet she'd grant you a boon."

Medvedev whirled around and jabbed a finger into her sternum.

"Ow," she said.

"He's not of the Nation."

"He's a Templar…we need them. The Lady needs them. If you help me get him out too, I'm sure they'll let you transfer back to the Legions. No more crimping my style with that sour puss of yours."

"You would have frozen to death on Koensuu without me," he said and then turned and walked off.

"Remind me to send Lieutenant Hoffman and his puppies a thank-you card before we leave Earth space…is that a yes?"

Medvedev flipped his visor down and stopped outside a metal door with a metal cross handle.

"There's no guarantee he'd come with us," he said. "He's pleaded not guilty to the treason charges."

"Charges he's not going to beat." Masha wagged a finger at him.

"Martyrs are useful."

"The Templar have Saint Kallen. They don't need her *and* Roland the Hanged. Or shot. Or spaced. What is the Terran punishment for treason?"

"We're not here for him." Medvedev pushed the door open a crack and glanced into the well-lit hallway beyond.

"No sense of gallantry," Masha huffed. "This mission is impossible. So what if we make it just a tad more impossible?"

"No."

"I hate you so much."

"No, you don't."

"A little! Phase two's shuttle arrives in eight hours. Be there."

Medvedev pushed the door open and went left. His partner went right.

****

Roland sat on a hard plastic bench, shifting his shoulders against his uncomfortable dress uniform and rubbing his wrists where the cuffs chafed against his exposed skin. The interior of his hood was getting stuffy, but the darkness reminded him of being in his armor's womb and didn't bother him.

"You're sure about this?" a female voice asked.

"Course I am. Are you?" said a man who sounded familiar.

"Just do it."

The hood came up and Roland blinked as his eyes adjusted. He was in a small holding cell. One of the Ranger guards stood outside the closed bars; the other was in the cell with him, unarmed.

The Ranger in the cell flipped up his visor and smiled at Roland.

"Jerry?" Roland asked.

"Told you he'd remember his old roommate." Jerry gave Roland a quick hug around the shoulders that the armor soldier couldn't return. "Haven't seen you in the flesh since the selection center in Phoenix…you've been busy."

"Was he really in an orphanage with you?" asked the woman Ranger from outside the cell. "He won't shut up about that. Says you still owe him like twenty bucks."

"Jerry? What the hell are you doing here? And…I think it was ten dollars."

"Debt's paid." Jerry leaned back against the bars. "Beer'd be on me if you weren't on trial and stuff. Gosh, told you going armor wasn't worth it."

"You don't remember us?" Valencia asked. "You pulled our asses out of the fire on Thesius. We appreciate the save."

"I'm sorry. I saw a lot of Rangers that day."

"Yeah, what a goat rope that was." Jerry shuddered. "I've had better drops and I've had worse."

"What happened back in the courtroom?" Roland asked.

"The network went belly up," Jerry said. "Protocol's to secure the prisoner—you, sorry—whenever so much as a fart happens out of sequence. We're heading back to the crater right now. Your trial's on hold until they figure out what the hell happened."

"Not like I had plans," Roland said. "You just came off the line. Why aren't you at an R&R center or at reconstitution training with your unit?"

"Genetic lottery." Valencia flipped her visor up and Roland traded smiles with her.

"We're true born." Jerry jerked a thumb at Valencia. "And Tholis rates only true born for the prison guards."

"Technically we're 'perimeter control specialists and personnel escorts,'" Valencia said, gesturing for air quotes.

"Because any proccie could somehow be tainted by the Ibarras," Roland said. "President Garret's circle of trust is pretty tight these days."

"Commo's tighter than Jerry's budget the night before payday," Valencia said. "Brass doesn't want anyone knowing there's a prison full of our proccies, Ibarran proccies…and two true-born armor."

"Morrigan." Roland perked up. "Is she OK?"

"Feisty." Jerry rubbed a thigh and winced. "She's with the Ibarrans. Leading prayers twice a day."

Valencia crossed herself and beat a fist against her heart.

"Catching up on old times is risky for you," Roland said. "What would this be? Fraternization?"

"What are they going to do?" Jerry asked. "Stick me in a hole on Mars and cut off all my comms? Look, Rolly-Polly—"

"Of all the things you could call me."

"You're not in your armor. I can get away with it. No one in the line units think you're a traitor."

"You were everywhere on Thesius," Valencia said. "We're not the only Marines who owe you our lives."

"It was my duty."

"This whole trial's a sham," Jerry said. "Most of us in the guard shacks think so. Major Lynch's a dick about it, but he's an officer, so what do you expect?"

"The guys assigned to the Ibarrans have been real squirrely lately," Valencia said, then lowered her voice. "You know what the Omega Provision is?"

"I do." Roland's mouth went dry. "Part of the Hale Treaty with the rest of the galaxy. No new proccies once the treaty was approved. They find any born after that, they're to be destroyed."

"All the proccies in your cellblock are OK," Jerry said. "Blood tests on all the Ibarran prisoners…something like nine out of ten are in trouble. Few from the original fleet that went AWOL, rest are on the chopping block."

"No." Roland shook his head. "We can't do this. President Garret won't. Murder is murder. Proccie or not."

"The brass have feelers out," Valencia said. "Looking for those in the guard force that are…that'll obey any order."

"No one on Earth knows." Roland raised his cuffed wrists. "Not anyone that can help. Phoenix has the whole situation on lockdown. By the time we…we need to get the word out."

"Back to your 'whole situation on lockdown' point," Jerry said. "No contact beyond the crater. Automated supply runs. We're all flushed down the memory hole."

"I have a lawyer." Roland lifted his head up. "He's got outside access."

"You trust him?" Jerry asked.

"It's not like we're burdened with options." Roland shrugged. "What are you two prepared to do?"

Jerry and Valencia traded a nervous look.

"Well," Jerry said, frowning, "Mr. Black Knight-armor-paragon-guy. We were hoping you'd have an idea."

"My trial isn't important. My actions are my responsibility and I regret nothing. The Ibarran prisoners didn't choose when or how they were born—they can't be punished for that. Keep an ear to the ground and find out what they're planning for the Ibarrans. Feed the news back to me and I'll get it out through Finkledge. See if public pressure can't do something…or…no."

"'No' what?" Valencia asked.

"Colonel Martel and the Templar won't stand for this," Roland said. "When they find out—"

The two Rangers slapped their skull facemasks into place and Jerry hurried out of the cell. The cart shuddered slightly and Roland felt it decelerate through the bench.

"Out of time," Jerry said. "Game faces back on."

"We'll figure out what we can," Valencia said. *"Ferrum corde."*

Roland leaned forward slightly and touched his fist to his chest.

"Ferrum corde."

****

Cha'ril moved a metal pick to one side of an empty wooden bowl. She stepped back and double-checked the angle, then clicked her beak and rolled the pick back a quarter inch.

"How did Mother do this?" she mumbled. Cha'ril glanced over her shoulder and saw a data slate on the frame around the cushions that formed the room's nest bed. She abandoned the table setting and hurried across the apartment. Living quarters for joined Dotari felt almost palatial after living so long inside her armor's womb and the bunks on the *Scipio*. The living quarters built into Mount Olympus struck her as being designed for comfort, which was not a concern of the Armor Corps that controlled the extinct volcano and the planet.

She swiped across several images of a traditional Dotari dining table, double-checking that every utensil was in the proper place. She looked up in horror when she realized the waste bowl for shells was on the wrong side.

The door opened with a swish and Man'fred Vo came in, holding a stack of wooden steamers by a twine handle.

"Cha'ril, your mighty hunter returns." He placed the steamers on the table.

"My joined," she said as she grabbed his face with one hand and turned his gaze to her. They touched foreheads and Cha'ril moved the shell bowl to the correct spot.

"I have such news." Man'fred Vo helped her sit down, then took his spot next to her, their shoulders touching as he unwrapped the steamers. "Such incredible news from the home world!"

"I have news as well," she said shyly. "But you go first."

"Father sent a priority message that just cleared the Crucible this morning. You know of the *Breitenfeld*'s deep-space mission?" he asked.

"The one the humans tried to keep secret? Of course."

"Uncle Lo'thar was there with Admiral Valdar. They found a Golden Fleet and brought it back to Dotari Prime. The phage," he said, plucking out a steaming gar'udda nut and feeding it to Cha'ril, "has been cured."

Cha'ril stopped chewing mid-bite, then looked over at their nest.

"The disease killing everyone—" he popped another nut into his mouth and cracked it loudly "—is in remission. My niece Trin'a is up and walking again. The Dotari on the Golden Fleet are all engineers and scientists and doctors—useless in a fight. You'd think they'd never seen a gauss cannon before. But they're all carrying the antibodies we need to beat the phage. Incredible, isn't it?"

"When did all this happen?"

"Perhaps a month or two ago." He clicked his beak. "The Council of Firsts are keeping things quiet until they're certain the phage is cured. Lo'thar told my father, of course, who wasn't supposed to tell me. And I'm not supposed to tell you. So you don't tell anyone either."

"Yes," she said, her eyes darting from side to side, "if the phage is cured, then the pheromone blockers will come back. There's no threat of extinction and…"

"Wait—are you angry with me?" the pilot asked. "You don't want to have our joining dissolved, do you?"

"Do…you?"

"No." Man'fred Vo kneeled beside Cha'ril and held both her hands. "I'm joined to the most beautiful Dotari I've ever seen. Everyone is so jealous. We're just beginning as a joined pair, but I would never petition to have this dissolved while we're still—"

"I'm pregnant."

"You…are?"

"My body's going through more hormonal shifts than I knew were possible." She grabbed a steamer, tossed away the lid, and smelled a plate full of baked grubs. "If you try to eat any of my *orikin*, you will lose a finger…and the blood tests all came back positive. I'm carrying your child."

She stuck her thumb talon into a grub and pulled it off with her beak, staring at her joined as she chewed.

"We need—" Man'fred Vo looked around. "We can't—not on *Mars*. I mean…you and I need to…" He fell back on his seat.

"You're taking this well," she said.

"My darling." He got up and hugged her. She kept munching on the *orikin*.

"I'm happy…" she said. "Just imagine if your father had sent that message a few weeks ago."

"I wouldn't be as happy as I am now," he said.

"Good. Good. Now I want you to go get me more of these grubs."

Chapter 10

Roland, his body braced in a push-up position, felt sweat dribble down his face and watched a drop fall from his nose onto an exercise mat.

"Halfway down and hold!" Adams called from the front of several ranks of prisoners, all in the front-leaning rest. There were groans and more than one curse directed toward the Strike Marine leading the physical-training session.

Roland's arms shook as he lowered his body even with his bent elbows. Fire burned in his muscles as Adams counted down from ten, then counted back up once she reached one. Most of the formation collapsed before she got to five again. Roland kept his focus, knowing he was conditioned well enough to endure.

"Recover!" Adams shouted as she popped her feet up next to her hands and sprang up. She winked at Roland as he got to his feet. He was the only one that managed to keep pace with her. Adams looked up at a snooper droid, then to the catwalk around the prison's perimeter.

"Group, atten-shun! Fall out, you weak bunch of pogues. Strike Marine PT isn't for any of you. Except one." Adams picked up a towel and wiped it across her forehead.

Roland put his hands on his hips and exhaled, tiny drops of sweat flying off his lips and into the air.

"Not bad, sir," the Strike Marine said as she walked up to him.

"You get the count?" he asked.

"The guards change shifts every four hours." Her eyes darted toward a pair of power-armored men on the catwalk, their faces hidden behind skull visors. "Those two aren't line troopers. See the way they walk? Stiff legs—normal for someone new to frontline gear and real Rangers don't prop their weapons over their waist. They should have the stock tucked into their shoulder."

"What about the guards on the Ibarrans?"

"We get glimpses," she said. "They're all in Ranger gear with no rank or name tags. The ones assigned to the Ibarran cellblock move like Strike Marines or Rangers. Guess they think we're less of a threat. Though any Devil Dog wearing GI Joke equipment has got to piss them right off."

"I'm sure if any of those Rangers could've fit their

head in the jar to pass Strike Marine quals, they would've done so," Roland said.

"Strike Marines don't need Halloween masks to be scary," Adams grumbled. "We're quiet professionals."

"Group six, report to the mess section," boomed through loudspeakers. "Group six, report to the mess section."

"Thought chow wasn't for another hour," Adams said.

"Odd," Roland said as he walked toward the center of the cellblock and Adams kept pace. "Well, I don't want to miss my reconstituted bowtie pasta drowned in oil."

"Might be turkey cutlets." Adams shrugged.

Roland got to the line forming at the food dispenser and waved enlisted soldiers ahead of him in line.

"How does chow work for you tanks?" Adams asked.

Roland gave her a sideways glare. "What did you call me?"

"The armor. I meant the armor. Sorry." She lowered her head slightly.

"Amniosis has all the nutrition we need. Eating actual food is almost a treat these days. Looks like I'll get used to it." Roland let Adams step in front of him and he took his spot in the back of the line.

He held his palm up to a reader and a drawer opened

with a ding. A single tray with steaming mashed potatoes and what looked like a shoe insert drenched in gravy waited for him. He took the tray out and felt a piece of paper underneath the left side.

Keeping his composure, Roland sat down next to Adams. Boucher set two cups of water and one of what looked like weak orange juice next to Roland's tray.

"Bug juice is a bit off today. Sorry, sir," Boucher said.

"Thank you." Roland took a bite of the potatoes and glanced up. A snooper drone drifted overhead.

"So we were on the *Kid'ran's Gift* doing a sweep and clear in case any banshees were still alive," Adams said. "And Rocha decides to eat one of the Dotari's gar'udda nuts right off the tree. Jackass breaks out in hives and Booker had to jab him with an antihistamine."

"I need some top cover," Roland said quietly and tucked his fingertips next to the side of his tray where he'd felt the paper.

Adams' head bobbed from side to side in thought, then she got up and stood behind Roland. Hooking a finger into the elastic band holding her hair in a bun, she pulled it away, shook her hair out, and leaned over Roland, pressing her chest to his back and letting her hair drape over his face.

"Can I get an autograph?" she asked a bit too loudly.

Roland slid the paper out and recognized Jerry's

handwriting on the small slip of paper: OP 72HRS.

Roland brought his hand holding the paper past his mouth, then gave Adams a pat on the cheek. She pulled away and sat back down, working her hair back into a tight bun with practiced ease.

Boucher stared at the two, his mouth agape.

"He'll let you have one too," she said.

Roland cut an end off what smelled like Salisbury steak and took a bite.

"You get it?" Adams asked.

Roland nodded.

"Where'd it go?"

Roland chewed harder.

"Oh. Now what?"

Roland took a sip of water and swallowed with some difficulty.

"I have a court date in the morning," he said. "That might be enough time."

Chapter 11

Finkledge raised his arms wide as Roland entered the holo room.

"Hell of a time for a system update, eh?" the lawyer asked as Roland sat down. "Interrupts proceedings, wastes all sorts of time. Another ding against telepresence court and ammunition for an appeal, at least."

"I want to testify," Roland said.

Finkledge looked at Roland like he'd just grown a second head.

"Sorry, did you just say you want to torpedo your defense? You don't even have to get on the stand to plead the Fifth. The prosecutor asks me if you're willing to take the stand and I get to 'nope' that idea right into—"

"You heard me."

Finkledge squeezed the bridge of his nose.

"The prosecution hasn't even rested their case. You can't testify today unless you're a witness for the prosecution. You know how that looks? The defendant providing hostile testimony against *himself*? This is courtroom 101 stuff. As your legal counsel, I strongly advise against this."

"Noted. Let's go." Roland motioned to the small control panel on the edge of the desk next to Finkledge.

"If you were a Marine, I might try to explain this to you in crayon, but you're armor. Let me try this again." The lawyer took a deep breath. "If you—"

Roland snapped out of his chair and grabbed Finkledge by the wrist, ignoring shouts from guards that burst through the door and his own lawyer's rather feminine cries. Roland slapped Finkledge's hand against the controls and the courtroom materialized around them.

"You tell them or I will," Roland said and let the other man go.

"Counsel?" the center judge asked.

"I will send you a very strongly worded letter about this," Finkledge hissed, "explaining just how stupid this is. Mostly so that I don't get disbarred." He went to the judges' bench and two of the prosecutors hurried over.

Roland looked at the gallery and saw Colonel Martel, Tongea, and General Laran in the front row. The prosecutors returned to their desk, buzzing with excitement.

"Is the court to understand the defendant wishes to testify…now?" the center judge asked.

"Yes, your honor," Roland said.

"Your counsel has made you aware of your rights?" asked the judge on the left. "Specifically about not incriminating yourself?"

"I am aware."

"Let that be reflected in the record," the center judge said and looked to the witness stand, which was an incorporeal projection for Roland. "Can the holo techs do something about this?"

The room froze, dematerialized, then snapped back into place with Roland sitting in the witness stand. His table clipped through the judge's bench and Finkledge phased through the judge's bench like a ghost.

"Counsel," the judge said, waving his gavel at Finkledge, "are you trying to peek up my robe?"

"No." The lawyer stepped out of the bench and held his hands up awkwardly. He looked at his desk beside the prosecutors', which was now a holographic projection. "I'm not sure what I should…"

"Stand in the corner for all we care," said the judge on the right. "Just don't get in the way."

A guard from Roland's location came over carrying a Bible. Roland swore on it, and the guard carried the other chair over to the defense's holographic bench and set it in place for Finkledge, who sat down quickly, trying to preserve what little remained of his pride.

Moore stood up and smiled at Roland, a glint in her eyes like a shark scenting blood in the water.

"Chief Shaw," she said, "please tell the court the nature of your time with the rebel Ibarran faction."

"Obj—no?" Finkledge was halfway out of his chair when Roland stopped him with a raised hand.

Roland looked at Colonel Martel. "The Omega Provision is in effect," Roland said. "Part of the Hale Treaty. The Ibarrans we captured on Thesius are two days away from—"

"Stop him!" General Laran shouted.

"Being murdered for no other reason than being born the wrong way!" Roland projected over the chaotic din in the courtroom and all three judges banging their gavels.

Finkledge ran for the real table where Roland sat and lunged for the control panel. Roland kicked the table leg and sent it skidding out of Finkledge's reach. The lawyer tripped over his own feet and hit the ground.

"All the Ibarrans from the *Narvik* are there," Roland said to Martel. "We are Templar. We cannot let—"

The holo courtroom fizzled away in static.

Finkledge rolled over, his meager ribbon racks torn

loose from his uniform. "Well...maybe you bought yourself a mistrial."

"It's not about me," Roland said. "It's about preventing a tragedy. Stopping a civil war that our enemies want."

"Unless it relates to your case, just stop talking." The lawyer got up as a pair of guards entered the room. "You say too much, I'll end up in whatever hole they've got you in too."

A guard slammed a hood over Roland's head.

****

Colonel Martel stood with his hands resting on the wooden beam separating the gallery from the rest of the courtroom. General Laran was a few chairs away, her gaze locked on the empty witness stand where they'd just seen Roland's holo projection.

The judges and prosecutors were huddled together at the bench, the judges' tone on the verge of shouting.

"Is it true?" Martel asked the general.

"I don't know where he got that information." Laran crossed her arms over her chest.

"But it is true," Tongea said. "The Ibarrans are going to be executed. No trial. No due process—"

"The Hale Treaty *is* due process," Laran said. "There are factors you don't understand."

"They don't matter," Martel said.

Laran's gaze snapped to the head of the Templar Order.

"Martel, I want all the soldiers of *my* Armor Corps in Carius Auditorium in one hour. No suits. Am I clear?"

"Yes, ma'am." Martel nodded.

She spun around and pushed through the nervous-looking representatives from the intelligence division.

"It's a trap," Tongea said.

"She's no fool," Martel said. "She trusts that our honor is greater than our pride."

"No question there. Order the recall?"

"Do it…Templar to wear their tabards and sword belts. I need to visit my armor first."

Chapter 12

Aignar reached up and caught a baseball with a gloved hand. He grabbed the ball with the other, felt the tight leather against his touch, and worked his grip harder. He reached back and threw it to a towheaded boy, who miffed the catch and went chasing after the ball as it bounced through short grass.

He flexed his toes, the feel of sweat brought on by the summer heat bringing a smile to his face as—

Knock knock

Aignar jerked awake and fumbled with the blanket covering him. Both his arms ended in metal caps just below the elbows and no matter how many years of practice he had, getting out of bed was always an ordeal.

"Aignar! It's me," Cha'ril said through the door.

Aignar sat up and swung his too-short legs over the side of the bed. He fit the end of his stump into a receiver in a boot and pressed it home with a snap. His other amputated leg clicked into the other boot, the cybernetic foot already inside.

The knocking intensified.

Aignar wanted to shout for the Dotari to be patient, but he couldn't. He'd removed his false jaw when he went to sleep and deactivated his throat speaker.

"Aig-*nar!*" Cha'ril banged harder.

He went to a pair of holsters fastened to his desk where his hands waited for him. He jabbed his right nub into the holster and it locked against the cap, his anger growing as the Dotari kept knocking. He hit the closed metal fist of his prosthetic against the handle and the door flew open.

"Fina—" Cha'ril stared at Aignar's face, his bottom jaw missing, the gap covered by a tight veil against his flesh.

"I…I forgot. I'm sorry."

He rolled his eyes and pointed the stump of his other arm to the well-made—and empty—bed where Roland used to sleep. Cha'ril sat down. Plugging in his other arm, Aignar removed a box from his desk, unlatched it with a metal finger, and flipped the top up.

Cha'ril, the normally gray skin around her eyes flush with blood to the point of being maroon, turned away from her lance mate.

Aignar removed the veil and snapped his prosthetic jaw into place. He squeezed buttons on either side of his throat speaker and it came on with a whine.

"Are the Kesaht attacking?" he asked.

"No."

"Is something on fire?"

"No."

"Then you had better have a damn good reason for waking me up at…oh dark thirty. Don't Dotari need to sleep too?"

"Roland's been arrested for treason," she said.

Aignar's brow furrowed in confusion. He pecked at a data slate, then squinted at a message.

"Gideon has to testify. He left me in charge," Cha'ril said. "There's a message from him with a time stamp of—"

"I see it." Aignar pushed the slate away. "Did you hear anything else? A specific reason?"

"His fighting for the Ibarrans on Balmaseda isn't enough?"

"Roland was fighting the Kesaht, not us…I swear nothing happens this early in the morning."

"Do you think the Ibarran we rescued on that moon had something to do with this?" she asked. "Roland was angry about the Omega Protocol after he spoke with her."

"I don't think the Omega deal is law…officially. We shouldn't talk about him."

"He's our lance mate. He's in jail. You wouldn't shut

up about him when the Ibarrans had him. Why don't you care anymore?"

"Because courtrooms, that's why. I don't know how the Dotari legal system works. Is there a lot of stick fighting and spitting involved? Don't tell me. I've had enough cultural enrichment for a while. We are witnesses, my Dotty friend. If we talk about the case and muddle details, it's all sorts of bad for justice. And us."

"Then why weren't we called to go with Gideon?" she asked.

"Beats me…why now, though?"

The color around Cha'ril's eyes faded away and her quills stiffened slightly.

"I think it's the Omega Provision," she said. "I was searching around the Internet, and there's nothing on them anywhere. Humans are so bad at hiding things. You don't want the enemy to know something, do a deception operation. At least then there's a moose-hole for people to get lost in."

"Moose?"

"Something of interest that can't be found anywhere? It must be very important to hide."

"If the Omegas are a real thing," Aignar shrugged, "then there are some implications."

"The Ibarrans must have millions of procedural

individuals that are in violation. What will the Terran Union do?"

Aignar punched the side of a small refrigerator and the door popped open. He took out a chilled smoothie with a straw, then worked a knuckle against the side of his jaw. It snapped open a half inch.

"What will the Dotari do?" he asked.

She clicked her beak in frustration and picked at the bedsheets.

"The older generation will accept destroying the Ibarrans," she said, "because tolerating their existence means the end of the Hale Treaty…probably all-out war with the rest of the galaxy. Dotari civilization was caste-based for centuries. We had to be. The voyage from our home world to Takeni—where I was born—was difficult. Every colonist was ranked according to their usefulness to the fleet. When a ship's systems failed, those at the bottom of the list were sacrificed for the whole—sacrifice a few dozen or lose tens of thousands because no one wanted to die? The void was a harsh place to make such decisions.

"We carried on the tradition once Takeni was settled. Famine? Guess who didn't eat. No room in the bunker during a radiation storm? We knew who'd be left outside. To sacrifice a part to save the whole is very much a part of who the Dotari are…who we used to be."

"What changed?"

"Humans." Cha'ril ran the claw on her thumb along her other fingernails, making small clicking sounds. "You brought a very old form of morality to Takeni when the *Breitenfeld* saved us from the Xaros. 'Women and children first.' Such a notion…but it saved my life. A team of Strike Marines proved they were willing to die for this belief, and once we were resettled on Hawaii and we found ourselves living on a planet with plenty of space and plenty to eat…"

"Things changed."

"My father was a high-lister, my mother a much lower caste. I was destined to go no farther than my mother, but then Ari and Caas…"

"The Dotari armor that fought at the last battle of the Ember War," Aignar said. "They have statues in Armor Square."

"They were orphans. Orphans weren't even on the ranking lists. Any Dotari adult that adopted an orphan lost rank instantly and they'd never gain it back."

"Harsh."

"Takeni was not suitable for us. Our population was slowly declining even after we made landfall, but that place doesn't matter anymore. We have our home world again." She clicked her beak in a gesture Aignar knew meant frustration.

"But Ari and Caas, the orphans, they volunteered to join the armor program once that Doctor Eeks of yours figured out a way for us to take the plugs." She touched the back of her head, her thumb talon making a *tink* against the metal. "For orphans to be there at the final battle, to strike the death blow against the Xaros Masters…it brought the old ways into question again. How many worthy Dotari had been thrown away because of a list?"

"Dotari your age won't agree with killing the Ibarrans to stop a war?"

"I was a worthless baby to the Firsts," she said. "My mother and I were left behind to the *noorla*, the Dotari twisted into Xaros shock troops, but human Strike Marines decided I was worth saving—for no other reason than I was just a baby. *I* do not agree with the Omega Provision. Neither does Man'fred Vo."

"Haven't seen your husband—joined, whatever—in a spell."

"Yes, he needs to speak to you." Cha'ril touched her stomach briefly, then set her hands in her lap.

"Wait. Why?"

"Because you were our *ushulra*."

"What does that mess have to do with…wait, are you pregnant?"

Cha'ril's face lit up. "You know the tradition?"

Aignar slammed his smoothie down so hard the top popped off and grayish liquid splashed onto his table and wrist.

"You've been joined for like…ten minutes and he already knocked you up!"

"There was some knocking. Coffee beans are incredible for the libido."

"I got my wife pregnant during our honeymoon and it was a—it wasn't bad because we got Jonathan. But we were not ready to be parents. Divorce is a miserable thing and—wait…" Aignar shook liquid off his hand and stopped to collect his thoughts. "I'm happy for you both," he said. "Very happy." He lifted a metal finger up, then pressed it against the side of his nose.

"I'm on medical leave until I lay," she said. "So you're in charge of the lance."

"I'm in charge of myself. I think I can manage that…what happens with your…laying?"

"The egg will fully develop in another three weeks. Then, my cloaca will—"

"Skip that part," Aignar said. "Are you coming back?"

"The egg will remain in a crèche until my term of service is complete, then it will be hatched. It's a long time to wait, but at the end…"

"I didn't know Dotari could do that. Humans have

forty weeks, then that baby's coming whether you're ready or not."

"Man'fred Vo is very excited. I wish I could tell Roland."

"The look on his face would be precious. We are all still Iron Dragoons, even if we're cast to the four winds." Aignar took a sip of his breakfast.

"I report to the Dotari hospital in a few hours. I need something from you." She stood up and opened his closet.

"What, exactly?"

She sniffed at the clothes, then pulled a box off a shelf. Inside were the ceremonial robes he wore when he officiated her and Man'fred Vo's ceremony.

"Aha!" She tucked the box under her arm. "It's for my nest. For good luck. Are you going to fight me on this?"

"Nope! Take it. You want more of my laundry?"

"This is all I need. I will send you pictures of the delivery, as is human custom."

"Your egg! Just your egg. When it's all clean and pretty-looking. If you send me pictures of—I don't even want to imagine—it'll be weird between us forever. Understand?"

"Tell Gideon for me."

"Sure. Can't wait to explain all this to him. I'm sure it'll go over like a lead balloon."

"Goodbye, *ushulra*."

"Congratulations." Aignar raised his cup in a toast and Cha'ril left. "Kids," he said, setting the glass back down. "Either they're getting married or getting arrested. It's like I never left the Rangers."

****

Lieutenant Commander (retired) Freeman lugged a suitcase down a berthing hallway, his eyes passing over number plates until he reached 137. With a sigh, he pressed a fob against the reader. The door jittered open slightly.

"Come on…" He whacked the fob against the doorframe and the door slid open to a dark room.

"Nothing works on Mars," he mumbled and the lights popped on. A blond woman in work overalls sat with her legs crossed on his bed. She gave him a come-hither wave.

Someone pushed Freeman forward so hard he pitched forward onto the carpet.

"Sorry," the woman said as Freeman heard the door shut.

He looked back and a monster of a man set his luggage into a closet.

"What the hell is this?" Freeman asked.

"I'm Masha, he's Medvedev, and we're here for your

kidneys," she said.

Freeman froze.

"Stop it," the big man said.

"You're supposed to play it up. Tell him the bathtub's already full of ice. You are just no fun at all," Masha said.

Freeman drew in a deep breath.

In a flash, Medvedev pulled a pistol from under his shirt and leveled it at Freeman's forehead.

"No fun, but he is dead serious," the woman said. "We're not here for your kidney, Maxwell Freeman, Terran Union Navy—retired. Supposed to be retired. You had a nice corner-office job in Saint George working for an automated construction company until a week ago when you were suddenly and inexplicably recalled to active duty."

"How do you—"

Medvedev motioned to a chair across from Masha. Freeman looked down the barrel, then crawled into the seat.

"We know plenty, Mr. Freeman. We know about your time on the *Europa* during the Ember War and we don't blame you for choosing a quieter life after all that was over—not that then Admiral Garrison ever wrote you stellar performance reports."

"That man was a tyrant," Freeman said, wagging a finger.

"We also know why you were recalled from

retirement," Masha said. "Seems you're true born, and that puts you in a unique position in Earth's current political situation."

"Breaking and entering. Kidnapping. Now you've violated the Naissance Act by even discussing how I was born. Who are you two and what do you even want from me? Should be pretty obvious I'm nobody," Freeman said.

"Don't sell yourself so short. You're very important, Mr. Freeman." Masha leaned forward and cupped her chin. "Especially for a particular someone."

Medvedev tossed a data slate onto Freeman's lap displaying pictures of him with a woman his same age hiking together, selfies with the Phoenix skyline in the background, her in swimwear floating in an inflatable tube.

"Salina? Do you know where she is? What happened to her?" Freeman asked.

"She's here on Mars." Masha perked up. "Such a story between you two. Meet at a conference a few months ago. Whirlwind romance. Then she just vanishes off the face of the Earth."

"Senior Chief Salina Humboldt was 'reassigned' to Mars," Medvedev said. "The Terran government found reason not to trust her."

"You mean our government?" Freeman looked at the big man, then to Masha. "Oh no...oh no...this can't be happening. You're…" His voice fell to a whisper.

"…Ibarrans, aren't you?"

"We're here to save your Salina," Masha said. "Earth will never let her out of the hole they stuck her in. She can either rot in prison to the end of her days…or you can help us get her out."

Freeman looked at the data slate and a smile crept across Masha's face.

"You won't…you won't hurt anyone?" he asked.

"No." Masha made a face. "If there's any sort of an…incident…during our operation, then there's all this back-and-forth of blood for blood and 'you broke my stuff now pay for it.' Who needs that?"

"Help us and you can go with her," Medvedev said.

"To where?"

"Home. Her real home," Masha said. "Navarre is a lovely place. Beaches, fine mountain views. You'd think you were in British Columbia. The two of you will love it. Or go back to St. George and live in your tiny little apartment. Alone. Forever."

"You're serious?" Freeman asked. "You can do this?"

Medvedev holstered his pistol.

"We are duly sworn agents of the Ibarra Nation," Masha said. "Of course you can trust us. Lady Ibarra sends her respects and—" she reached under a pillow and brought out two devices—one identical to his key fob, the other a tooth "—she sends the most wonderful toys. The key fob has an IR broadcaster and the tooth has a quantum dot communicator."

"I don't understand," Freeman said.

"You have been assigned to the brand-new Crucible gate over Mars," Masha said. "As a true born and as one with a history of distinguished service on a void-ship bridge, you'll be working the command center."

"OK..." Freeman shrank into his chair as Medvedev pulled a pair of dental forceps from his pocket.

"She'll explain the rest after the not-so-fun part is over," Medvedev said.

Chapter 13

A diamond-shaped drone flitted over between blood red boulders, hesitated just above pink sand, the repulsors stirring up a weak cloud, then shot straight up. A gauss barrel emerged from the center of the drone and it swung around.

A single bullet sliced through the thin air and blew through the drone with a muffled crack of plastic.

Aignar bent his gauss cannon arm at the elbow and scanned the surrounding field of rocks that reached up to his armor's waist servos.

"Range complete," sounded in Aignar's ears. He turned his helm to his lance commander.

"Sir, that was only table II. We not doing table VI?" Aignar asked.

"Range control shut us down," Gideon said. "General recall notice for all Armor. Dragonfly's inbound."

Aignar cycled gauss shells out of his cannons and cut the power to the magnetic coils.

"The Kesaht hit something big?" Aignar asked.

"Recall code is magenta…not diamond. Admin issues," Gideon said.

"Must be some issue to cancel a live fire. There's a whole squadron on field exercises in the next valley." Aignar scanned the horizon for the dust cloud that would signal the Dragonfly's approach. "Cha'ril's going to end up missing one heck of a slideshow."

"Pregnancy." Gideon strode up a small hill, one foot on the crest. "Of all the things to take a soldier off the line. You fought to get back to this after your injury."

"Cha'ril's got a bit less of a recovery period to look forward to than what I went through." Aignar flexed his armor's hands. "One hopes. You have an idea what the recall's about?"

"There's a reckoning," Gideon said. "We can't put it off any longer and there's no perfect solution. You know the Omega Provision."

"Only what Roland mentioned. He got it from the Ibarras, so that makes it suspect. Bird on approach. 107 degrees." He pointed to a shimmer in the atmosphere in the distance.

"Acquired. Good eye. Pickup positions." Gideon

stepped aside, turned away from the oncoming aircraft, and held his arms out perpendicular to his shoulder. Aignar matched his posture a few yards to one side.

"IR lock with bird confirmed," Aignar said.

"What Roland knows of the provision is…correct," Gideon said.

Inside his womb, Aignar's stunted legs kicked out in surprise.

"I only know Colonel Hale from the stories," Aignar said, "but agreeing to Omega doesn't sound like something he would do."

"It was added without Hale's knowledge. Those who agreed to it obviously never thought we'd have to enforce it," Gideon said. "And I believe that's what this recall is for."

"Now? We're going to carry it out right now?" Aignar's head locked back as the Dragonfly swooped over them and massive clamps locked against their armor, hoisting them into the air and tucking them beneath the aircraft's forward fuselage.

"It's possible," Gideon said. "Will you do it?"

Aignar hesitated.

"It's not an easy decision at first," Gideon said. "Ibarras' proccies should be just like ours, but they're not. You saw Stacey Ibarra on Oricon. You read Roland's report of when he saw her lose control on Navarre. What kind of person is she?"

"She's insane," Aignar said. "Clearly insane."

"And what kind of an army would the insane create?" Gideon asked.

Aignar thought back to Balmaseda, where they encountered Ibarran civilians that had a near fanatical devotion to Stacey Ibarra.

"While we fought the Kesaht on Oricon," Gideon said, "Ibarran sleeper agents took over our fleet's artillery ships and fired on the Kesaht. Ibarra triggered them with a phrase planted deep in their psyche…every one of them died soon after the battle. Again, as Stacey Ibarra designed."

"Even if all their proccies are tainted, do they have to be destroyed?" Aignar asked.

"They are fanatics. Loyal by design and not by choice. Stacey Ibarra would not risk free agency in her soldiers. They cannot be reasoned with."

"I understand you, sir. It's just the Ibarras seem interested in tending to their own garden. If we go all-in on the Omega Provision, we're declaring total war on them. They're no pushovers in a fight either." Aignar received an alert from Chief Henrique, the lance's maintenance chief, that he and Gideon were to separate from their armor as soon as they landed. He activated the shutdown sequences for his targeting computers.

"The rest of the galaxy won't tolerate the Ibarras," Gideon said. "No matter the Terran Union's position. The aliens on New Bastion have little to no concept of separate factions within other members. They had hundreds—if not thousands—of years of unity before the Ember War ended, and most of them never trusted humanity, even after we killed off the Xaros for them. They'll hold us to choosing between New Bastion and the Ibarras. It'll be war with one side or the other."

"Then there's the Kesaht," Aignar said. "My son's eleven years old. I don't want him to grow up in a world at war. I want him to worry about a mortgage. Soccer games, taxes—not if the Vishrakath will shell his foxhole…not fearing his own children will be taken by the Kesaht."

"If we side with New Bastion against the Ibarras, it will end quickly," Gideon said. "Then the Kesaht will fall. All it will cost us is to put down rabid dogs."

"They're still people," Aignar said.

"We kill a few hundred now or lose millions in a fight against the rest of the galaxy in wars that will never end. Every soldier prays for peace. Templar or not."

"I miss fighting the Vishrakath on Cygnus. It was simple there. See an upright ant? Shoot an upright ant. Don't get shot in the process. Though I did screw up that last part."

The Dragonfly crested over a ridge and Mount

Olympus came into view. Running lights from shuttles and cargo haulers danced around the dead volcano. Massive metal doors in the miles-high escarpments rang as the volcano slid open and the Dragonfly flew across the red plain.

****

Gideon stood in an armament bay as servo arms whirled around his armor, removing ammo packs and blowing out tufts of red dust from the grooves and bends in the plates.

"Iron Dragoon," came from behind. He stepped out of the bay and stood face-to-face with armor two feet taller than his own, the helm bristling with antennae, the plates perfectly pristine and an oversized single-barreled gauss cannon on the arm. The Terran Armor Corps crest glinted with gold inlays across the breastplate.

"General Laran." He beat a fist to his armor in salute.

"I need soldiers ready to kill Ibarrans," she said. "Kill them…and their allies."

"Traitors deserve only one fate." Gideon felt his blood rush with excitement.

"I knew you were true. What of Aignar?"

"He…may hesitate," Gideon said. "I've not trained him well enough. The Templar—"

"That's enough. I've identified a number of other armor that know what loyalty means, and you're to lead them," she said. "Task Force Iconoclast."

"When and where?"

"You'll report to the *Ardennes* soon. I have another task for you in the meantime," Laran said.

"The Ibarrans' foot soldiers can die. They don't concern me. What of their armor? What do you want of them?" Gideon asked.

"If they surrender, they surrender. If not, you'll treat them as any enemy. Terminate them. And Stacey Ibarra…dead or alive. Makes no difference to me. Come…*Captain* Gideon."

Chapter 14

Aignar worked his way past armed security posted outside Carius Auditorium. He flashed an ID card strapped flush to his left forearm to an MP waiting outside a tall wooden door.

"Biometric authorization." The MP held a slate out to Aignar.

Aignar looked at the palm reader, then to the MP, and then let his metal hand flop against the slate.

"Oh…" The MP checked Aignar's ID card, then opened the door. "Apologies, sir."

"One of those days," Aignar muttered as he entered the auditorium, self-conscious of the clumsy clomp of his boots as he made his way to the back row that had a few empty seats. He got a good view of the backs of the heads of the hundreds of soldiers present. All had armor plugs in their skull. All stood.

To one side of the seating area was a swath of white tunics, the Templar. They made up nearly a tenth of those present, with a few of the order spread out across the rest of the auditorium, adherents keeping close to their lance who were not fully Templar.

Carius Auditorium was cavernous. The stage at the front was dwarfed by a massive holo screen. Unit crests as tall as a man for active armor squadrons and regiments took up the left wall. Crests the size of shields for individual lances filled the right wall, and all were draped in black cloth for lances lost in battle.

The auditorium could hold up to five thousand, slightly more than every armor soldier in the Corps. Deployments and operations kept much of the armor away from Mars, but Aignar estimated nearly three thousand were present—a significant percentage of the Terran Union's Armor.

On the stage, General Laran stood behind a lectern.

"Armor," she said, "I am honored to be amongst so many of you. The Union needs us. All of us. Earth and her colonies stand at a crossroads. The consequences of our choice have not been as dire since the day Colonel Carius called armor to the final battle against the Xaros."

Aignar sidestepped down a row of seats to a gruff-looking man with short blond hair. His left shoulder bore a black Teutonic cross on a yellow field for his lance insignia.

The man turned slightly to Aignar and he saw captain's bars. The captain looked like he was about to admonish Aignar for being tardy, but a glance at Aignar's prosthetic hands seemed to calm him.

"A bit late," Aignar said quietly. "Had to put my face on."

"You've not missed much," the captain said. "Gershwin. Eisenritter lance."

"Aignar with the Iron Dragoons."

The other three members of Captain Gershwin's lance leaned forward to get a look at Aignar.

"You must know the Black Knight," Gershwin said. "Is he here?"

"What? You haven't heard?"

A shush came from a few rows away and Gershwin turned his attention back to the general.

"…why these orders are so important." She touched a button on the lectern and a wall of text appeared on the holo screen above her.

"General Order 99," she read, "as signed by President Garret of the Terran Union, hereby declares that all procedural entities created after the ratification of the Hale Treaty are not protected by the laws of the Terran Union and possess none of the rights enshrined in our Constitution."

A murmur spread through the assembled armor and Aignar felt a cold pit forming in his stomach.

"As such," Laran added an edge to her tone, "any such entities in violation will be destroyed by Terran Union forces on contact." She whacked a data slate against the lectern to quiet the room.

"There are a number of sub clauses that you can review on your own time," Laran said. "We are soldiers of the Terran Union, and we will obey this order—"

"We will not!" Colonel Martel stepped up onto the stage, his Templar tabard and his sword's brass scabbard gleaming in the lights. "This order is a violation of the Union's Constitution and is illegal. We serve to protect humanity, not cull those the rest of the galaxy fears."

The auditorium was deathly silent as the Corps commander and the Templar leader squared off.

Gershwin raised the flap on a breast pocket and light glinted off a lens.

"Stand down, Colonel," Laran said. "You have your orders."

"I will fight the Ibarrans on the battlefield," Martel said. "I will slay any that raises a hand against the Terran Union, but I will not murder anyone for how, or when, they were born."

"Then it's a mutiny?" General Laran spat. "Who else is with him? Who else will refuse to follow the orders of your commander?"

Martel grabbed the hilt of his sword. Almost as one, every Templar in the room drew their blades with the hiss of metal on metal. Martel flipped his sword tip down and drove it into the stage.

"I'm with him!" someone shouted from the non-Templar crowd.

"As am I!"

Laran touched her forearm screen and the back wall opened with a groan of hydraulics. Three suits of armor stood in a chamber, and Aignar's heart fell as he recognized Gideon on the left.

The center armor's rotary cannon swung up and locked against its shoulder, but the barrels didn't spin.

"Then you are all under arrest," Laran said.

MPs rushed out from behind the stage, shock batons in hand. Aignar's heart ached as the first rushed toward Colonel Martel. Aignar was certain the man would fight...but the Templar raised his hands in surrender, leaving his sword embedded in the stage.

"She planned this," Gershwin muttered. "All of it."

The MPs slapped cuffs on Martel and frog-marched him behind the stage. Tongea and other senior members of the order were arrested. None of the Templar resisted.

Aignar's breathing quickened as anger flooded his mind.

"This isn't right." He stepped away from Gershwin, but the captain grabbed him by the collar and yanked him back.

"Stop," Gershwin said. "What will you accomplish if you join them?"

Aignar lowered his head to his chest and looked at his metal hands. "If I'm not armor…then I'm nothing," Aignar said.

Gershwin closed the flap on his pocket and covered up the camera lens.

"Martel is honor-bound, stubborn as an old mule," Gershwin said. "But he's no fool. And you don't have to wear Templar white to agree with him."

"Then what do we do?"

"Not every battle's won with gauss cannons and fury," the Eisenritter said. "Stay quiet. Wait…and keep your mouth shut, eh?" He gave his hidden camera a pat.

"No choice there," Aignar said and he tapped a finger against his throat speaker. He watched as the rest of the Templar were led away in chains.

****

Chief Henrique held a vault door open for Aignar as he walked as fast as he could manage on his prosthetic feet.

Aignar stepped over the threshold into a cemetery where a dozen suits of armor stood in maintenance bays, all shaped like coffins around the armor. A team of technicians huddled around a single suit. Aignar took the stairs to the catwalk that ran parallel to all the armors' chests.

"*Saiam de la! Movam suas bundas antes que elas esmaguem seus cranios!*" Henrique called out from the doorway. The techs set their tools down and scurried out the open door.

Aignar stopped in front of Gideon. "Why?"

"Loyalty," came from Gideon's speakers. "Roland turned on us because he was Templar. Nicodemus. Morrigan. Bassani. All betrayed Earth for their worthless beliefs. Now that cancer is removed from the Corps."

"Sir…they're not traitors! They fight for Earth, for humanity. Just because they follow Saint Kallen—"

"Is exactly why they had to be cut out!" Gideon shouted so loud it made Aignar wince. "There is no place for divided loyalty in the Corps. We fight for the Union or we are traitors."

Aignar snapped his hand into a fist and banged it against the railing. "How do we beat the Kesaht without the Templar?" he asked. "Are General Laran and President

Garret really going to keep them out of the war?"

"Yes," Gideon said. "And they'll know about every battle they chose to sit out. The Templar will be known as cowards too afraid to fight by the time it all ends. If they choose to enforce the Omega Provision…then maybe they'll be let loose."

"They kill Ibarran proccies and violate their oaths or they sit back while others fight the battles…which is against everything the Templar stand for." Aignar shook his head. "They can't really win, can they?"

"It doesn't matter to me," Gideon said. "You've made your choice. Or do you want to join them?"

"I am armor," Aignar said.

"Good…but you're going to their prison anyway."

"Wait. What?"

"As a courier, not an inmate. General Laran needs armor she can trust. I volunteered you for an assignment while I'm on a separate mission," Gideon said. "You'll get your instructions soon."

"Where are you going?"

"I'll tell you once I return. Send the techs back in here. Laran needs me for a briefing."

"Always ready, sir," Aignar said and went down the catwalk to the stairs.

"Always ready, Iron Dragoon."

Chapter 15

Keeper swiped a data feed around her holo tank, dropping it on the tank wall directly behind her. She opened a photoreceptor in the back of her head and read off the data as her normal "eyes" took in more information from a half-dozen screens floating before her.

Her true form was that of a Xaros drone, the last drone in existence, she assumed. She carried that moniker around for years after the Ember War, but the *Breitenfeld* and a team of Strike Marines had come across a drone controlling a Dotari colony fleet in deep space. That drone had been destroyed and now Keeper hoped she truly was the last drone. The galaxy had suffered enough.

The mind of a human woman named Torni ruled the drone body now. In her drone form she could fly, manipulate electromagnetic waves, process raw omnium from matter, and form disintegration beams through her stalk arms. Keeping her human form was somewhat limiting, and like it or not, the mind inside the drone was used to operating through two arms and two eyes. Pulling data through other locations affected her hold on her shell.

Besides, shifting into a drone in front of the Ceres Crucible's unwitting bridge crew would spark a riot and be a burden to explain to everyone. President Garret and a few other key personnel knew what she really was, and that was enough.

A priority data packet slipped through the noise and came to her attention—an interception from the Vishrakath listening post.

"Hello? What's this?" She opened the packet and skimmed through Kesaht lithographs—a blend of intricate calligraphy on the inside of a circle, mirrored by more crude marks that echoed cuneiform on the other side of the circle. She picked out a Crucible gate designation and tossed it into the tank.

A star near the galactic core pulsed.

"Nunavik? There's nothing there…doesn't matter." The data packet pulsed with a question:
DELETE?//FORWARD?

Keeper deleted the message. The Terran Union would deal with Stacey Ibarra and teach the galaxy a human lesson: if it must be done, a man shoots his own dog himself.

****

Admiral Lettow paced across a line of a dozen armor soldiers on the *Ardennes* flight deck. Commanders Paxton and Kutcher kept pace, each holding a small stack of data slates.

"Wing commanders report a ninety-five percent operational rate on the Condor bombers," Paxton read. "Which is—"

"Yesterday they were green across the board," the admiral snapped. "Why the change?"

"Priority personnel transfer to 22nd Fleet engaged in the Wolf Star sector," Paxton said. "Personnel for casualty replacements to units in contact can't be fought. We were a buffet for crews needing to fill out their rosters before we got this mission."

"A mission we shouldn't be waiting around for," Lettow said.

"Making us wait is a species trait," said Kutcher, the ship's intelligence liaison. "If they were on time, it would signal some manner of distress."

"My ship, my cultural mores," Lettow said.

"I can teach them some manners when they arrive," Gideon said at the fore end of the line of armor.

"Maybe not?" Kutcher looked up at the armor. "You're here to intimidate and show we're serious about the mission. Not that I wouldn't mind going to see Ambassador Ibanez and explaining why you caused a major diplomatic incident. Still, no. Just give me a war face…just like that."

"If he steps on you, I'll write it up as an accident," Lettow said.

An oblong ship half the size of a Mule flew up and halted just beyond the open hangar doors. The ship looked like a meteor had been hollowed out and engines added to it. The forward section had irregularly sized windows, like the eyes of some mutated spider.

Gideon loaded gauss shells into the double-barreled cannons on one arm and his rotary weapon snapped up onto his shoulder.

"That's not necessary," Lettow said as the ship floated through the force field. Landing gear extended from the bottom of the rocky hull and it set down a few yards from the admiral.

"It might be," Gideon said.

"You don't like them," Kutcher said. "They don't like you. Let's all agree to hate each other quietly and with no bloodshed. Yeah?"

Lettow gripped a wrist behind his back and waited as a trio of Vishrakath exited their shuttle. The aliens were insect-like—six-foot-tall ants that walked upright on four legs attached to their bottom segment. Lettow had been told that their skin covered a skeletal shell and could change hues to blend in to the environment. The alien in the center bore a wide sash of woven metal and several jeweled badges.

Azure eyes flicked around independent of each other as the three came to a stop a yard from Lettow.

"I am to ask for permission to board this vessel," the middle alien said. "Though I am already here."

"Permission granted," Lettow said. "I am Admiral Lettow. Welcome aboard the *Ardennes*."

"Horva. We will take up positions on your bridge."

"No," Lettow said firmly.

The Vishrakath's clawed feet scraped at the deck. "By the agreement Ambassador Ibanez reached with brood sire Wexil, we are to have full—"

"Full observation rights," Kutcher spoke up. "And you will. In a wonderful chamber we've set up that conforms to Vishrakath environmental needs. Our humidity requirements are much lower than yours. Can't have you uncomfortable during your stay."

"You will not stick us in a cell and expect us to take your word for what happens," Horva said. "That is not the agreement."

"Your facility will have full sensor data," Lettow said, "and a holo mirror to all my communications with anyone *not* in the Terran Union. Ibanez and Wexil did not agree you would look over my shoulder during this entire observation."

"Unacceptable," Horva said. "The Terran Union agreed to allow observers to prove you are not in league with the Ibarrans. You could alter the data coming into this facility you've created."

"Which is why we have other observers." Lettow raised a finger in the air. Gideon stepped aside, startling the Vishrakath. An enclosed hover chair with a clear upper section floated over. Inside, bubbles clung to the glass and an alien inside leaned through dark-blue water.

This kind of Ruhaald always struck Lettow as some sort of creature from a dark lagoon, except that this one had a mermaid's tail instead of legs.

"I am Rhysli of the Ruhaald diplomatic corps."

The other alien observer was taller, with a wide build and in thick armor. Its purple-skinned head was encased in a clear helmet, and it had tendrils in place of a mouth.

"Septon Jarilla, of the Ruhaald Expedition and I render the appropriate greeting."

Both aliens were of the same species, which fascinated Lettow. Rhysli was of the aquatic facet, while Jarilla was amphibious but required a good deal of moisture to be comfortable. Lettow had heard of a third Ruhaald offshoot, giants that lived deep within their planet's oceans.

"We will be on the bridge to confirm your data,"

Rhysli said.

"My mission is to kill or capture Stacey Ibarra," Lettow said. "You'll see that the Terran Union is not protecting or aiding them in anyway. Kutcher, show the Vishrakath to their chamber."

"We have these nice hats for you." Kutcher removed three large hoods from a pocket. "Strictly a formality while you move through the ship. Would you like me to—"

Horva hissed like a rattlesnake about to strike.

Gideon's rotary gun spun to life.

"Formalities that are optional." Kutcher pointed a finger up at Gideon but the barrels kept spinning. "Do follow me." He stuffed the hoods back in his pocket and the Vishrakath followed him away.

"Deceitful creatures," Rhysli said. "Never to be trusted."

"When the intelligence officer works for you, one must give them the benefit of the doubt," Lettow said.

"I spoke of the Vishrakath," the Ruhaald said.

"Sir," Paxton said, touching an earbud, "we've got a hit on the Ibarrans."

"Just in time." The admiral looked up at Gideon. "Your team ready for deployment?"

"We are always ready," Gideon said.

Chapter 16

Roland watched as drones buzzed overhead and flew to the empty cellblock. Clipped shouts from the guards echoed over the walls and Roland heard bars slamming shut.

"New arrivals," Adams said from across the chessboard she shared with Roland.

"How long since anyone else's been put in here?" he asked.

"Other than you and the Ibarrans, sir?" Boucher asked. "Maybe…two months?"

"Fifty-nine days," Adams said. "I was one of the last."

"You hear those slams? Lots of cells getting occupied," Boucher said. "Maybe another Ibarra ship was captured?"

"If the Omega Provision's being enforced," Roland said, stroking his chin, "seems like a lot of excess trouble for prisoners they're just going to kill. Navy voids people for capital punishment, don't they?"

"That's right," Boucher said.

A drone swooped down and shined a light on Roland.

"Prisoner Shaw, report to Guard Post Bravo immediately. Prisoner Shaw—"

Roland grabbed a black knight on the chessboard and moved it.

"Checkmate," he said to Adams.

"Good luck," Adams grumbled as she stared at her doomed king.

Roland went to the guard post, a reinforced shack built into the base of the crater wall connected to a lift up to the main guard post. A chamber made of thick bars buzzed next to revolving door. A trio of Rangers with shock batons waited on the other side for Roland. By their height and build, Roland knew none were Jerry or Valencia.

Roland opened the door to the chamber and stepped inside. It locked shut and a Ranger grabbed him by the front of his overalls and jerked him forward. Cuffs and a hood came next, both applied with more speed than finesse.

"My trial back on?" Roland asked.

Guards grabbed him beneath both arms and dragged him away.

"I wouldn't be in a hurry for that to start back up,

traitor," one said.

Roland felt his boots drag over a rough surface, then he was manhandled into a cart for a ride that lasted a few minutes. The guards escorted him into a quieter area, and he heard the buzz of drones in the air around him. There was a slam of a cell door and his cuffs and hood were removed.

He was alone in a small cell—a single bunk and latrine. He spun around and found Morrigan in the cell across from him. Behind bars to her left was Tongea; to her right, Martel knelt in prayer.

"I always thought General Laran was a ladder-climbing, conniving bitch," Morrigan said. "But at least I've someone to talk to now."

Roland pressed his forehead against the bars and tried to look down the long line of cells around him. He saw shadows move in some, while hands and arms rested on the bars of others.

"Tongea," Roland said, "this wasn't what was supposed to happen. When I told Martel about the Omega—"

"General Laran shut off Olympus from the rest of Mars and the Crucible," the Maori said. "Couldn't get word back to Earth or anyone else."

"The Ibarrans," Roland said, grabbing the bars. "If you're in here…how're they going to survive?"

"They all know what's coming," Morrigan said. "They're not afraid of it. They serve Lady Ibarra to death, no matter where it comes from."

"We can't just sit here and—" Roland kicked his bunk and pain shot through his foot. He sat down, feeling alone and useless.

"What did you do while you were in her jail?" Tongea motioned to Morrigan's cell.

"I…prayed. Kept my faith in Saint Kallen that a solution would arise," Roland said.

"Then keep the faith." Tongea rapped his fist twice against the bars. "Templar! Evening prayers!"

Cell doors rattled as the Templar beat their fists against their cells.

Roland went to a knee and took a deep, cleansing breath. He glanced up and saw Morrigan, her knee bent and head bowed.

"*Salve, Kallen, ferrum corde…*" echoed through the cellblock.

****

Freeman stood in an elevator with a handful of other naval personnel. He kept his eyes glued to the control panel, willing his body to stop sweating so much.

"You believe this crap?" a woman asked. "I was on a Pathfinder cruiser, doing planetary surveys, then *whammy*. Get your ass to Mars. Not even Mars proper. Orbital control."

"Could be worse," another woman said. "This could be an indefinite-duration assignment. Oh wait, it is."

The elevator stopped and opened into a large room shaped like a bowl. Tiers rose up from the depression at the bottom, the lower levels full of workstations, the upper rows bare. A dais in the bottom of the room supported a large holo tank inside of which was a semi-opaque, well-built woman with blond hair and a well-lined face.

"Second watch," said a lieutenant commander as he made his way to the top of the stairs to the lift doors. "Welcome to Grinder-M. Freeman? Sir, I need to take care of a formality." He held up a scanner clamp. He put it on Freeman's fingertip and a light on top flashed green.

"You're true born," the officer said. "Can't believe we have to check that, but here we are. You're with Keeper in the tank. Rest of you, get checked, then I'll show you to your stations."

Freeman wiped sweat away from his forehead and rubbed his tongue against the molar the Ibarrans had transplanted into his jaw. Their promises that the communications were untraceable and undetectable didn't make him feel any better as he descended to the dais.

The hologram of Keeper touched a screen and pulled up a map of the galaxy. Her hands tapped icons for Crucible gates and information leaped up onto the holo, far faster than Freeman could process it.

He cleared his throat.

For a second, he could have sworn Keeper's skin shimmered with fractals. *Just a connection error*, he guessed.

"Finally," Keeper said. "Managing the Ceres Crucible and Grinder-M is a tax on resources. Get in here."

"Sorry, Miss…Keeper, is it? I used to drive starships, not juggle wormholes," Freeman said.

"It's both harder and easier than it looks." Keeper's holo vanished, but her words continued through the speakers. "Hop up."

Freeman put a shaky hand on the top of the dais and climbed up with little in the way of grace. Once he was back on his feet, he saw the stairs on the other side.

"Grinder control is simple," Keeper said as a dozen new screens popped up around him. "The most important thing is authorizing or declining wormhole formation. You'll go through that first in training modules I made for you and other operators at colony Crucibles. Twelve hours each. Should take you a month to be fully qualified. Start working through your qualifications. I'm on Ceres and can handle most of Grinder-M's functions through the Crucible network."

"So I just—"

"My focus is needed elsewhere. I'll pop back in and check on you." There was an audible click as she closed the channel.

"Back to school," Freeman murmured as he looked around and found a blue-ringed data port, right where Masha said it would be. He wiggled his fake tooth and brushed a hand over a thumb drive in a pocket.

I miss you, Salina. We'll be together soon.

****

Masha left footprints in the red sand as she hurried down a cut to a creek bed that had been dry for millions of years. She took cover beneath a rock outcrop and looked up at the pink skies.

Breath fogged against the inside of her helmet as she took a box off her belt and opened it. Trapped air burst out and inside was a small device the size of a hockey puck and a tarnished shell casing. She waited as the puck stirred to life. Metal arms unfolded from the top and it bobbed up and down in her palm.

"You ready to go to work?" she asked.

The device touched an arm to her gauntlet screen and

text flowed across her visor.

"You got it. Fly, my pretty." She tossed the device away and it bounded across the red soil, kicking up little tufts of dirt with each jump in the weak gravity.

"Masha?" came over the IR in her helmet. *"Where'd you go?"*

The spy took the shell casing out of the box and lifted it over her head.

"Look what I found!" She turned just as three men came into view. "You think it's from when the Xaros attacked?"

"Buddy teams, Masha," said a tall man as he shook his head. "This is an orientation walk. You know how bad it looks if Mars Search and Rescue loses someone out here? The Pathfinder contingent already thinks we're nothing but amateurs."

"But the Pathfinders don't have a war relic, do they?" Masha twisted the shell casing, letting sunlight wink off it.

"It might be from the Chinese occupation," another man said. "Gauss weapons don't use shell casings."

"So this is even *more* of a relic?" Masha clutched it to her chest.

"Beginner's luck," a woman said. "I've been hiking out here for months and haven't found a damn thing."

"Great, that's all great." The leader glanced at his

gauntlet screen. "What's even more great is that Commander No Fun just posted the alert roster. We're all on duty in six hours. Time to head back."

Masha looked back and didn't see any sign of the device she'd let loose. She smiled and gave a quick salute to the horizon.

Chapter 17

If there was one thing Aignar didn't miss about his time in the Rangers, it was being stuffed into a Mule up to his neck in cargo and other people. The Mule he was in brought back a number of bad memories of air sickness and squad mates that hadn't showered in weeks.

The cargo pallet locked down in front of him provided a big brown wall of boredom to stare at during the flight. The document pouch in his lap was locked, and he'd been forbidden to carry anything electronic on the flight.

The mountain of a man in a black jumpsuit sitting next to him had slept the entire flight, a trick Aignar used to know back in his infantry days: any time not spent fighting, eating, or actively engaged in work was an opportunity for some shut-eye.

Waking the sleeping bear next to him for the sake of

conversation was not how one made friends in the military, so Aignar kept to himself.

He glanced at his screen-less forearm out of habit, then looked down the row of cargo pallets and across the other passengers to where the crew chief should've been sitting, but that person was missing too.

"I hate drone Mules," Aignar said.

"You're surprised?" the big man grumbled and Aignar almost shot out of his restraints in surprise. The man raised his head, then stretched his arms—the width of Aignar's legs—up over his head.

"Can't trust them," Aignar said. "Who knows who's been mucking about in the code. We crash, there's a pilot to blame. If this thing plows into a mountain because the terrain readers went on the fritz, whose butt do I kick? You kick. You look like the bruiser kind."

"I'm a simple drone tech." The man rapped the back of a hand against a cargo pod. "Got to drop these new units off to Tholis. If it makes you feel any better, I know enough about the Mule's autopilot I'm not afraid."

"If it craps out?"

"There's still a manual override."

"I am armor. I am not a pilot," Aignar said.

"Why is armor going to some Martian bolt hole?"

"I could tell you," Aignar said, tapping his document

pouch, "but then I'd have to…just not tell you."

"Sorry, I should know better than to ask."

"You're not in service coveralls. What did you do before you went civilian? Eat and lift cattle over your head?" Aignar asked.

"Lots, but drone work pays the best. You stay safe once we land."

"It's a prison and I'm on the right side of the bars. Should be fine. I'm Aignar."

"Medvedev." He held up a fist and Aignar gave it a bump. "We're about to land."

"How can you tell?"

"Flight time was ninety-six minutes. It's been ninety-four."

"You counted in your sleep?"

Aignar felt the Mule begin its descent and gave the big man next to him a double take, then held his metal hands over the document pouch as the Mule made a too-rough landing.

"I want my armor back," he muttered. "Shoot me out of a torpedo? Fine. I'd rather walk back to Olympus than do this again."

The landing-pad dome closed over the Mule and air rushed in to pressurize the space. A minute later, the Mule's back ramp lowered and armed guards hurried up the ramp.

"All personnel form a single line for inspection!" a guard shouted.

"I have to break out my cargo," Medvedev said, unbuckling from his restraints. He grabbed the top of the pod and pulled himself on top. "No extra pay for all the extra work."

"Bet you make more in a week than I do all year." Aignar whacked his fist against his restraints and they came loose. He filed down the narrow passage and clomped down the ramp where passengers stood in line, stretching out as the guards checked IDs. A guard held a small device with a tube up to the mouth of the first one off the Mule.

"Chief," said Major Lynch, waving Aignar over to the other end of the ramp. "You're a VIP. Don't need to waste time in line."

"Appreciate it." Aignar glanced back at the other line. "Doing a blood-alcohol test?"

"Naissance inspection," the major said. "True-born-only duty station. Security concerns. Real pain to find qualified personnel, but such is the way of things."

"Same as it ever was." Aignar held up his forearm with his ID card attached to it and Lynch waved a guard over.

"She'll take you to the prisoner," Lynch said. "This Mule cycles back to Olympus in four hours. You're on it or you stay here until the next one…in sixteen hours."

"Got it." Aignar looked at his escort. "Lead on."

****

Outside Tholis prison, Masha's device crept up the crater walls. It froze as a sentry drone swooped past, then continued its climb. Once it reached the top, it scrambled up the dome along a swatch of metal connecting the segments of the crater's cover.

The device halted a few yards short of the apex, its internal sensors working overtime. One thin limb reached out and inserted a needle tip into the metal over the seam. There was a spark as the device disabled a motion sensor before it skittered up and into the mass of antennae on top of the dome.

Tiny filaments shot out from the device and latched on to the prison's communication hub, then the device settled down as its coloring changed to blend in with the windswept dust clinging to the dome's surface.

****

Medvedev guided a cargo pod down the ramp rails and adjusted the anti-grav lifts to slow the cargo's momentum. He pushed it to a wide yellow stripe on the tarmac a few feet shy of the dome and brought it to the ground.

"Hey you." Lynch waved at Medvedev from the Mule. "Inspection."

"Right right." Medvedev walked back to the Mule in no particular hurry. "You know I'm paid by the hour, right? Maybe have some of your staff give me a hand?" He went right past the proffered breathalyzer and back into the Mule, unsnapping a strap on the next pod and tossing it over to the other side of the Mule. He pulled a handle on the pod's cradle and it shifted a few inches away from the third pod.

"You know I can deny this shipment and then whatever contract you're on will be in a world of hurt?" Lynch asked as he entered the cargo bay and stopped short of the pod. "Inspection. Let's go."

Medvedev reached deeper between the two pods.

"Damn release is always a pain," he said.

"Private," said Lynch as he rolled his eyes and waved a guard over. The guard, who looked like he'd been on his feet for the better part of two days, held the nozzle up to Medvedev's mouth. Medvedev blew into the tube, then stretched his arm lower.

"Uh…got an error," the guard said. "Genre reader says you're a proccie, but your naissance file says you're not."

"I know what I am." Medvedev pulled a silenced

pistol out from between the pods and shot the guard between the eyes. He put two rounds in Lynch's chest and a third in his head before he hit the ground.

The Ibarran agent pulled a handle on the side of the cargo pod and the front fell open. Inside were three legionnaires in matte-black combat armor, red Crusader crosses on the front of their visors and on their shoulders. Air and water lines fed into their helmets just beneath the chin.

Medvedev touched a control panel and the legionnaires awoke with sudden intakes of breath.

One ripped the lines away and stumbled out on rubbery legs. He looked at the two corpses, then at Medvedev.

"You started without us," he said.

"Inevitable," Medvedev said.

"Where is your pet?" the legionnaire asked.

Medvedev stripped off his coveralls, revealing a thin pseudo-muscle layer used with power armor. He reached into the pod and removed a black breastplate.

"She's doing her part. We do ours." He attached the breastplate and caught the Terran Ranger–pattern gauss carbine one of his fellows tossed to him.

"For the Lady," a legionnaire said.

"For our Nation." Medvedev slapped a magazine into

his weapon.

****

A guard holding a cup of coffee walked into the landing pad through the air lock, stopping to ponder the three cargo pods next to the idle Mule, and sipped his drink.

"Captain Lynch?" the man asked. "Lieutenant Colonel Izuma's trying to reach you on the IR."

There was a sound like squirrel chatter to the guard's side. He looked over just in time to see a rifle butt smash into his face. The blow knocked him out cold and he fell into a legionnaire's arms.

Medvedev, now in full armor, rushed to the air lock and pulled a canister off his belt. He banged the bottom against his thigh and threw it into the guard post. The canister bounced off the observation glass overlooking the Terran military cellblock and landed in a technician's lap, hissing as invisible gas expelled into the room.

The technician went slack and collapsed against her workstation. The gas spread through the guard post and personnel were knocked out before they knew what was happening—except for Jerry Marris, who was in his Ranger power armor. He slapped his visor down the instant he saw the first technician collapse, sealing his armor and switching to internal air tanks.

Jerry keyed an emergency channel and ducked behind a file cabinet.

"Control, this is Post Alpha. We've got an emergency." He looked at the shock baton in his hand and the empty gauss pistol holster on his thigh. The arms locker was on the other side of the post. Looking up at a pane of glass, he saw a pair of legionnaires moving from the air lock to the control room.

"Control?" he whispered into his mic. All he heard back was static. He switched to a backup frequency and was about to speak when Medvedev reached around the file cabinet and grabbed Jerry by the wrist.

Medvedev pulled him into the open and paused, almost surprised to see an armored Ranger.

Jerry activated his shock baton and jabbed it into Medvedev's crotch. Electricity crackled out of the baton and danced around Medvedev's pelvis. The Ibarran locked up, his cry muffled by his helmet.

Jerry grabbed the carbine in Medvedev's hand and tore it free. He flipped it around and aimed at another legionnaire who had peeked his head up from the workstations in response to Medvedev's cry.

Jerry pulled the trigger, but the weapon didn't fire.

A blow struck him in the kidneys, and enough force

traveled through his armor to send a jolt of pain through his body. He leaned forward with a step, then whirled around to strike with the butt of the carbine.

Medvedev caught Jerry by the wrist again and swung the Ranger into a file cabinet with a bang. Bracing himself against Jerry, Medvedev pinned the carbine between their bodies, the skull visor reflected in Medvedev's mirror-faced helmet. Medvedev worked his finger into his weapon's trigger well.

Jerry twisted his right wrist to the side twice and a bayonet popped out of his forearm housing. He jabbed Medvedev in the face, sending a spiderweb of cracks across the helmet but failing to penetrate it.

Medvedev pulled back and raised his arms to ward off another stab. Jerry chopped a hand against the legionnaire's gun hand and a single bullet fired with a snap, blowing a chunk out of the wall.

Jerry shoved Medvedev back against a railing and thrust his bayonet at the legionnaire's throat. The blow stopped well short, caught by another legionnaire who jabbed a thumb against the side of Jerry's helmet and pressed the emergency release for his skull visor. It popped off and Jerry held his breath as he tried to elbow the new attacker.

A kick from Medvedev hit the Ranger square in the testicles and Jerry took an involuntary breath. He collapsed to the ground a moment later.

"You've been away from the Legion too long," Labaqui said as he helped Medvedev to his feet. "Couldn't even beat one of their dog soldiers."

"I had him." Medvedev aimed his carbine at Jerry's head and paused. He tore the power packs away from the armor, then used Jerry's own cuffs to bind him to a rail post.

"Jamming still holds," called the third legionnaire from a workstation. A data line ran from the back of his helmet into a port. "I shut down the trams, but the drones are still operational. The virus your pet gave us isn't working to specs."

"Then we adapt," Medvedev said. "Ubera, get to the food processors and load up our gifts. I'll get the contingency plan ready."

"Medvedev," said Labaqui, jabbing at a holo display only he could see, "there's a complication. More prisoners than we anticipated. Many more." He pinched a spot of air and tossed it to Medvedev.

Medvedev looked over the data splayed out on the inside of his helmet.

"I need to contact Masha. Now."

****

Nicodemus stood sentinel in his armor next to Stacey Ibarra as orbits of light circled around her. This wasn't his first journey into a Qa'Resh site, but the sheer alienness of it all put a strain on even a seasoned warrior like him.

Stacey had been silent inside the data node for hours, shifting through a data base untouched for millions of years.

A priority message came through the quantum dot communicator in his helm.

"My Lady," he said as twirling bands of light reflected off her silver surface. "My Lady," Nicodemus repeated, increasing the volume on his speakers. The lights slowed down.

"You just cost me an hour's work," she said.

"We have a situation. A Terran Union vessel, a carrier, likely the *Ardennes*, just arrived in system and is on course for this city. I recommend we abort. The *Ebaki* is no match for a ship that size," Nicodemus said.

"They tracked us here?" Stacey said. "How?"

She raised her hands like a conductor and the light around her changed into a latticework. "This place is…attuned," she said. "Every ripple in the fabric of reality recorded and stored. The magnetar caught the Qa'Resh's interest so long ago…they must have thought this distortion field could open a path to a different dimension. The idea failed, so they went with another option for ascension…"

"My Lady, we must abort," Nicodemus said. "The Union will send their armor to kill you. There are only three of us here to protect you."

"Now, now…what's this?" A swirl of golden lines formed a mirror of her face. "A graviton echo after the new arrivals…emanating from this planet."

"Your Templar are true, My Lady," Nicodemus said. "We would never betray you."

"I know…I know. It's from our ship. Relay to Commander Spiner to send a distress call back to Navarre. Then I have instructions for how to find the tracker."

"We're not leaving?" Nicodemus asked.

"I'm so close, my dear. So very close."

Chapter 18

Aignar and Valencia walked down rows of cells, all shimmering with one-way privacy screens. The Templar within couldn't see out, but Aignar could see them, and to walk free past so many battle-hardened men and women of conviction filled him with shame.

"You hear that?" Valencia asked.

"What?"

"Sounded like a gauss rifle." She looked up at the guard post over the cellblock and touched the side of her helmet. "If some pogue had *another* negligent discharge, Major Lynch will make all our lives so miserable I'd be better off in one of these cells."

"Just one?" Aignar asked.

"Yeah, and the comms are quiet."

"Probably a negligent discharge." Aignar stopped at

Morrigan's cell. The Irishwoman was doing handstand push-ups, her feet braced against the wall, and was the only prisoner he'd seen without the Templar's white tabard.

"This block's only Ibarran," Valencia said. "Got a real mouth on her too. Can't tell what she calls us, but her tone ain't friendly. You ever heard Irish-accented Basque? Sounds like a drunk schizophrenic screaming in cat. She always calls me a 'gobshite.' I think it's a compliment."

"Morrigan…I've heard so much about her, but I'm not here to see her," Aignar said. He gestured to a plastic chair set in front of Roland's cell. The soldier slept on his cot.

"The Black Knight's all yours," Valencia said and tapped a code into her gauntlet screen. The privacy field on Roland's cell fizzled away.

Roland sat up and blinked at Aignar.

"What're you doing out there?" Roland asked.

"What are you doing in there?" Aignar sat in the chair and tapped stiff fingers against the document pouch. "Treason. You're on trial for treason. I don't know why I asked."

"And the Templar are here because they refused to go along with the Omega Provision." Roland got up and rubbed sleep from his eyes. "If you're not in a cell, then—"

"You're one to judge!" Aignar snapped. "Behind bars and still raising all kinds of hell for me and the lance. You think I'm like Gideon, ready to crush every Ibarran proccie I can find? I'm not." He raised a hand next to his face and the fingers snapped up and down randomly. He covered his wayward hand and stared daggers at Roland.

"What would I have in one of these cells? Not my armor. Not my son."

"A clear conscience."

"Fuck you." Aignar rose out of his seat. "The Kesaht are still out there. Battles in seven different systems. The colony on Syracuse is under siege right now. A phase-one golden world with twenty-five million people on it and our fleets are cut off. Every last armor squadron and lance is being sent to the front lines right now, and you and your chanting buddies are doing what? Three hots and a cot. All because of your damn pride, though you've got it a bit worse than the rest, I'll admit that."

Roland leaned his forearms against the bars.

"You went to see Saint Kallen with me."

"Shut up."

"That meant nothing to you?"

"It changed after one of your Templar friends cut me in half!" Aignar shouted. He seethed for a moment longer, then tossed the document pouch through Roland's bars.

"That's from your lawyer and that's the only reason I'm here. See what you've reduced me to? A courier. And I can barely do that with these damn claws," Aignar said. "If you'd get your trial back on track so I can do something a bit more useful with my time, I'd appreciate it. Close him up."

Valencia tapped the side of her helmet and looked from the cell to the guard post.

"Why is nothing working today?" she asked herself.

"I'm done here." Aignar turned away, then looked over his shoulder. "Cha'ril is pregnant. Thought you should know."

"Pregnant?"

"When a man and a woman really love each other, one night—"

A drone crashed against the floor and bounced against Roland's cell.

"What the hell?" Aignar looked up as more drones fell out of the sky, raining down on the cellblock.

"Think there's a problem." Valencia slapped her visor down and looked toward the end of the row as two black figures came running around the corner.

"Ibarrans." Aignar gave Roland an accusing glance.

There was a snap of gauss fire and the barrel of Valencia's rifle exploded. She shrieked as the capacitor overloaded and sent a shock up her arm. Reeling back, she knocked Aignar off-balance and into Roland's cell.

Aignar saw the sidearm strapped to Valencia's thigh

and leaned forward to grab it, when Roland caught him by both elbows.

"Don't!" Roland shouted. "I don't know what this is, but don't get yourself killed for nothing."

Aignar struggled, but he couldn't break free from Roland's hold on him.

A black-clad legionnaire leveled a gauss carbine at Aignar while the other flipped Valencia over, ripped her suit's battery packs out, then cuffed her while her body still twitched from the electric assault.

"Black Knight?" asked Medvedev, who was drawing down on Aignar.

"That's me," Roland said. "Don't hurt my lance mate. He's with us in his heart."

"The hell I am!" Aignar jerked an arm loose and elbowed Roland in the sternum through the bars. He swung his free arm at Medvedev and landed a punch to the side of his helmet. His fist bounced off like he'd hit a statue.

Medvedev swept Aignar's legs out from under him and the armor soldier landed hard. Medvedev put a boot on Aignar's chest.

"You'll stop right now," Morrigan ordered as her cell door slid open and she strode out. The other legionnaire beat a fist to his heart in a quick salute.

"This one has iron in him," Medvedev said.

"And you'll not take it," Morrigan said.

Aignar breathed hard through his nose, looking from Medvedev and the Ibarran armor to Roland.

"I don't know anything about this," Roland said. "I swear it."

Morrigan conversed in Basque for a few moments with the legionnaires, then nodded.

"Roland," she said, "you're about to know something. This is a jailbreak. For me and every Ibarran in this hole. I don't think it'll work and we'll likely all die in the attempt, but it's better than rotting away down here. You can come with us. I vouched for you once. I'll do it again to our Lady, and I'll see you keep your armor. Stay in your cell or join the Ibarra Nation once and for all. Choose quick, *cara*. We're on a schedule."

"Roland, they're all trait—" Aignar's voice caught as Medvedev pressed his foot against his chest.

"Stop!" Roland shouted and Medvedev relented slightly.

Roland looked from side to side, at all the Templar in the cells around him. He went to both knees and reached through the bars to touch Aignar's shoulder.

"I am armor. I am Templar. Earth…doesn't want that from me anymore. We cannot escape what we are, what we know is right." Roland drew his hand back. "I'll go with you,

Morrigan, but you'll take us all."

Medvedev touched the side of his helmet and the bars to Roland's cell slid to one side. He stepped into the passageway, as did the rest of the Templar.

"I hope they're easier to convince than you," Morrigan said.

"Well met." Martel touched his fist to his heart when he recognized Morrigan.

"Colonel," she said, "it's been…a minute since we've seen each other. We've time for an elevator pitch. The Ibarra Nation extends a welcome invitation to serve in her armed forces for the good of all mankind."

"We prayed to Saint Kallen for a solution," Martel said. "Who am I to argue with how those prayers are answered?"

"Lovely." Morrigan hit Medvedev on his arm and he removed his foot from Aignar's chest. "The Lady's intelligence service promises us a way off Mars. I'm all for making an Irish goodbye of the situation."

There was a clap and a missile shot overhead, the engines burning like an ember as it wobbled up and down, then veered toward Guard Post Charlie. Gauss fire snapped out and the missile exploded short of its target, raining debris against the glass observation windows and sending smoke billowing up and against the top of the dome.

"That's a problem," Medvedev said. "That was supposed to kill most of the guards securing the *Narvik*'s crew."

"You only brought one rocket?" Morrigan asked.

"The other is spoken for," the legionnaire said.

"There are a hundred Rangers and Strike Marines in that guard shack," Roland said. "How many did you bring?"

"Three," Medvedev said, "but we'll have more soon." He handed an earpiece to Morrigan and sprinted back toward Guard Post Alpha with the other legionnaire.

"Three?" Roland asked. "Did I hear that right?"

"Aye," Morrigan said. "Colonel Martel, we need to get your Templar to the lifts as soon as our transports arrive…I don't recommend keeping our heads down in the cells, on account of the Earth dogs might get control of the network again."

"Tunnels connect the guard posts," Roland said. "We should be safe in there."

"Tongea," Martel said, "we form up by lances. Roland, get us out of the line of fire. We're armor…just all rather crunchy at the moment."

"Yes, sir." Roland looked down at Aignar, who was propped up on his side.

"Just kill us both," Aignar said, motioning to Valencia.

"No." Roland shook his head. "You're coming with us for now. You've got plugs in your head. The soldiers at Charlie will be gunning for any and all armor…but her." Roland grabbed Valencia by the carry handle on the back of her shoulders and dragged her into his cell.

He removed her helmet and set it on his bunk. Her face was wet with tears, her eyes wide with fear.

"I…my arm doesn't feel right," she said.

"It'll pass," Roland said. "I'm sorry. This is the best I can come up with right now."

"Say a prayer to Saint Kallen for me?" she asked. "All I ever wanted to do was meet Templar in person. Now they're all around me and it's…not how I envisioned it. At all."

"I will. For you." Roland touched her face and removed the slate off her gauntlet. He left the cell and hit a key to lock it behind him.

****

Masha sat in the cockpit of a Destrier transport, the much larger cousin to the ubiquitous Mules. The view of the massive doors for Olympus hangar Sigma-Nine hadn't changed in the hours since she'd come on duty. Her copilot swiped through an ebook on a data slate.

The Ibarran spy checked a clock again, then drummed her fingertips against her thighs.

"You need the latrine, use the latrine," said Padilla, the copilot. "We're not under alert condition alpha. We can move around."

"Fleet standards for mission receipt to wheels up is two minutes," Masha said. "Keep forgetting Mars is a bit different."

"Dirt-side assignments are just a bit easier than void time." Padilla stretched and leaned forward to look through the viewing panels built into the floor of the cockpit. "The techs finish maintenance on the forward landing gear?"

"They left an hour ago." Masha checked the time again. Medvedev was overdue to report, a delay that was very unlike him.

"Mobile, this is action." Medvedev's words sounded in her ears, transported through bone conduction through the false tooth in her jaw.

Masha ran a hand down a thigh and pressed a button on a small device in a hip pocket.

Red lights flashed on Padilla's control panel.

"Electrical fault in the forward gear," Padilla sighed. "Bet the techs got lazy and didn't reset the breakers. They always forget that. Want me to call them back?"

"We're a hangar queen until the fault clears," Masha

said. "It'll take those grease monkeys more than five minutes to get back and fix it, and I don't want to explain to Commander Hard-Ass why his alert bird is off-line on my first day on the job."

"Yeah, he's a dick. I'll flip the breakers." Padilla got out of her seat and left the cockpit.

Masha waited a moment, then clicked her jaw twice.

"Action, go."

"Phase one complete, but there's a complication. Total head count for evac is now 312," Medvedev said.

"Sorry, did you say '312'?"

"The Terrans imprisoned all their Templar here. You said Lady Ibarra would want the Black Knight. I assume she'd want any other armor we could evacuate as well."

"That's very open-minded of you, Medvedev. I am talking to Medvedev, aren't I, not one of the smarter legionnaires we snuck in?"

"That is more than we planned on taking home."

"A lot more…let me think. I can get two hundred in my Destrier." She looked out a side window to two more of the large transports on the flight deck. "We're going to need a distress signal from Tholis. A big one."

"We shut off all communications."

"I know what I did, Medvedev. Thank you very much. Then we need to *un-shut* them off for just a bit…and we'll need pilots. The doggies in the other birds are in for a surprise and I doubt they'll be eager to join us. You have the wire-guided munitions with you, right?"

"*Two.*"

"Not four?"

"*Not enough room in the cargo containers.*"

"Excuses, now I'm getting excuses…here's what you need to do."

****

Strike Marine Lieutenant Colonel Izuma scrolled through a data slate. He shook his head at the proposed list of new personnel assignments and swiped left on any and all that had no combat experience. Just why the Bureau of Personnel thought data-integrity technicians could manage Ibarran fanatics was lost to him,

He touched a room-temperature cup of coffee and sneered.

"Orderly?"

"Sir?" A private that looked like he was old enough to start shaving last week appeared in the doorway.

"Why hasn't Major Lynch from Post Alpha sent over his daily situation report?" Izuma asked.

"I sent the request twenty—"

"Why is my coffee cold?"

"I made it for you an hour—"

"Why aren't you fixing these issues?"

"Do you...the coffee or—"

"Move out!"

Izuma snickered as the junior soldier almost jumped out of his boots to comply. Why the desk jockeys hadn't found him a decent senior NCO to serve as his first sergeant was starting to grate on him. Most of the combat soldiers assigned to him were young—children when the Ember War began. Using only true-born humans for this assignment might have briefed well to the senior staff, but he had to run his cellblock with almost no midlevel leadership.

"Sir?" The soldier stuck his head around the corner.

"You didn't even come back with coffee."

"There's a problem," the soldier squeaked. "We can't raise block Alpha."

"For the love of..." Izuma got out of his chair and snapped a pistol belt around his waist. He strode into the command center and went to a mix of soldiers, sailors, and Marines huddled around a workstation.

"Well?" Izuma asked. "I have to show you all how to work a damn radio too?"

"Negative, sir," a Strike Marine said. "All connections to posts Alpha and Bravo are green. They're just not answering."

Izuma put his hands on his hips and looked through the window to the post across the crater.

"Didn't a shuttle just land at Alpha's pad?" the colonel asked.

"Yes, sir," someone answered. "Not due to lift off for another three and a half hours."

"Raise Olympus," Izuma said.

"Aye aye," the commo Marine said. He tapped at the controls and frowned. "That's weird. We're making the handshake to Olympus control, but there's no data going back and forth."

"Are we being jammed?" Izuma asked.

"This is more of a system fault."

Izuma grabbed a sailor by the shoulder. "You. Get into the barracks and get everyone out of their bunks and in full riot gear. Not a drill." He grabbed another. "You. Get the QRF in here." He half shoved the sailors away. "Comms, get me the floor patrols."

He took a micro bead off his belt and pressed it into an ear.

"They're all off-line," the tech said. They looked out the windows and saw a pair of Rangers standing between the rows of cells holding the Ibarran prisoners. One Ranger tapped the side of his helmet while the other waved to the guard post.

"Power armor," Izuma said, "everyone. Open the arms locker and load live ammo. We're under attack."

****

Adams kicked at a fallen drone. A slight smell of smoke from the exploded missile tickled her nose and she almost felt like she was back in action with her old Strike Marine team.

"What was that?" Boucher asked, his eyes wide with panic. "Are we—who's—should—"

Adams grabbed him by the back of the neck. "You want me to cut your head off so you can finish your chicken impression?" she asked.

Boucher froze up.

Speakers in the fallen drone whined with feedback and Adams covered her ears.

"Prisoners," Medvedev's voice came from the drones. "The Ibarra Nation calls you home."

"Kiss my ass!" Adams shouted at the drone. "I am a Strike Marine! *Terran* Strike Marines, you traitor." She kicked the drone in the repulsors and sparks shot out.

"For Earth!" Boucher punched a fist in the air and repeated the words. The prisoners joined in the chant and added a number of expletives directed toward the Ibarras.

"Guillotine," Medvedev said through the drones. "Tecumseh. Geranium. Circus."

The chant died down and Adams felt lightheaded. She wobbled against a mess table and a sudden pain grew between her eyes.

"The Ibarra Nation fights for the Lady," Medvedev said.

"For the Lady," Adams repeated as a sense of calm washed over her. She looked at the Terran Union flag on her uniform with disgust and ripped it off.

The food station in the middle of the mess area rose out of the floor and the drawers popped open, all stuffed with loaded gauss carbines and pistols. Labaqui walked through the throng of prisoners and up to Commander Strickland.

"What does the Lady will?" Strickland asked the legionnaire.

"Who's combat trained and experienced?" Labaqui tapped a thick pouch on his waist. "I need a security element."

"Her." Strickland pointed at Adams, who ran over to the food dispenser and drew a carbine. She reloaded the weapon and slipped two magazines into her pockets. More prisoners took up arms.

"Rescue is on the way," Labaqui said. "Get everyone else to the elevator and wait." He slapped Strickland on the shoulder, then ran toward the wall separating the cellblock from where the crew of the *Narvik* were held.

Adams struggled to keep up with the legionnaire. She wasn't sure if it was the armor or the conditioning that helped the Ibarran move so fast. The red Crusader cross on his black armor held her gaze, the sight filling her with hope and excitement.

Deep in her mind, a sense of wrongness scratched at her consciousness. She shook the feeling away and caught up to the legionnaire at the wall where rows of razor wire discouraged any notion of going over the top.

Labaqui opened the pouch and drew out a roll of burn cord.

"Strike Marine, you know how to breach?" he asked.

"I'm cross-trained." She took the end of the cord and drew it out. "Diamond-shaped entry? Our people should still be in their cells. If we go for frag and—"

"No choice." Labaqui tapped his muzzle against the rock wall. "Feldspar composite? The Terrans use a spoil compactor to build this?"

"It was like that when we got here." Adams pressed the burn cord against the rock, and adhesive built into the outer layer glued the cord in place. "Water charge?"

"You have an IV bag?" a prisoner said from where he crouched next to a closed cell. "Pathfinder," he said, giving a quick salute to the Ibarran.

"If we use enough cord—" A rifle shot sounded across the prison and Labaqui stumbled forward.

"Sniper!" Adams called out as she caught Labaqui before he could fall over. The new Ibarrans took over and one pointed to Post Charlie.

Labaqui grunted and grabbed Adams by the waist. He shoved her aside and swept up his weapon, sinking to a crouch just as another bullet snapped over his head. He fired from the hip once, then braced the carbine against his shoulder and let off two more shots.

Across the prison, a Ranger pitched off the catwalk and fell into the *Narvik* cellblock with a crunch of broken armor.

Labaqui's right arm went limp at his side and he cursed in Basque as rivulets of blood ran down the back of his arm from a broken armor plate. He locked his carbine on his back and picked up the roll of burn cord, slapping it into the middle of the diamond Adams had almost finished as he waved his good arm at the cells.

"Fire in the hole!"

Cell doors—all the cell doors—slammed open. Adams ducked into the first opening as Labaqui stood just outside the cell, shielding her from the burn cord.

"Sir?" she asked. "Don't you want to—"

The burn cord ignited and a blast wave smacked against her head. A cloud of dust roiled past Labaqui and into the cell.

The legionnaire darted away. Adams heard the crunch of heavy boots on rocks and hacking coughs from her fellow prisoners.

"*Korrika egin!*" Labaqui shouted. "*Exekutatu nire ahosta!*"

Adams wasn't sure how she could suddenly understand Basque, but she knew the legionnaire was calling for the Ibarran prisoners to run to the sound of his voice. She ran through the clearing dust and saw the legionnaire standing atop a section of collapsed wall. Dark figures emerged from the fog, coughing as Labaqui waved them over.

The Strike Marine bumped into an Ibarran sailor, his uniform torn and singed from the *Narvik*'s crash. He looked at her with fear in his eyes.

"Keep going." Adams turned him toward the back of the cellblock and jabbed him on his back with her carbine's stock. She charged up the slope as Labaqui kept shouting.

On the other side, dozens of Ibarran sailors rushed out of their cells and toward the legionnaire.

A bullet snapped past Adams' head and struck the wall next to Labaqui.

"Contact!" Adams slid down the other side of the hill and stopped herself by bumping into the side of a cell. The Pathfinder thumped against the wall next to her.

"Turcotte," he said.

"You puffies better be good in a fight." Adams quickly peeked around the corner and saw more Ibarrans rushing past.

Gauss shots rang out and someone cried out in pain. A sailor stumbled forward, clutching her stomach. She fell in front of Adams, blood pooling beneath her.

"They're not even armed," Adams said as she reached out and grabbed the woman by the collar, dragging her out of the line of fire. A blood bubble formed in the woman's mouth and she swiped a hand across Adam's shirt. The woman went limp and died before the Strike Marine could do any more.

"God damn it." Adams stood and set her carbine to full auto. "Puffy, with me."

Gauss shots snapped through the air as Labaqui returned fire. Adams saw which way his rifle was oriented and shouldered her weapon.

"Three…two…go!" Adams swung around the corner and stepped over a dead sailor. She saw a Ranger duck behind a cellblock and pulled the trigger on her carbine, emptying the entire magazine into the cell wall, blasting through the rock and kicking up puffs of vaporized rock.

She ran forward, slapping a new magazine into the weapon, and went into a feet-first slide past the gap in the cells. Three Ranger guards stood in the passage. One had his hands pressed to the front of his visor, while the other two didn't seem prepared for an unarmored prisoner to come into view.

Adams opened fire, using the weapon's recoil to pull the aim across both Rangers. She stitched bullets across one's chest, then took the other in the throat. The one hit in the chest staggered back, his armor taking the brunt of the impact and proving strong enough to keep the bullets from penetrating. He gripped his rifle and swung it toward Adams.

She slid to a stop and saw the ammo counter on her weapon flash zero.

Turcotte shot the staggered guard through the damaged armor plate and the enemy collapsed.

"Get up!" The Pathfinder swung his weapon at the Ranger clutching his face. The Ranger looked up. One eye socket of the skull visor was broken out and a bloody eye looked right at Turcotte. The guard slapped the Pathfinder's carbine aside and swung a punch that missed Turcotte's head but broke a chunk of the already damaged wall out.

Adams got her feet under her and jumped at the Ranger, swinging her carbine like a club and whacking him on the back of the head. The blow glanced off and Adams heard the creak of the pseudo-muscle layer beneath the Ranger's armor plates as he swung his bulk around. His fist caught her on the arm and the blow sent her flying. She landed hard on her shoulder and skidded into cell bars.

Pain lanced up through her arm and breathing suddenly became very difficult.

The Ranger drew a pistol from a holster and shot Turcotte in the stomach. The Pathfinder fell with a yowl, arms clutched to the wound. The Ranger swung his weapon to Adams.

"Hey," Labaqui said.

The Ranger glanced to his side just in time to see the legionnaire's shoulder bash into his face. The Ranger made a brief flight into cell bars and fell to the floor. Labaqui raised a foot and stomped the Ranger's damaged helmet. The visor shattered and there was a crunch as the Ranger's skull fractured.

Labaqui pulled a grenade from his belt and lobbed it toward the guard shack at the base of Post Charlie.

"Can you move?" he asked Adams.

"Turcotte…" she said, waving to the fallen Pathfinder as she grabbed a cell door to help her up.

"He won't survive," Labaqui said.

"Doesn't matter," Adams said.

"Pathfinder…wouldn't leave you to die."

"Noted." The legionnaire tossed Turcotte over his shoulder and ran back to the breach. Adams followed with agony in every step from her badly broken arm and cracked ribs.

Drops of blood left a trail behind Labaqui, and Adams wasn't sure if it was from the legionnaire or the Pathfinder.

****

Izuma twisted his helmet into place and joined the IR network formed between him and the rest of his power-armored troops in the guard post. He sat with his back to a workstation at the fore of the post's command center, keeping Martian rock between him and Alpha.

"Status?" Izuma asked.

"They've got snipers in Alpha," one of his Strike Marines said. "Not armed with a rail rifle, but he's a good enough shot to tag us if we stick our heads outside the post."

There was a snap as a gauss bullet cut through the windows and drilled through the wall into Izuma' office. The top of his wooden desk blew into splinters, a spiderweb of cracks marking where the round penetrated.

"Sonsabitches, that was an antique," Izuma said.

Izuma did a quick count of fighters on the network. Twenty-five power-armored individuals, another six coming on line from the armory. Not knowing how many enemy he faced was proving to be a planning obstacle.

"Sir," said a Ranger sergeant as he scooted over next to Izuma, "the Ibarran prisoners are escaping to cellblock Charlie."

"Doesn't matter. This is Mars. They get outside, they'll last thirty seconds before they suffocate and die. They ain't going nowhere," Izuma said.

"They have a Mule," the sergeant said.

"One. They have one Mule for what? Two thousand?"

"Then they're here for VIPs? Use the rest of their tube babies as cannon fodder?"

"I wouldn't put it past the Ibarrans," Izuma said.

"Missile!" someone shouted.

"Volume fire!" The sergeant popped up, weapon ready.

Izuma was a beat behind the sergeant. He saw the missile arcing up and away from his guard post…flying straight for the dome.

"What in the hell…"

"Brace for decompression!" The sergeant threw himself on the floor.

Izuma stood still and watched as the missile exploded against the dome. Fault lines wove up the composite glass and alarms blared through the prison...but the dome held.

A realization struck Izuma.

"Commo! The automated alerts should be screaming to Mount Olympus, right?"

"Yes, sir," said the tech, getting up onto his knees at the workstation. "That message went through...I can piggyback on the line, get some help."

"Do it." Izuma ducked back down just as a sniper bullet burst against the glass. He looked over at the doorway to the logistics rails. An idea came to him.

"Strike Marines, Rangers," Izuma said, "you ready to take this fight to the enemy?"

"Hoah, sir," the sergeant said.

Chapter 19

Alarms blared in the Destrier's cockpit and Walker fumbled her e-reader away in surprise. Masha snapped on her flight helmet, brought the ship's engines online, then raced through the preflight checklist.

"Not a drill, that's for sure." Walker touched a screen and tossed a file onto the forward HUD. An icon flashed on a location well south of Mount Olympus. "Does Mars Command have a screw loose? This can't be right. Restricted zone. No orbital tracks over that area at all…they're sending *us* to make a rescue?"

"Not just us," Masha said. "The whole ready flight of three Destriers…medical teams are loading. Wheels up in sixty seconds."

Warning lights warbled around the bay doors as the massive metal plates slid aside. The force field separating the hangar from the deadly Martian environment shimmered as blown dust swept over the energy wall.

"But there's nothing out there," Walker swiped across a screen with video feed around their aircraft. "The whole flight would only launch for something as big as a disabled cruiser or a mass-casualty event at one of the macro cannons."

A scarlet text box popped up on every screen and the HUD.

"Delay?" Walker shook her head. "Delay for security teams?"

"To hell with that," Masha said. "Command pushes the panic button and they want us to sit around and twiddle while they find some jarheads?" She dismissed the alert and opened a channel.

"Crimson flight, this is call sign Gezur," Masha said. "Standard search-and-rescue protocols are in effect. Whoever's in trouble needs our help right now, not when our ducks are in a row. I'll take point. Wheels up in five."

"Commander Hard Ass is calling us," Walker said. "Pretty sure he's about to countermand your order."

"Bah." Masha powered up the repulsor engines and the massive shuttle lurched forward. "Let that lard ass try and squeeze into a flight suit and come find me."

The Destrier slid through the force field and blasted off into the red skies.

"You may get the record for fastest time between in

processing and out processing the squadron," Walker said.

"Well shucks…" A half smile crept across Masha's face. She bit her teeth together with a quick code. "ETA is nineteen minutes."

"I know that. I'm looking at the same flight path you are," Walker said, slightly annoyed.

"Confirmed," Medvedev said through the quantum dot communicator in her tooth. *"By the Saint, I pray your patsy delivers. Else this prison will be our home, and we've already proven to be poor houseguests."*

"Faith the size of a mustard seed and all that," Masha said and clicked her teeth five more times.

"What?" Walker asked.

"Is that you?" Masha heard Freeman ask with a muffled whisper. *"Is it time?"*

"Saint Kallen, save all sinners from the fires of Hell," Masha said. "Forgive blackened souls. Help them to see the light."

"I didn't know you were religious." Walker crossed herself quickly.

"Got it…I got it," Freeman said. *"Just get Salina out of there and remember to take me with you."*

Masha increased the Destrier's elevation as they came up to a ridgeline and leaned forward to look up at the Martian sky.

"Never hurts to ask for a miracle," Masha said.

****

Freeman's hand trembled as he drew a small data drive from a pocket hidden in his sleeve. He looked around the Crucible's control room through the dais' holo panels, wondering which of the crew was braver and smarter than he was.

He swallowed hard and snapped the drive into a port.

Power failed across the control room. Holo screens snapped off and the lights became erratic strobe lights. The bridge crew sat at empty workstations, like they'd all reverted to children at an analog elementary school and were staring at their teacher on the dais.

"Emergency reboot!" Freeman shouted and reached down to touch a still-working panel out of sight from the rest of the crew. He tapped in a nine-digit code and the entire command center lurched to one side, tossing Freeman against the railings.

"Wormhole realignment!" A crew member pointed to the circular view port in the ceiling. The gigantic thorns that made up the smaller Crucible gate realigned, and a white plane formed in the gate's center.

"That's not on the schedule." Freeman reached under

a control panel and jiggled a wire, doing his best to look busy.

"Alert Mars Command!"

"Everything is still off-line," a commo tech responded.

The wormhole aperture widened suddenly and a massive ship appeared, perilously close to the bridge. Freeman ducked out of reflex and looked up, mouth agape, as rocket pods attached to the carrier ignited and the ship accelerated toward Mars.

Screens flickered to life and Freeman lost his focus as he was inundated by a mountain of data and shouts.

A vid capture of the ship popped up in front of him, the computers designated the ship with a red hostile icon, and a callout box zoomed in on the name painted on the blue and white hull.

The *Warsaw*.

The rocket pods fell off the carrier as it swept toward Mars.

"That's an Ibarran ship," a crewwoman said. "What the hell are they doing?"

"Not our problem," Freeman said. "Get this station back online so we can bring in help from the Ceres Crucible."

Just don't do it too quickly, Freeman thought.

****

Admiral Makarov gripped her armrests as the *Warsaw* dipped into Mars' atmosphere. Heat shields flared as pink skies formed around the ship, the upper band the dark of the void. Two key officers flanked the admiral while the rest of the bridge crew focused on their stations in open-topped bays just below her command platform.

Makarov longed to go to the deactivated holo table behind her, but the g-forces pressing against her entire body were an unpleasant reminder of just how rough this mission was going to get.

"Shields are holding," said her XO from his station to her right. "Vector in line with projections."

"Give me a course plot and timer to our exit window," Makarov said, and the *Warsaw*'s projected path wrapped around Mars and traced back to the Grinder. "Gunnery, status on our insurance policy?"

"In place," said a stern-faced woman from Makarov's left. "Shall I bring it online?"

"Don't tip our hand just yet. We'll see—"

"Admiral, we're being hailed by Mars Command," came from the crew bay.

"We'll see how they want to play this." Makarov doubled-tapped a key on her armrest and the holo of General Laran came up on the inside of Makarov's visor.

"Ibarra Nation ship," the general said, "you will take up orbital anchorage immediately and surrender or I will blow you out of my sky."

"I think not." Makarov tapped her armrest with her fist to get her XO's attention, then pointed to the deck. "We're here for our citizens. The ones you're about to murder."

Laran shook her head. "The Terran Union did not create this situation, but we have the strength of will to see it through, to preserve the peace. Did Stacey Ibarra dump you out of the tubes with any ability to reason, or am I talking to a stump?"

"We serve the Lady," Makarov said. "Her will is ours. Don't test it."

"I remember your…namesake," Laran said. "A hero of Earth. For Ibarra to spit on that legacy by churning out some sort of cheap imitation to—"

"My mother would have gone to Navarre with the Lady," Makarov said. "And she would never have left any of us behind. I'm not interested in surrendering. You'd just kill us all as 'unauthorized productions,' wouldn't you?"

"It would be my duty."

"Well, then let's not pretend I'm in any hurry to surrender this ship," Makarov said. The *Warsaw* rattled as it descended. Even with Mars' thin atmosphere, the stress of sliding through the skies was taking a toll on her ship.

"Really hope the landscape hasn't changed since we planned this mission," the XO said, "or else this will go down as the most embarrassing rescue attempt in history."

"I'll make you a deal, General," Makarov said. "You sit on your hands until we leave with all our people and no one gets hurt."

"I am armor."

"You are a disgrace," Makarov cut the transmission.

"Rail batteries on Arsia Mons coming to bear," the gunnery officer said.

Ahead, a line of fire snapped across the ship's flight path as a hypervelocity round ignited the thin air with its passing.

"Guns?" Makarov asked.

"Shot went four hundred meters over our direction of travel," she said. "In line with projections, we're below defilade. If we keep this altitude, they shouldn't be able to hit us."

"They built Mars as an anvil," Makarov said. "Meant to punish anyone that got into a fight overhead. General Laran and the rest of the planet didn't plan on a guest sneaking through the keyhole of their shiny new Grinder and ducking beneath their defenses before they could react. The rail batteries are all built into elevated positions to engage orbital targets, not a ship flying with her belly scraping against the ground."

"I'll feel more smug once we're back through the gate," XO said. "There are still four more things that have to happen perfectly or this'll end in a complete disaster."

"*Ferrum corde,*" Makarov said.

"*Ferrum corde,*" the bridge crew intoned.

****

General Laran reached into a holo tank with all of Mars projected within and turned the planet around with a pass of her hand. The *Warsaw*'s flight path, current location and projected course around the red planet flashed with priority.

Her staff, and the crew of the command center, waited silently as the general studied the situation.

"Ground batteries?" the general asked.

"None can engage," replied an army officer, somewhat sheepishly. "Not until they try to break orbit."

Laran swiped through a menu and icons for combat air patrols around Mars populated the holo. Her hands tapped the fighter patrols and dragged them to points along the *Warsaw*'s projected path. She shook her head as estimated flight times popped up next to each proposed route.

"Our fighter coverage is too thin and their ship is moving too fast," Laran snarled. "Bastards did their homework on us."

"Their end game has to be to rescue their personnel at Tholis," her chief of staff said. "If they wanted to destroy the prison and kill the prisoners, they could have done that from the Grinder with a single rail battery salvo."

"Land their carrier? No, they'd never make orbit again." Laran picked at her bottom lip. "They have to take in the prisoners while they're still on the move." She zoomed in on Tholis and touched the dome. Status reports sprang up in the holo: a solid red box for the facility's communications, a blinking amber one for its life support.

"No contact with the guard force," the chief of staff said. "Some sort of structural integrity issue triggered the emergency evac protocol. The S&R flight en route hasn't responded to hails either."

"Clever," Laran said. "They're using our own standard operating procedures against us."

"We can scramble fighters from Olympus. Take out their transports," said a void force officer from the crowd of staff.

"While they're empty?" Laran asked. "The Ibarrans are bold, but they've handed us an opportunity. If we scratch the S&R, then there's still a prison full of problems to…solve, and Makarov might feel inclined to lash out if she realizes she's on a fool's errand. No. They'll be most vulnerable while their people are trying to get aboard the *Warsaw*. We strike then. Take them all out with one blow."

Laran zoomed the holo tank out and swiped a palm across the planet. Icons for warships in orbit blinked.

"We have artillery ships at anchor," she said. "Alert Trebuchet and Ballista squadrons to charge up their rails and work up a firing solution for…here." The general drew a box along the *Warsaw*'s projected path back to the Grinder. "They can fire without leaving their anchorage. Don't alert the Ibarrans by moving any of our ships to intercept. But we need another angle of attack. Ready interdiction fighters with capship missiles. They're to engage as the Ibarrans break orbit…we should see them burn up from here."

"Yes, general," said the void force officer as he looked down at his forearm screen. "I'll have the alert fighters' load out changed right away…just one thing. The alert fighters are all piloted by Dotari."

"Is that going to be a problem?"

"I doubt it…they're all from the *Ardennes* joint squadron. They've tangled with Ibarrans before."

"Then ready the launch. Makarov's going to stick her head right into our noose," Laran said with a smile.

Chapter 20

"Medic!" Adams shouted as she limped out of the lift and into guard post Alpha.

Roland looked over as Labaqui carried Turcotte in and set him down against a wall. Blood stained the Pathfinder's front and dribbled down the legionnaire's back.

"What the hell are you people doing?" Aignar asked Roland from where they stood at the opening of the tunnel leading to post Bravo. The Templar lined the tunnel walls behind them.

Roland watched as Adams checked Turcotte's pulse, then began chest compressions with one arm.

"Stop this," Aignar said. "They'll listen to you, Roland. Put a stop to all of this."

"How?" Roland asked no one. "Adams is a Strike Marine, dedicated to Earth. Why are she and all the other prisoners suddenly—"

"The Ibarrans did this," Aignar said. "Another one of their tricks. They've done it to you, to them…am I the only one here that realizes how insane you all are?"

"Wounded to the Mule!" Medvedev shouted from command center. "All wounded to the fore, now! Labaqui will fly you out!" The big legionnaire went to Adams and pulled her away from Turcotte then handed her off to a group of *Narvik* crewmen. He knelt beside the Pathfinder and closed the dead man's eyes.

Adams wiped blood from her mouth and swiped her hand against the wall, leaving an arc of red. She went to the hangar, cradling her broken arm.

Medvedev hurried over to the Templar's tunnel and banged a fist to his chest, saluting Colonel Martel.

Roland tensed up. Seeing Ibarran legionnaires in their combat armor up close brought out combat instincts—instincts confused as he questioned where his loyalties lie.

"We have a way off world," Medvedev said to Martel. "Three more Destrier transports en route. The crew of the *Narvik* leaves first. Then the rest of our people."

"Our people," Roland thought.

"You think Mars Command is going to let four transports full of escaped prisoners and—" Martel swallowed hard "—and the rest of us just leave?"

"The *Warsaw* will carry us home," Medvedev said.

"How can—"

"That one." Medvedev leveled a knife hand at Aignar. "Why isn't he in a cell?"

"I'm not a prisoner, bucket-head," Aignar said. "I mean, I'm *your* prisoner. Not a prisoner of this prison so that makes—"

"Secure him with the others." Medvedev tossed a set of cuffs to a prisoner with a carbine then thrust his hand toward a group of guards cuffed to handrails at the far end of the guard post.

"Get your filthy hands off me," Aignar said, swatting away the prisoner's grasp.

"Aignar..." Roland gripped his friend by the elbow and stepped between him and Medvedev. "This is hard enough."

"Is it?" Aignar pulled his arm free and walked toward the bound guards, his boots clomping against the deck plating.

The guard with the cuffs looked between Roland and Aignar and shrugged.

Roland caught up with Aignar and the rest of the liberated prisoners watched as the two armor made their way across the post.

"You can put a stop to this madness," Aignar said.

"If I could, what would that accomplish?" Roland asked. "We know what's going to happen to the *Narvik*'s crew. Omega Provision. And the…others? They're not with the Terran Union anymore. What will Earth do to them?"

"Deprogram them. Undo what the Ibarrans have done." Aignar's gaze stuck on a group of former prisoners clustered around a doorway leading to the prison grounds. All had weapons trained on post Charlie.

"I don't know if that's even possible," Roland said. "During the Ember War something similar happened. Naroosha changed proccies in their tubes…Marc Ibarra had them all killed."

"You're running into the arms of monsters guilty of the exact thing you're afraid Earth will do," Aignar said. "What did they do to you, Roland? If they changed something deep in your head, I can forgive you being an out-and-out traitor. Don't tell me this is what you want."

"Marc Ibarra is not Stacey Ibarra. The Lady—I mean—"

"Rolly Polly?" Jerry looked up from the outer edge of the mass of guards. Both of his hands were cuffed to a railing and he struggled to raise his head in his unpowered armor. Roland left Aignar's side and went to his old roommate from his childhood orphanage as the former prisoner with the restraints urged Aignar forward.

"Jerry? You OK? Anything hurt?" Roland asked.

"My pride," Jerry said, shifting uncomfortably, "and my balls. Mostly my balls right now. What was that other armor guy talking about? Where's Valencia? Why aren't you…"

"She's safe." Roland looked out over the prison to where they'd left the other guard. "She's locked up in the Templar cell block. Listen, Jerry…things are all screwed up right now."

"You saved my life on Thesius," Jerry said, his face contorting with emotion, "and now you're with them? These bunch of traitors?"

"They're not…" Roland knelt next to Jerry and crossed his arms over his bent knee. "I am armor. I am Templar. The Union—the Union turned its back on what I swore to defend."

"The Union is the Union, Roland," Jerry said. "We fight for all mankind." He shrugged a shoulder with the Ranger unit crest painted on the pauldron. "You're going with a bunch of tube babies and the Ibarrans? What happened to you?"

Roland's hands balled into fists and he looked back to the hangar entrance just as the air-lock doors closed. Medvedev had one hand to the side of his helmet, his head bowed slightly as he listened to someone. The last of the

Narvik's crew and the former prisoners around him looked resolute, sure of their purpose.

"You haven't seen what I've seen, Jerry," Roland said. "They're not what you think."

Jerry looked at his bound wrists then back to Roland. "There are bodies in the hangar," Jerry said. "Dead Rangers, all my brothers, out in the yard. I think they're my enemies and they haven't disappointed me yet."

"The Kesaht—"

"Hate us anyway," Jerry said. "The Vishrakath are looking for an excuse. So are the Naroosha. The Haesh. Just because I'm a grunt doesn't mean I don't know what's going on out there. They get away and what happens? We lived through the Ember War when we were kids, Roland. You remember the bunkers? How scared we were? That's what's coming again."

"So I should leave them all here to die? That's not what I've sworn my life to."

"To hell—" Jerry lowered his voice. "To hell with you. You think a higher loyalty to some…damn it. I prayed, you know that? I prayed for the first time in years when the damn Rakka were about to rip us to pieces. I prayed to Saint Kallen and then you showed up. Now you're telling me you being all Templar and stuff means you have to be a traitor? Help me figure this out, man, because I don't know if it was what the tubies used to knock me out or what, but I can't put the pieces together on this."

"It shouldn't *be* this way," Roland said. "We should be side by side against the galaxy, but here we are, killing each other. This is what Earth's enemies want—division, a civil war in the hope some damn piece of paper protects the future."

"Just go, bud." Jerry looked away. "I should never have let you fill up Hale's drinks that night back at Deco's. That put all sorts of stupid ideas in your head…now look where we are."

"You should've parked yourself in some macro cannon out beyond Pluto," Roland said. "Would've been a lot safer for you."

"Second group!" Medvedev shouted as warning lights spun to life around the air lock. "Second group, prepare to embark!"

"That you?" Jerry asked.

"No." Roland stood and looked over the guards bound to the railings. Those that had their heads turned up regarded Roland with scorn. Aignar was at the far end, his back to Roland. He fought the urge to go and explain himself to his lance mate. The conversation with Jerry made him realize just how futile that task would be with Aignar.

"What're your buddies going to do with us?" Jerry

asked.

"They don't—we don't want you." Roland stood up. "Stay safe."

"Not really an option right now," Jerry smirked.

Roland went back to the Templar tunnel. He leaned a shoulder against the rough rock and crossed his arms over his chest.

"There is an answer," Tongea said as the older man stepped up next to him, his hands clasped behind his back.

"I…don't know it yet. I have a feeling…" Roland said, touching his heart. "But this," he paused and touched his head, "hasn't caught up to it."

"When you were the Ibarras' prisoner and you learned of the Kesaht attack on one of their colonies, did you hesitate to volunteer?" Tongea asked.

"No…easy decision."

"You gave no thought to how it might end for you if the Terran Union learned what you did?"

"It didn't matter."

"If Aignar or your old friend were there with you, would you have chosen any differently?"

"No." Roland took a deep breath and emotions came loose from his heart.

"What is your choice now?"

"There is no choice. I am Templar. We fight for the

future. One we won't live to see."

"Nicodemus and Morrigan were right to lend their names to you for the vigil," Tongea huffed. "If they hadn't, Martel and I would have."

"Thank you, sir."

"There is no thanks for what is earned."

****

Masha banked her Destrier over the prison and watched as the dome over post Charlie rolled into the ground, revealing a Mule. The Mule rose a few yards off the ground and then blasted away into the sky.

"Where the hell are they going?" Walker asked.

"Olympus is that way." She pointed to the northeast, almost opposite the direction the Mule had flown.

"First transport with wounded is away," Makarov said through her dental implant.

"Bento," Masha said to the pilot of one of the other two Destriers, "this is Gezur. Land and board as many evacuees as you can."

"Gezur, what's the status of the prison?" Bento asked over the IR. *"The guard force isn't broadcasting a distress."*

"You see those cracks in the dome? Whatever did that damage must have slagged their comms," Masha said.

"I'm in tight-beam contact with the warden. You're secure to land."

"You are?" Walker flipped through channels and gave Masha a confused look.

"Roger," Bento said. *"Setting down now."*

The other craft landed and Masha bit her lip as the dome slid up from the housing and just barely cleared the large transport's hull.

"Rickets, you're up next," Masha sent to the second transport.

"This is the weirdest day," Walker said. "We haven't had a single demand for a sitrep from Hard-Ass since we took off. There should've been some spittle and screaming after you blew off the request to delay for a security element."

"Small favors, eh?" Masha's heart pounded as she glanced at the mission clock. The pickup window to the *Warsaw* was getting smaller every second.

Walker frowned and clicked a switch several times. "We don't…we don't have any contact with Olympus. I just sent an IFF ping and got nothing back, but the channel reads green."

The dome opened and the Destrier inside lurched into the air slowly.

"Bento," Walker said into the flight's channel, "give us a passenger count. Standard reporting, let's go."

"Rickets, get in there," Masha ordered and cut the flight channel.

"This is all wrong," Walker said. "Why can't I hear—"

Masha drew a pistol off her chest in a flash and pressed the muzzle to Walker's faceplate. The other woman froze, her eyes wide with shock.

"Everything is going just fine," Masha said. "Now...I don't really *need* a copilot right now. So you can either deactivate your station and cuff yourself to your chair with the handy-dandy bracelets I tucked under your seat or you will never have another problem again. Pick. Flying this bucket and holding this gun are a bit much for me right now."

"You're...you're one of them," Walker said.

Masha tapped the muzzle against Walker's visor.

Walker raised her hands slowly. Then snapped a hand toward her commo panel.

Masha's pistol cracked and blood splattered against the cockpit windows. Walker slumped against her restraints, her head lolling over a shoulder.

"I hate heroes." Masha holstered her pistol and shut down the copilot's controls.

****

Aignar rolled his metal wrists from side to side in his cuffs and glanced over at the former prisoner holding a carbine. The man had his attention on the door to the air lock where Medvedev was taking a head count as prisoners filed past him. Prisoners led aircrew into the guard post at gunpoint and locked them up with the rest of the guards.

A pilot was forced down next to Aignar and shackled to the handrail.

"What the hell is going on?" Rickets asked. "We touch down and some monster in black armor's in the cockpit seconds later with a gun in our face."

"The Ibarrans are checking out early," Aignar said. "Anyone know what's happening out there?"

"We got a life-support alert," Rickets said. "Holy crap, are those the Templar over there? Why aren't they hog-tied like us?"

"Explain later. Fight now." Aignar kicked a helmetless Ranger's leg, the blow of his boot against the armor startling the man awake.

"Soldier, I'm less than useful with a rifle." Aignar wiggled his metal fingers slowly. "If I get you a battery pack and a weapon, you need to take control of this situation."

"That plug in your skull mess your brain up?" the Ranger asked. "Even if I was loose, I—"

"The regiments get soft since I was in?" Aignar leaned over to the Ranger. "You've got one real threat—the legionnaire. Take him out then you're dealing with pogues that aren't in armor. How many more you want to get away?"

"You got your cart before the horse." The Ranger rolled his eyes, then pulled the chain between his cuffs against the handrail.

"I saw where they dumped all the gear they stripped off the guard force." Aignar nodded to an open office door a few yards away. "Suit batteries. Pistols."

"Lot of good that does us," the Ranger said.

Aignar craned his neck around and saw two armed prisoners talking with each other, both pointing at the Templar and the last of the Ibarran turncoats walking into the hangar. Neither were watching the guards.

He grabbed a wrist with one hand, then unsnapped his prosthetic from the socket below his elbow.

"That's kind of gross," Rickets said quietly.

Aignar tilted his detached arm down, and it slid out of the cuffs and onto his lap, leaving one hole empty. He brought his other arm down, quickly re-snapping his arm back into place, then rolled onto his elbows and knees and crawled into the open office, moving on his elbows and knees—which were flesh instead of metal—to soften the sound.

He looked toward the prisoners that were supposed to be watching him and saw they were still distracted. If his mouth could move, he would have smiled. He looked back into the office as he crossed over the threshold and almost bumped into the back of a prisoner's legs.

"I'm taking one of these Ranger P9s," the man said. "They always got the best gear. You think we'll get something better once we get home?"

He turned around and looked through an empty doorway, a pistol held in one hand.

"Carl?"

Aignar brought a foot around and planted it on the floor. The prisoner looked down just in time to see Aignar's metal fist rise in an uppercut. His head snapped back and he crumbled into Aignar's arms as the pistol clattered against the floor.

"Damn it!" Aignar looked through the doorway and one of the guards flashed him an OK sign. He let the unconscious man slide out of his grip and his head bounced off the floor. Aignar shrugged. On the desk were piles of pistols, magazines, power packs and a single carbine.

Aignar picked up the pistol from the floor, then clamped a hand onto a magazine and worked it into the weapon. He struck the loose magazine against his thigh and the weapon cycled a bullet into the chamber. He popped a trigger finger open then tried to pull it toward his palm. The finger jittered.

"If I was in my armor…" He tucked the pistol into the back of his waistband and picked up a power armor battery.

The Ranger shook his head quickly and Aignar waited, the cuffs swishing against one wrist.

Chapter 21

Admiral Lettow suffered through the habitual wave of vertigo that came with a wormhole passage. Considering that, to make the journey, he and his ship were crossing a quantum bridge between two points thousands of light-years across without being smeared into electrons or passing through a nightmare dimension full of demons, he considered himself lucky.

He looked out the *Ardennes'* bridge windows and froze. Space, the void, was white, an infinite expanse of blazing white.

"Radiation alert!" Paxton announced. "Shields holding but we've got maybe ten minutes before we start taking rads."

"Admiral..." Behind the admiral at the command and control holo tank, Jarilla unlocked the mag plates on his exo-armor and grasped at the air with overly long fingers. "Ruhaald do not have the same radiation tolerance as humans. The effects on us will be—"

"You have ten minutes before you're allowed to panic." Lettow pulled up his ship's sensor suite and got a mountain of scrambled data. Swearing, he got out of his command chair and noticed striations in the great white around the ship and bright pinpricks of light in the distance. They were inside a nebula, one that could stretch out for light-years.

"XO, what's out there? Are we sure the Ibarrans are even here?" Lettow activated the holo tank and it fizzled to life. The Crucible gate with his ship in the center was well imaged, but what was around that came in broken and distorted.

"Radiation is wreaking hell on our scanners," Paxton said. "We're working through spotter feeds from around the ship now."

A minute ticked by. If the two Ruhaald observers were getting nervous, he couldn't tell. A message request from the Vishrakath contingent popped up, but he swatted it away.

A black ball of a planet cut through with varicose lines of red lava appeared forward and below the Crucible gate. A shadow in the nebula formed on the near side of the planet and Lettow's brow furrowed as he tried to make sense of all this.

"Fascinating," Rhysli said, raising her enclosed chair flush with the holo table. "This system is moving through the nebula. It must be a rogue star. One so close to the galactic core is—"

"Sir," Paxton interrupted, running over to the holo table, "there's a magnetar star fifteen astronomic units away. It's flooding the nebula with radiation. If we get in the planet's wake, our shields will hold."

"Conn, get us in low orbit, best speed!" Lettow ordered.

"Aye aye!" came from the bridge and the *Ardennes* lurched forward. A course projection came up in the holo tank. The carrier would reach safety with two minutes to spare.

"Rad levels should slack off the closer we get," Paxton said. "Not that I suggest we slow down."

"We can make the return trip to the Crucible easy enough," Lettow said.

"Why are the Ibarrans here?" Rhysli asked. "I get ahead of myself. Why did the Xaros build a Crucible gate here?"

"The Xaros built gates in only two places," Jarilla said, "over habitable worlds or in systems with archaeotech—

civilizations dead before the Xaros arrived."

"Nunavik isn't exactly ripe for colonization," Lettow said, shifting the holo tank to the planet. Swaths of the surface came into clear focus as cameras from around the ship sent video to the tank for processing: active volcanoes and obsidian-black terrain riven through with lava flows.

What are they here for? Lettow wondered, then asked, "XO, any sign of the Ibarrans?"

"We got a hit from the graviton wave generated by our arrival," she said, and in the tank a cone extended from the Crucible to Nunavik, encompassing the whole planet. "They got a head start on us. My guess is they're in low orbit to keep out of the radiation."

"We'll find them," Lettow said. "It'll just take some time."

"By the depths," Rhysli said.

In the holo, an ivory and gold circle appeared. Lettow directed more cameras to the area and zoomed in. The area covered over a hundred and twenty miles, nearly the size of metropolitan Phoenix back on Earth. On closer inspection, the gold lines became buildings, all radiating out from a central dome.

"Fascinating," Rhysli said, "the radius is ten kilometers. The builders gave it an area that echoes pi. This could be a Qa'Resh location. They worked mathematical constants into their architecture on other planets."

"How is it still here?" Paxton asked. "The Qa'Resh vanished millions of years ago. This planet is like Io."

Jarilla reached into the tank and tried to manipulate the view with his eight-tentacled hand. Bubbles floated from his mouth tendrils and he pulled three tentacles back to match a human hand. The view shifted to the edge of the city…and Lettow watched in amazement as terrain moved beneath the circumference.

"The city is moving," Lettow said.

"Keeps it out of the lava and the radiation," Paxton said. "Not bad."

"Long-term study of a magnetar moving through the galactic center would—" Lettow stopped the Ruhaald.

Paxton touched her forearm screen and tossed a file into the tank. The view shifted over to a human drop pod not far from the central dome.

"Got you," Lettow said. He swiped through shifting data readings then opened a channel to the commander of his embarked Rangers. "Major Haskell, how long can your men function in that environment? The city's out of the worst of the radiation, but the levels are still far above normal."

"Maybe seven minutes before our absorption layers fail," the major sent back.

"Stand down," Lettow sighed. "This isn't a suicide

mission. Augment the counter-boarding and damage-control parties as the chief of the boat sees fit." He closed the channel.

"Guess it's up to the armor," Paxton said. "They're built for harsh environments like this."

"I don't like having only a single option," Lettow said. "It makes you predictable and vulnerable, but it's not like we're spoiled for choice right now. Captain Gideon?"

"Task Force Iconoclast stands ready." Gideon's icon popped up in the tank.

"Load drop pods," Lettow said. "I'm letting you off the leash before we make orbit. If we can't detect the Ibarrans on sensors in this mess, they won't see your approach."

"We will not fail." Gideon cut the channel.

Lettow stepped back from the holo tank, emotion roiling behind his eyes. This wasn't like Balmaseda where he led a mission to remove an Ibarran colony as peacefully as possible—a mission he carried out that led to a tacit truce with the Ibarrans when it came time to fight the Kesaht. This was a decapitation strike. This was an overt act of war. There was no turning back from this.

"You have concerns, Admiral?" Jarilla asked.

"No," he said. "My orders are clear. Stacey Ibarra's reign ends now."

Chapter 22

Roland felt vibrations through the floor as the hangar dome opened. All the *Narvik* crew and most of the prisoners had evacuated, leaving Medvedev and a handful of turncoats remaining along with the Templar.

Medvedev handed Roland a carbine.

"What's next?" Roland asked.

"Last chance out of here," the legionnaire said. "Then it's up to the Saint if we make it home."

"The Saint…" Roland turned to Tongea. "Her tomb is here on Mars. Who will look after it? After her?"

Tongea frowned. "It's not just the Templar that revere her," the Maori said. "A good deal of the military does too. They wouldn't disturb her."

"It's a tomb," Colonel Martel said. "Relics of the final battle against the Xaros are buried there. Laran wouldn't dare—"

Medvedev raised a hand.

"Our ride landed. Hangar is pressurizing. Get ready to move." The legionnaire went back to the air-lock doors.

"Aignar," Roland said to the other two Templar. "He could be reasoned with. Maybe he'll—"

"Where is he?" Tongea said.

"In the back." Roland motioned with his carbine. "You can see his hands…or not."

A light wobbled over the top of the tunnel entrance. Roland leaned to one side and down the curved passage. Templar shifted uneasily from side to side.

"That's the arrival light," Tongea said.

"It's on the other side too." Martel pointed across the guard post to the shut doors of the tunnel leading to Charlie.

The sound of a high-speed cart racing down tracks sounded through the opposite doors.

"Incoming!" Roland dived forward just as the other tunnel doors exploded. A concussion slapped against Roland's head and a hunk of a metal door ripped through a workstation next to him, killing a pair of prisoners guarding the catwalk entrance. Smoke filled the air, choking Roland.

Pain crept into his feet. He looked down and saw that both his feet were on fire. He kicked at the floor and slapped the flames away, burning his hand against the red buckles of his boots. Hacking and coughing as more smoke entered his lungs, he pawed through the growing darkness for his weapon.

His eyes stinging against the caustic air, he swung his carbine toward the observation windows and willed his weapon to fire.

I'm not in my armor! he thought.

He pulled the trigger, emptying the magazine into the window, and heard coughing all around him…then a cracking sound. As the glass broke apart in a rain of crystal knives, smoke billowed out and into the dome, clearing the air slowly throughout the guard post.

Roland blinked tears from his eyes and saw the round counter on his carbine flashing double zeros. His ears roared with tinnitus from the explosion, and he was acutely aware of what a difference his armor made on the battlefield.

Another carbine lay a few feet away, a severed arm still gripping the handle.

Muffled shouts fought through the ringing, but he kept his focus on the weapon. Even out of armor, he knew he needed a weapon to be useful in a fight. He crawled forward, the smell of soot and blood almost gagging him.

Roland reached for the weapon, and a gauss bullet snapped past his face and sliced across the top of his arm. He cried out and fell onto his stomach as another round passed through where his head had just been.

"*Ferrum corde!*" Medvedev shouted.

A dozen power-armored Strike Marines and Rangers rushed through the blown doors.

Medvedev leaped off a workstation and speared a Strike Marine with his shoulder. The legionnaire's sudden attack caught the Union troops flat-footed and he rolled into the middle of their group. He jabbed a carbine into a Ranger's neck and blew his throat out, then swung the dying soldier into another Strike Marine, knocking her off her feet.

The legionnaire slapped a rifle aside and grabbed the Ranger by the wrists, pulling him across his body with a twist of his hips. The Ranger stopped a bullet meant for Medvedev's heart and flopped to the ground.

Izuma snapped his Ka-Bar out of his forearm housing and hacked it against Medvedev's forearms, cracking the armor plate and forcing the legionnaire to drop his weapon. A Ranger kicked Medvedev in the small of his back and sent him stumbling forward. Izuma pulled his knife arm back and rammed the blade into Medvedev's stomach, piercing the armor.

"Templar!" Martel shouted. "Charge!"

A roar filled the air and the unarmored Templar thundered out of the tunnel.

Roland snatched up the carbine with his good arm

and struggled to his feet as gauss fire erupted from the Union troops.

The forward ranks of the Templar fell, riddled with bullets. A melee broke out as Templar charged over their dead and wrestled with the Union troops.

Tongea wrenched a Strike Marine's muzzle up, straining against the armor's powered muscles just long enough for another Templar to crush the butt of her carbine into the Marine's visor.

Roland almost tripped over a dead Templar and veered toward a scrum of his fellows beating Izuma with bare fists and hunks of rock. Blood poured down the split flesh of his arm, but the pain was lost in the adrenaline haze.

A Strike Marine toward the fore of the fight threw off a Templar, crushing bones against the wall. Roland braced the carbine barrel over his bloody arm and fired, hitting the Strike Marine in the chest and staggering it back.

Martel, a broken Ka-Bar blade in his bloody hands, stabbed the knife into the Strike Marine's neck with a roar.

Roland felt his collar tighten and he went reeling backwards. He crashed against a desk and fell against a file cabinet in the post commander's office.

Aignar stood over him, pistol in hand and aimed at Roland, shaking his head slowly. "No, Roland. You're not getting away from this," Aignar said.

The sound of the fighting tapered off and shouts for help echoed across the room.

"Aignar..." Roland held up his bloody arm and grimaced as the pain caught up with him. "This is all wrong."

"You're right." The pistol in Aignar's grip quivered. "You're not above the law. I don't care what you believe or what we used to be. You are not getting away from this."

Roland looked his friend in the eye...felt a part of his soul wither away...then raised a foot and kicked Aignar just below the knee where his prosthetic foot met his real leg. The limb snapped free and Aignar twisted forward as he fell. Roland rolled aside and Aignar fell hard. Roland grabbed Aignar's gun hand by the wrist and twisted it twice, just as he'd seen Aignar do to release the limb. The hand came loose smoothly and Roland tossed the weapon and the arm away.

Aignar made a pitiful cry and reached for his hand with the stump.

Roland got up and took the pistol out of Aignar's detached hand. He looked back at his friend, who struggled to cross the floor with his remaining limbs.

In the main room, Templar lay dead, their bodies intertwined with dead power-armored Union soldiers.

Roland made for the door when Aignar grabbed him by the ankle. "No...you're not...getting..." Words crackled out of Aignar's throat speaker.

Roland pulled his foot free and roared as he kicked Aignar in the face. The other Iron Dragoon's head smacked against the floor and he lay still.

"Aignar?" Roland, horrified at what he'd just done, touched Aignar's shoulder.

Aignar looked up, his false jaw swinging free from a socket. A bloody, ragged breath gurgled through Aignar's exposed throat. He reached out for Roland, his metal fist bouncing off the Templar's chest.

Roland backed away, his breath heaving as he saw his old friend in such a state.

Aignar slammed his remaining hand to the ground and inched forward, looking at Roland with hate in his eyes.

"Traitor," Aignar said, blood flecking his broken jaw as he crept forward. "You are a...traitor!"

"I'm not." Roland shook his head. "I'm sorry, Aignar." Roland backed out of the door, and a mournful cry followed him.

Martel and Tongea dragged Medvedev to the air lock, both Templar bloody and struggling to move the man in his armor. Medvedev had one hand clutched to the knife wound in his abdomen.

Roland ran over and reached behind the legionnaire's head. He found two buttons and pressed them home. The armor plates on Medvedev's arms, legs and shoulders fell away. Tongea let go and crumpled against a wall.

"Get him," Martel said, nodding at Tongea, as he dragged the legionnaire into the hangar toward a Destrier with its ramp lowered.

Roland guided Tongea upright and got the Maori over his shoulders. He took a hard step forward, then another.

"Kallen," Roland said, "*ferrum corde*..." He broke into a run and stomped up the ramp.

"Anyone else?" asked a prisoner with a bloody face.

"No." Roland knelt and set Tongea against the bulkhead. The ramp rose and locked against the Destrier.

"Medic?" Roland asked, but Tongea wasn't the only one in need.

A pair of prisoners worked on Medvedev, his chest armor cracked open, blood oozing from the stab wound.

Templar were strewn across the cargo bay, all bloody and battered.

Roland looked down at his arm, still oozing red.

Tongea's breathing was shallow. He wheezed with every exhale.

"Sir, stay with me." Roland felt moisture against his leg. A pool of blood spread out from the Maori.

"Not now." Tongea shook his head and blood dribbled from the corner of his mouth. "She...the Saint cried for me. I'll die in my armor. Not like this." He grabbed Roland by the collar with strength. "Not. Like. This."

The hand went slack and fell to Tongea's side.

"Medic!" Roland caught Tongea as he slumped to the side.

****

The drop pod burst through a plume of volcanic smoke and ash, hurtling toward the Qa'Resh city. Two more followed, each spaced several kilometers from the other. Rockets flared from the first, arresting the downward velocity so fast it would have snapped the spines of any normal humans inside.

The pod slammed into a wide boulevard and a metal panel swung down like a drawbridge. Gideon charged out, gauss cannons loaded, scanning for targets. The buildings along the street had white walls, ghostly light blue hues shifting beneath the surface seemed to mimic the nebula filled sky above. The gold roofs glittered for reasons Gideon didn't care to understand. There was no obvious pattern to the size of the buildings; some were as wide as a Mule, while others stretched on for hundreds of meters. All had a single iris for a door at ground level, twice the height of an armor soldier.

Gideon charged toward a building and took cover

against a corner. The rest of his cobbled-together lance, Pak and Thomas, both from lances torn apart by the Templar detention, pulled security around him.

His HUD fizzled with radiation, making long-distance targeting difficult. The building wall seemed to react to his presence as ripples of white matching his outline rose up from where the wall melded into the ground.

Gideon leaned back from the building and shot a pigeon drone out of the launcher on his back. An IR channel connected him to the other two lances on the ground.

"Hell Fighters, Black Watch, report," he sent.

"Boots on the ground."

"No sign of the enemy."

"Move toward the central dome. Send a drone if you make visual or hostile contact," Gideon said. "The Ibarrans have their armor here—you all saw the drop pod. We are not here to talk them down. We are here to end them. Gideon out."

He pulsed a command to the drone and it fell onto a sparkling gold roof.

"Qa'Resh architecture." Pak almost poked the wall but restrained himself at the last moment. "The laws of physics tend to be a bit…wonky."

"Three-sixty security," Gideon said. "Assume the Ibarrans can be anywhere until you've got them dead at your feet. Follow me."

He made his way down the boulevard, checking corners and moving at a bounding over watch across open space.

I hope you're here, Nicodemus, he thought. *You and I have unfinished business.*

****

Trepidation crept into Masha as the *Warsaw* came over the horizon and a dust storm billowed in the carrier's wake. Flying a Destrier nap of the earth was a heart-racing task; how something as big as the *Warsaw* managed to do so at slightly more elevation was a feat Masha did not want to attempt herself.

"*Evac 3, this is Makarov,*" came through a tight-beam IR laser. "*Enemy defenses are moving to engage. We're adjusting pickup.*"

"*Warsaw*, you're coming in too fast. The plan was for me to approach from behind and land through the aft bay."

"*That was the plan. Now you're going to maneuver for an overtake,*" Makarov said.

Masha caught her breath.

"That's a negative, *Warsaw*. If either of us fouls up our merge vectors, the explosion will be phenomenal," Masha said.

"Then don't screw up. Do it right and we go home. Screw up and kill us all. Or you can stay here."

Masha looked at the copilot she'd killed. "Murder and espionage trials are for amateurs," she said. "Send the telemetry data."

Instructions flashed across her HUD.

"Oh boy…" Masha flipped a switch on her flight stick. "Attention everyone, this is your captain speaking. We are in for a rough landing. I suggest everyone buckle up. Barring that, the more flexible of you should consider sticking your head between your legs and—"

"Don't you dare kill me with incompetence," Medvedev sent through her tooth. *"I'm going home to the legion…only if you don't kill me first."*

"When you ask so nicely," Masha sighed and fired the Destrier's afterburners. The big ship accelerated forward and she banked the craft through waypoints on the HUD. A screen popped up displaying the rearview from her plane and the *Warsaw* raced up behind her like a leviathan from the deep about to swallow her whole.

Masha's jaw clenched as she cut back on the engine power. Her throat went dry as the cavern of the *Warsaw*'s flight deck crept closer. In theory, she could guide the Destrier into the hangar and land, like taking off in reverse.

"Almost there," Masha mumbled.

A fighter streaked past her nose and Masha shrieked in surprise, yanking back on the control stick. The Destrier lurched up. The aircraft, half in and half out of the hangar, smacked against the ceiling, bounced off and then belly-skid across the flight deck in a shower of sparks.

Masha killed all power to the engines and braced herself against her seat as a groan of metal on metal filled her ears. The transport tipped to one side and she heard a wing break away. The view in her cockpit swung around and came to a bone-jarring halt.

A crewman on a catwalk looked at Masha through the glass, his jaw open. Masha gave him a playful wave.

"I don't seem to be dead yet," Medvedev sent.

"Any landing you can walk away from, right?" Masha unbuckled her seat belts and tossed off her helmet. "Teddy bear, you know where I can hide from the admiral? I doubt she'll appreciate what I've done to her flight deck."

"You're doomed."

"And you're welcome."

Corpsmen rushed out of side passageways and pointed into the cockpit. Masha jerked a thumb at Walker and waved fingertips across her throat. She pointed back to the cargo bay and kicked her feet up onto the instrument panel.

"Sorry, Walker, that's the game."

****

Man'fred Vo flipped his Eagle fighter into a barrel roll and dove into a canyon as a storm of antiaircraft fire from the *Warsaw* blasted overhead. His flight suit tightened against his legs and midsection, keeping blood in his brain as g-forces pressed against his body.

"Six, what the hell was that?" asked his human flight commander.

"We can't fire on the Ibarran ship," the Dotari pilot said. "What was the problem?"

"You almost caused a crash when that last Destrier linked up to the carrier."

"Almost? I should have flown closer." Man'fred Vo pulled his Eagle's nose to the sky and accelerated straight up. The long anti-ship torpedo on his fuselage dragged against his fighter's maneuverability in atmosphere and he clicked his beak in annoyance. He'd rather take a rail cannon shot on a target like the *Warsaw*, but it was still in enough atmosphere to throw off the ballistics.

His wingman, a human that insisted on being called "Nero" while they were in the air—against the Dotari tradition of simply going by their numerical ranking in the squadron—fell in on his wing as Man'fred Vo leveled out, cruising away from the *Warsaw*.

"Flight, vector to one-seven-niner and spin up your missile's tracking," said the squadron commander. "Enemy ship's gaining altitude…and we've got rocket pod ignition. Set for hook terminal guidance."

The Dotari pilot entered a quick command into his weapon's panel and dove back toward Mars. Six plumes of light blazed off the *Warsaw*'s aft as the rocket pods attached to the carrier pushed it beyond the grip of Martian gravity.

Four Eagles swung back and traced the Ibarran ship's path from dozens of miles away. The missiles would have the best chance of striking their targets with a wake attack as the interference from the rocket pods was sure to degrade the ship's point defense tracking. The missiles would hook around the ship's flanks at the last second, avoiding the immense heat emanating from the rocket pods.

As Man'fred Vo gripped his control stick, his mind wandered to Cha'ril and their egg, then he refocused on the readings on his HUD. Even with his fighter rattling at top speed, the *Warsaw* outpaced the Eagles.

"We're going to lose the shot," Nero said.

"Mark tone," said the squadron commander. "Angle final vector by sequence and launch on my mark."

The Dotari locked his missile on the *Warsaw*, setting it

to swoop up through the ship's underbelly. He'd never taken out a target this big before. Cha'ril would be so proud.

"Break, break!" Nero shouted.

A column of fire slammed through the atmosphere ahead of his fighter. Man'fred Vo banked hard and a wave of superheated air slapped his fighter like a fly caught in a hurricane. Alarms blared through his helmet as Mars tumbled around and around.

"Cha'ril!"

****

"What the hell was that?" Laran demanded. The fighters that were on the verge of attacking the *Warsaw* had all gone off-line.

"Multiple hits on rail battery emplacements," said her chief of staff as damage icons sprang up around a wide circle on Mars…all the cannons that would have had line of sight on the *Warsaw* as it broke for the Grinder.

"From where?" Laran zoomed her holo tank out, looking for an Ibarran ship that must have come through the gate.

"There's some ionization," said the gunnery officer. "It reads like rail cannon strikes."

"Not from the Ibarrans, the angle's impossible…have

the artillery ships fire when ready," Laran said. "That ship isn't leaving."

"General, reverse ballistics coming in." Her chief of staff tossed a file into the holo tank. The trace on the projectiles that had knocked out the fighters and blasted the ground cannons all came from Mars' orbit...along the *Warsaw*'s original course over the planet.

"Impossible," Laran said as she pulled the holo's viewpoint along the route and found spent thruster pods surrounded by bits of debris. She zoomed in. The "debris" were all uniformly shaped into tubes, some burning with heat. She went in closer. Mag coils ran around the tubes.

"They're launchers..." Laran went pale. "They seeded launchers behind them when they arrived. Order the artillery ships to break anchor. Evasive maneuvers, now!"

An alert pinged in the holo tank. The general touched it and her face fell as the ships at anchorage fed damage reports into the system. All were off-line, the long rails of their launchers wrecked by kinetic impact...four of the eight ships destroyed.

"How many launchers do they have left?" Laran asked as Mount Olympus rumbled with impact. The holo wavered in ad out.

"Hail for you, ma'am," said her chief of staff. "It's Admiral—"

"Put it through." Laran braced her hands against the tank rim and looked up at Makarov.

"How many do I have left?" Makarov asked. "Enough to crumble Olympus? Just enough to slag your command center? Want to find out?"

"Doesn't matter if you kill me." Laran raised her gaze. "You'll pay for this. We will hunt you down to the galaxy's edge and see you all burn for—"

"The only reason I haven't atomized you is Saint Kallen," Makarov said. "Her tomb is there. We will be back for her bones and if we can't have them, we will take your head. Call off anything else you might have after us. I don't want to kill anyone else today."

The transmission snapped off and Laran hunched forward, her head bowed.

"Ma'am?" her chief of staff asked.

Laran raised a hand, held it next to her ear a moment, then set it back on the railing.

"Ready my shuttle," she said. "I'll explain this to President Garret myself."

****

A cry went out through the Grinder's command center as crew pointed up through the wide view port in the ceiling to Mars. Flashes of exploding ships in orbit and tall plumes of smoke and ash like volcano plumes filled Freeman with dread.

What am I doing? The Ibarrans didn't promise any of this, he thought.

Freeman lifted a thin chain necklace out of his jumpsuit and fished out a sweat-covered key. He opened a panel on the dais and flipped open a clear plastic latch.

"Hard reboot in three." He plugged the key in and twisted it hard to one side. All power through the command center shut off and plunged the room into near darkness; only pale starlight and Mars shone through. A moment later, illumination came back.

"At least the lights work," Freeman said just before the holo tank sprang back to life around him.

"Freeman!" Keeper appeared in a holo screen.

"Oh…it's you," he said. *Not part of the plan.*

"We got a light-speed message about the Ibarra attack so my information is dated," Keeper said. "What's the situation? I can't open a gate to your station *or* an exit point anywhere near Mars to send reinforcements."

"There's…I've got a quantum scrambler field up," Freeman said quietly, checking to see that none of the crew were listening too closely to him as they struggled to get their stations working again.

Fractals shimmered over Keeper's face. "You what?" she asked, her demeanor stern.

"Freeman! We're on final approach to the gate," Masha sent through his tooth receiver. *"We have Salina. She's safe but she's injured. Get us home, now!"*

"Opening wormhole now." Freeman twisted his hand around in the holo tank and pulled up a map of the galaxy. He tapped in a code and the Crucible in the Sagittarius arm pinged.

"Stop this," Keeper said. "I don't know what they promised you, but it's a lie."

"What we do for love, right?" Freeman said as the Grinder's enormous thorns crisscrossed against each other.

The *Warsaw* appeared in the distance, engines burning straight for the Grinder. Panic broke out through the crew as the ship barreled down on them. A wormhole formed in the middle of the Grinder and Freeman looked away from the bright white circle.

"Remember to activate the timer on the data scrambler to hide our destination before you join us," Masha sent.

"Freeman," Keeper's face lost all color then snapped back to normal, "you don't know the Ibarrans like I do. This—"

The *Warsaw* roared through the wormhole and vanished.

"Abandon ship!" Freeman squeezed the data drive still plugged into the control panel and heard a click. A vibration went through his fingers and the final programming Masha gave him went into the system.

"Sorry, Keeper." He gave the woman a quick salute. "I've someplace else to be."

The wormhole collapsed into a point and winked out of existence.

"What?" Freeman pushed Keeper's box aside and tried to reactivate the wormhole, but the controls were frozen. "No, no, no! She promised!"

"Where did they go?" Keeper asked calmly. "Do the right thing."

"How am I supposed to—" Freeman's hands shot to his mouth. The false tooth the spics had given him felt like it was on fire. The quantum dot disintegrated, sending purple smoke pouring out of Freeman's mouth. He collapsed to the ground and lost feeling in his mouth as the toxins in the smoke entered his lungs.

Freeman crawled to the edge of the dais and reached out to a horrified crew member for help. With one last, hacking cough, he slumped over and fell off the dais. His flesh went gray and cracked, crumbling into ash within seconds. His clothes settled to the floor like a deflated balloon.

Chapter 23

Cha'ril looked down at her bare belly and stroked it. She just started to show this morning and couldn't wait for Man'fred Vo to see it. The egg growing inside her would be ready in a few more days.

She cracked a nut in her beak and reached for another. Her mother told her she'd go through a few ravenous days, but the cravings were worse than she'd expected.

Cha'ril nudged the pillows of her nest bed around, smelling the scent of her joined.

From across the apartment, a data slate chirped with a call. She looked down at her swollen feet and debated against getting up. She was on medical leave. There was no routine matter worth getting out of bed. Cha'ril put a pillow over an ear and ate another nut.

There was a banging on the door.

"By the crystal winds of Takeni," she said as she sat up awkwardly, her swollen abdomen not helping her.

The banging intensified.

She trilled in Dotari, climbed out of the nest and almost waddled to the door. She looked through the peephole: two Dotari officers and a human, all in uniform.

The data slate kept ringing and Cha'ril chided herself for not dealing with that first.

Gripping the handle, she hesitated. Man'fred Vo was on ready-alert duty. Why would anyone come here for him? She half opened the door when a sudden sickness hit her stomach.

"Third armor Cha'ril?" the human officer asked.

"I am…not ready for guests," she said.

"We must discuss your rank," said one of the Dotari in their own language.

Cha'ril backed away from the door, her mind reeling.

The two Dotari came in then linked their arms at the elbow. She knew this from plays from her childhood, an old Dotari military tradition.

"No. It can't be," Cha'ril said.

The data slate kept ringing and the human officer cut away.

"Man'fred Vo is missing," one said in Dotari. *"His fighter was lost pursuing an Ibarran vessel off Mars. It was…many hours ago."*

"*The chance of his survival is low,*" the other added.

Cha'ril sat on the edge of the nest, hands to her belly.

"I don't know what you're saying," the human whispered into the slate pressed to his ear. "English please…Cha'ril? Not now. I—you do speak English. That's not polite…fine, and you don't know my mother."

Cha'ril opened her beak to speak, but nothing came out.

The human brought the slate over to his Dotari companions.

"Which button's for video? I can't read it."

One of the Dotari tapped the screen. The human frowned as the image changed, then he handed the slate over to Cha'ril, who didn't move.

"My star?" Man'fred Vo asked. He was in a dust-caked flight suit with a flight deck visible behind him.

"That's what he used to call me," Cha'ril said absently.

"My star, look at me." Man'fred Vo shook the slate he was using for the call.

Cha'ril snatched the device out of the human's hand. "Joined? You're alive?"

"Of course I'm alive. How else am I going to call you? S&R picked me up and I'm…I don't know where I am.

Some base that's not Olympus. I needed to call before the rankers showed up and—"

Cha'ril flipped the screen around and let Man'fred Vo see the pair of Dotari. One of the officers pulled a slate from his pocket and hissed at a text message.

"We're sorry," the other said. "We'll leave."

"You're not hurt?" Cha'ril asked as her apartment door shut.

"A little banged up. Nothing serious."

"You are dead!" Cha'ril snapped. "Do you know what I just went through?"

"Is it worse than being ejected from a burning Eagle and bouncing across Mars?"

Cha'ril's eyes widened and a series of chirps started in the back of her throat.

"Of course it was!" Man'fred Vo said. "I'll be back to Olympus as soon as I can. There's something of a situation going on." He looked to one side. "I have to go."

"You get back here so I can kill you," Cha'ril said. "I love you."

"I love you too." The slate went to the home screen.

She swiped a claw tip down from the top of the screen and read through alert messages.

"Roland was in the middle of all this. I'm sure of it." She called Aignar, but there was no answer.

Chapter 24

The central dome, made up of ruby-colored crystals that glinted sporadically, rose slightly above the next line of Qa'Resh buildings. The space over the dome wavered like air over a fire and Gideon wondered just what kind of ancient alien technomancy was at work.

"Clear to move," Pak said from across the street on the lance's tight-beam IR. Gideon rushed across, his audio receptors turned up to gauge the sound of his footfalls as he ran. The atmosphere was pure nitrogen and thick enough to convey sound. That the local atmosphere didn't match the rest of Nunavik was an observation he'd leave to Pathfinders and scientists to ponder.

Gideon stopped against a building adjacent to the dome structure and made his way down the wall. The dome had iris doors all around the outside and Gideon hesitated.

He remembered searching through the Qa'Resh facility for Aignar and Roland, a frantic dash through portal doors that followed no rhyme or reason to where they went next until he found them both...found their suits at least. Roland's had been cut open, the womb inside missing. Aignar's armor had been cut to pieces, the soldier inside left behind.

Getting out of the Qa'Resh structure with Aignar's womb had been much easier, as if the structure was helping them get out before it sank into the crushing depths of the gas giant the alien structure had floated through for millennia.

The thought of entering another maze didn't fill him with confidence.

The wall next to him rippled as he approached a corner, and the outline of an armor soldier oscillated past him...but this armor carried a sword.

Gideon ducked as an Ibarran armor swung around the corner and slashed a blade that would have cut Gideon's helm clean off had he been a split second slower. Instead, the sword chopped into the building and embedded itself several inches into the wall.

Gideon fired his gauss cannons and hit the Ibarran in the flank, shooting off sparks as the bullets ricocheted away. The other armor reeled back, but kept his grip on the sword.

Gideon unfolded the shield built into his left arm and rammed the edge toward the other armor's elbow. The

Ibarran let go of the sword just in time and lifted his arm out of the way. The shield impacted with the building, leaving a cut that bled a chalky substance as Gideon wrenched it away and charged his foe.

He felt hammer blows beat against his shield as the Ibarran unloaded his gauss cannons at Gideon. He punched his cannon arm around the edge of his shield and fired blind. The bullets shot through an iris in the dome building and vanished without a trace.

The Ibarran slammed both fists down on Gideon. Gideon got his shield up and stopped the blows, but the Ibarran grabbed the edge of his shield and twisted to one side with enough force to send Gideon flying.

Gideon released the shield from the anchors on his arm and it went sailing into the distance without the Iron Dragoon, then Gideon swung his arms around and hugged the Ibarran's arms against his torso. The helm of the Ibarran armor, adorned with a Templar cross, stared into Gideon's optics.

Gideon snapped his rotary cannon onto his shoulder and unloaded into the Ibarran's helm. Bullets ripped it apart in a split second and Gideon shoved his foe back and into a wall. The Ibarran clutched at his ruined helm, a bad reflex Gideon exploited.

Gideon's right hand pulled back into his arm housing

and a spike took its place, locking with a snap. Gideon punched the spike into the Ibarran's breastplate and felt it puncture the outer armor plate and sink into the pod beneath. Amniosis fluid gushed out like blood.

"Where's Nicodemus?" Gideon asked.

The Ibarran jostled from side to side for a moment, then went still. The soldier inside was dead. Gideon pulled the spike out and pushed the suit to the ground with disgust.

As the snap of gauss fire echoed through the air, Gideon looked around for Thomas and Pak, but they were nowhere to be seen. The buildings fouled the echoes, hinting at too many possible directions for the fire.

He shot up a pigeon drone and connected to his lance, his HUD showing them both two blocks away and engaged in a gunfight. Gideon ran down the street parallel to the central dome and reloaded his gauss cannons.

Turning a corner, Gideon found an Ibarran armor next to an iris, dragging himself on a mangled leg toward the doorway. With his back to Gideon, the Ibarran had a cannon arm trained in another direction and firing, a sword gripped in the other hand. Gideon hit the Ibarran in the arm and shoulder while focused fire from Pak and Thomas hit the armor in the back. The Ibarran collapsed to the ground.

Steaming amniosis spilled onto the ground. The Ibarran worked his sword tip into the ground and used it like a crutch to try to work his way to the iris.

"Pathetic." Gideon snatched the sword away by the hilt and put a boot to the Ibarran's head.

"Where is she? Is Nicodemus with her?" Gideon asked.

The armor's legs and shoulders began twitching, like a seizure was imminent.

"He's redlining." Pak put a hand on the back of the Ibarran's neck and data cables snaked out of his wrist and into ports at the base of the helm.

"Don't bother," Gideon said. "It's a death sentence either way."

"Gideon!" a familiar voice shouted.

The Dragoon whirled around. There, in the threshold of one of the dome's many irises, was an Ibarran armor soldier. Gideon recognized the combat posture, the way he held his cannon arm cocked to one side.

Nicodemus.

Gideon tapped the flat of his captured blade against his leg as Stacey Ibarra emerged from the iris, light glinting off her silver body.

Gideon and Nicodemus squared off for a moment. The two warriors needed no words. Gideon ran toward him and Stacey, breaking into a sprint and roaring a challenge.

"Captain!" Pak called out. "Wait!"

Stacey put her hand on the doorframe.

Gideon thrust his gauss arm at her but a hypervelocity shell from Nicodemus blew his weapon apart. Electricity from shattered capacitors arced up his arm, but Gideon kept running. He leapt at his quarry just as they pulled back into the iris and he fell in after them.

Gideon hit a floor and skid to a stop. Springing to his feet, he slashed his sword around then realized he was in a tunnel. A tunnel that must have been a mile long and ended in a small pinpoint of light. There was no sign of Stacey or Nicodemus.

The chronometer on his HUD blinked with an error. There was a ninety-second gap in time that his system couldn't account for.

"Damn you!" He struck his sword against the wall and a kaleidoscope of light rippled from the impact. The shape of armor and a woman on the wall moved away from the light end to a darkness at the other.

"Fifty fifty…" Gideon tore away the ammo belt to his lost cannon and took off running.

****

Fifty-nine bodies lay in a makeshift morgue. Body bags lay spaced out neatly through one of the *Warsaw*'s empty cargo bays, as if the dead were in formation and awaiting orders. Most bore white shrouds emblazoned with Templar crosses.

Roland knelt next to Tongea, one hand on the armor's shoulder as he prayed. Tongea looked fierce even in death, the tribal tattoos on his face set firm.

Roland finished his prayer and touched the bandage over his bullet wound. His lungs ached with each breath, and a dozen small cuts and bruises across his body were a constant source of pain…but the feeling in his heart was the worst.

He looked across the dead, but in his mind's eye he saw Aignar. He heard his friend's last word over and over again.

A throat cleared behind him.

Roland looked over his shoulder and did a double take.

The woman behind him had hair as dark as the abyss, skin almost alabaster and lips a deep red. The admiral pins on her collar didn't match her age—she couldn't have been much older than Roland.

"They all need the final blessings," Roland said.

"This can't wait," she said.

"It is my duty to—"

"My ship has a chaplain that can give last rites. If this

wasn't a life-and-death emergency, I wouldn't disturb you, Templar."

"Life and death…" Roland leaned over and kissed Tongea's forehead. "Plenty of death today."

"Lady Ibarra is in danger. She needs armor and she needs it now," Makarov said. "Morrigan said you are true to the cause."

Roland got to his feet slowly, pain dogging his every motion. "Lady Ibarra…will she honor them? What they sacrificed?"

"She loves us," Makarov said. "The Templar stand with her and she stands with the Templar. Must you ask?"

Roland looked at her, the bruises and cuts on his face evident in the bay's light. "My faith's been tested lately," he said.

"Lady Ibarra calls," Makarov said. "I will answer. Will you?"

Roland shut Tongea's body bag and draped a shroud over him. "I am armor. I am Templar…" He touched his bandaged arm.

"You need a suit," she motioned to him. "Follow me."

****

Roland leaned against the corner of a lift he shared with Makarov. His legs felt like jelly and the bulkheads were a sturdier alternative to standing.

"Makarov?" he asked.

"That's me. Perhaps you knew my mother. She was—"

"Commanded the Lost 8th," Roland said. "Fought off the Toth incursion. Jumped into deep space to slow down the second Xaros invasion. She succeeded, at the cost of everyone in the fleet. My father was on the *Midway*. Last minute reassignment before the fleet weighed anchor."

"My mother's flagship," Makarov nodded. "I didn't know about your father."

"War. My mother died on Luna when the Xaros smashed it." Roland worked his jaw as he looked to the deck counter.

"Let's get something out of the way, shall we? I know who my mother was. I know what I am. She was a procedural, as was almost everyone else in the 8th Fleet. Born from the tanks to fight for Earth. She was 'alive' for less than a year." She touched the side of her head. "But I know her, remember her from a childhood I know didn't happen, remember learning she died. I still love her and my heart still aches to think of her."

"You're young…for an admiral," Roland said.

"Accelerated training regimen in the tubes. Lady Ibarra needed fleet commanders. She didn't need a proccie with all that experience in a body ten years from retirement."

"Huh...I would never have thought of that." Roland shrugged his right shoulder, wondering if he had any joints that didn't hurt.

"The Lady does what must be done. The old rules for procedurals were dropped once the Nation came into being, though...I'm unaware of anyone as...unique as me."

"You were cast from a superior mold." Roland regretted the words as soon as he said them. "No, I mean—"

"Thank you." She opened a pocket on her uniform and withdrew a small piece of cloth in a plastic case. Placing it on her palm, she showed it to Roland. It was a bit of an old-style void suit with an admiral's rank insignia from the Atlantic Union, the military that fought the Ember War before Earth became the Terran Union.

"This was my mother's," Makarov said. "President Garret found her void suit on the *Midway*'s bridge. The Lady...secured this for me."

"Lucky you. I have nothing of my parents."

Makarov touched Roland's chest just above his heart.

Roland nodded slowly. He understood the admiral's meaning; he carried his parents with him.

"Save Lady Ibarra." Makarov pressed the case into

Roland's hand. "Then bring that back to me."

"I can't—"

"Going to reject *this* lady's favor? I thought you were the Black Knight."

Roland smiled, and even that hurt. "Keep this ship in the void and I'll return to you with…with our Lady."

"*Warsavo walcz,*" Makarov said.

The lift slowed to a stop and the doors opened to a busy cemetery. Technicians tending to a half-dozen suits of armor stopped working and watched as Roland stepped off the lift. At the far end of the cemetery was a suit of black armor, Templar crosses on the shoulder and breastplate, a sword hilt locked to the leg, the chest and interior womb open and waiting for him.

Roland strode forth, returning fist-to-chest salutes from the crew. When he stopped at his ready armor, the pain in his body faded away. He looked back to the lift and saw Makarov touch her fingertips to her lips just before the doors shut.

"About time," Morrigan said from the suit next to his.

"Who's with us?"

"Martel. The Black Star lance. Saint Kallen. Who else do we need?"

"Martel can barely walk." Roland stripped off his prison garb, foregoing modesty but for skintight shorts.

"He's under while he syncs with his armor. Meanwhile, you look like you poked a bear in the arse," Morrigan said.

"Doesn't matter. I am armor."

"We are the fury."

Roland climbed into the womb and the abyss closed around him. Amniosis rushed into the pod and he took it in, the atavistic biological response to drowning trained out of him. He fed the armor's umbilical into the plugs at the base of his skull and felt his armor form around him.

Vision fed into his brain and the pain of his flesh faded away as his suit became his body. He turned his helm from side to side, lifted his arms, then clamped his hands into fists so loudly is startled the technicians.

"How do you feel?" Morrigan asked.

"Whole."

Chapter 25

Gideon ran into a semicircular room with a dozen different irises, all wavering like disturbed ponds. He rapped the edge of his sword against the ground and followed two sets of footprints to the iris second from the right.

"Here goes nothing," Gideon muttered as he rushed through. A small room barely the size of a Mule cargo bay opened around him with another iris door on the other side. Stacey Ibarra was in the middle of the room, speaking with Nicodemus.

Gideon's momentum carried him forward and into Stacey. He scooped her up and tried to stop, but his feet slid across the floor and took them both through the portal. Through the undulating doorway, he saw Nicodemus' shadow barreling toward them. He stabbed the sword toward the door as Nicodemus darkened it…and hit nothing as the other armor vanished.

Stacey tried to wiggle out of Gideon's grasp. He grabbed her by the arm and hurled her into a curved wall. The wall cracked with the impact, but she popped right back onto her feet.

Gideon slammed the sword down in front of her, missing the tip of her nose by a fraction of an inch.

She stopped, then calmly regarded the Terran Union armor soldier and folded her hands across her waist.

"You must be Gideon," she said. "Nicodemus isn't the type to mistake someone."

"You…" Gideon wrenched the blade out of the floor. "This is all because of you. Nicodemus and Morrigan followed your worthless name. Became traitor because of you and your grandfather and that lie of a saint."

"You are more right than you know," she said. "I have heard a great deal about you, Gideon. Gideon the scar face. Gideon the failure."

"What did you call me?" He pulled the sword behind his back.

"The Toth crushed you. Left you full of inadequacies you thought you could conquer as armor, but then you couldn't measure up through training. Nicodemus had to carry you through the qualifications. Morrigan spent *days* teaching you something so simple as walking in armor."

"That's not true."

"Scores so poor that no lance commander wanted you, but Nicodemus and Morrigan refused any assignment until all three of you were incorporated into a unit together. Then you were taken off the line when you almost redlined."

"Stop it. You don't know what you're talking about."

"Then you finally began to show some progress as armor and what happened? Your lance left you behind. I don't blame you for feeling like a complete waste of—"

With lightning speed, Gideon swung his sword at her. The blade—with the force of shoulder, hip, and knee actuators—bounced off her arm.

Stacey Ibarra looked down at a deep gouge running from her shoulder to her elbow. Raw silver sparkled like the golden roofs of the Qa'Resh city. She squeezed a hand against the cut and her arm reknit itself.

"You have to try harder than that, scar boy."

Gideon roared and slammed a hand around her neck. He hoisted her off the ground and squeezed with all the power his armor could muster.

"That's the spirit!" Her mouth didn't move, but her eyes laughed at him. "You think I need to breathe? Quaint."

Gideon felt her neck crush ever so slightly, then she raised an arm and set it atop his. A crystal glowed in her fingers.

"This is a Qa'Resh data crystal. Want to see how it works?"

A flood of light struck his helm and Gideon's HUD went white. His armor's failsafe kicked in and shunted off all inputs to the womb to prevent his neural system from overloading and burning out his brain.

He was trapped in darkness, aware of nothing but his real body floating in amniosis and his beating heart. He reached up with his real hand, which felt numb, and fumbled with a panel buried beneath the womb's inner padding.

How did she know that? No. It doesn't matter. I am armor. I am fury. I will not fail.

He flipped a switch and his armor came alive.

Stacey was gone, but the light she'd hit him with had bleached a swath of his arm white. He picked up the sword and hurried through the lone iris door, his heart as full of determination and hate as ever.

****

Lettow's holo tank fizzled as he panned over the Qa'Resh city and glanced down at the radiation levels displayed on the tank rim. The *Ardennes*' shields degraded under the constant pressure of the distant magnetar and the irradiated nebula, but he still had several more hours before he needed to deal with the issue.

The thoughts of bone-marrow reconstruction and full blood transfusions for his crew were at the back of his mind, but if they could end the Ibarran threat right here and right now…

"Graviton detection," Rhysli said from the other side of the tank. The Ruhaald's long arms tapped against a holo screen Lettow couldn't see.

"Another Union ship," Jarilla said.

Lettow zoomed the holo out and found the new detection moving away from the Crucible.

"No IFF pulse," Lettow said. Camera feeds swept through the area and a grainy image of a carrier popped up. "It's human…not Union. The Ibarrans are here. Guns, work up a firing solution."

In the holo, the Ibarran ship jumped from side to side slightly.

"We can send salvos until the batteries are empty, Admiral," said his gunnery officer from a workstation adjacent to the holo tank. "Sensor data's fouled. At these distances and the speed she's moving…scoring a direct hit would be like trying to punt a football in Phoenix and have it go through the uprights in San Diego. While blindfolded. At night."

"I understand," Lettow said.

"We're liable to lose them in…aaand they're gone," the gunnery officer said.

The *Warsaw*'s last plot in the tank blinked, then the projected course turned into a dashed line.

"The Vishrakath contingent is asking for you," Paxton said.

"Stall," Lettow said, leaning against the holo controls with a hard look on his face. He sighed and ran a fingertip down a panel.

Horva popped up in the holo tank. "Admiral, why haven't you opened fire on the Ibarran vessel?"

"Because I don't waste ammo. If we bring the rail cannons into this now, the EM signature of them firing will be a nice big beacon for the other Ibarran ship in this system. Plus, we're in a dangerously low orbit. If the Ibarrans fire on us, they'll hit Nunavik if they miss. Low gravity. Lava. If they hit the surface with full-power rail shots, it'll kick up spall that could damage my ship. We'll wait until they're in orbit, try and engage them then."

"Ruhaald, has this coward been in contact with the Ibarrans?" Horva asked.

"What did you call him?" Paxton asked.

"He has not," Jarilla said. "A long-range radio signal would be lost in the nebula as would infrared. I thought the Vishrakath would send observers who know their head from their gaster."

"I find this difficult to believe. I will arrive on the bridge in—"

Lettow cut the channel. "Gaster?" the admiral asked.

"The orifice that secrets fecal matter," the Ruhaald said. "The human term is—"

"I got it." Lettow brought the holo tank back to the Qa'Resh city. "XO. We need to move away from the city, give the Ibarrans a clean shot at getting close. They know we're here—else they wouldn't have sent reinforcements—but they don't know where we are."

"Aye aye," Paxton said. "We'll almost be in knife-fighting range when we do find them. Risk a scout mission with fighters?"

"No. That's a death sentence. Alert Task Force Iconoclast of the development. Tell them we'll be out of IR range until we return to find and destroy this ship," Lettow said.

Always another wrinkle, he thought. *The Ibarrans never make things easy.*

****

Roland felt almost at home as his armor rattled inside a drop pod. He opened a channel to the other two armor in the pod with him.

"Morrigan, the Ibarrans—I mean us—there's no tactical insertion missiles for armor?"

"On strike carriers," she said. "Wouldn't use them here anyway. Guidance systems wouldn't work in this soup. Which is why I'm piloting this by eye so stop flapping your gums at me." She left the channel.

"How's your sync rating?" Colonel Martel asked.

"Eighty-five percent and rising, sir. Still some psychosomatic pain in my arm…nothing that can stop me from fighting," Roland said.

"You are Templar. Only death can keep you from a just battle. I will miss fighting beside Tongea. Now he stands beside the Saint," Martel said.

"How many did we lose, sir?"

"Too many. Another dozen are in critical condition. I asked for volunteers to this mission. Do you know how many asked to wear one of the six suits the Ibarrans had?"

Roland didn't hesitate. "All of them."

"All of them. You were the youngest Morrigan and I chose. You fight well enough, and the Ibarrans trust you to save their Lady far more than they trust me. The other drop pod has a lance that's fought together for years," Martel said.

"Who do think's down there hunting Ibarra?" Roland asked.

"No one I wish to cross blades with. Days ago we were brothers and sisters…now—"

"Ready for emergency evac!" Morrigan shouted. "Pack-assisted drop in three…*go h/freann leis.*"

Roland's drop-pod bay opened and he went tumbling through black smoke. His HUD blared heat and radiation warnings but he was more focused on trying to activate the jump pack bolted to his back. He wasn't sure of his altitude or how long until he came to a very sudden stop once he fell through this smoke.

He fired small maneuver thrusters attached to his legs and stopped his tumbling.

"Morrigan? Colonel?" he sent over IR, but it was lost in the smoke.

His instrumentation flashed error messages as he tried to gauge his altitude. Activating his pack too soon and burning it out too high could leave him without any means to slow down. He was armor, but terminal velocity and gravity were likely stronger than him.

A thunderclap sounded through the smoke and a pressure wave slapped him sideways. He came out of the volcano's plume suddenly and saw the Qa'Resh city rolling over and over as he fell.

He activated a range-finding laser and got a V-shaped curve of readings as the laser swept across the city and around Nunavik. He made the educated guess that the lowest reading was how far he had to go before he crashed, and he activated his jump pack.

Wings of fire shot past his legs and he bumped against the inside of his womb.

"—*ower! Lo*—" Morrigan came over the IR.

Roland cut the power in his pack and went into free fall. There was a shockwave of expanding air in the city below, and what looked like a laser beam shot past him.

Rail cannons. Armor in the city were firing their rail cannons at the Ibarran rescue force.

Roland rolled head down and reactivated his jet pack. He was no longer concerned about how fast he'd land. Now he desperately wanted to get out of the line of fire.

He banked hard and cycled the power levels in the jet pack. He knew how to throw off a rail cannon shot. The hypervelocity slugs were best at long range against steady targets and the capacitors had a recharge time of several minutes.

Roland swooped over the city and pulled up between rows of buildings. Ahead, a suit of Union armor was braced against the ground, rail vanes angled over the shoulder and aimed toward the sky. Roland flew slightly higher over the road and kicked his feet forward as he ejected the jet pack.

His feet took the Union armor in the side with a

crunch of metal. The Union armor's left leg tore free of the body, the anchored leg still standing in place.

Roland landed on top of the other armor and they slid forward in a shower of sparks. Roland slapped away the rail cannon vanes and a blue arc of electricity connected from the weapon's capacitor to his shoulder.

His true arm went numb as the electricity played hell with his systems. They slid into the side of a building and Roland went helm-first into the wall and fell next to the Union armor.

The one-legged armor swung his cannon arm toward Roland, but Roland punched the side of the cannon and knocked the aim off. Two gauss shells blew a chunk out of the ground next to Roland.

The Union armor rolled onto Roland and pinned his own cannon arm to the ground. Roland used his other hand to grasp the sword hilt locked to his leg. He jammed the guard under the Union armor's chin and activated the blade. It burst through the back of the helm with a snap as the graphenium lattice within the blade formed, locking the razor-sharp weapon into place.

The Union armor faltered as Roland popped his helm off with a twist of his sword. He drew the weapon back and bashed the pommel into the breastplate, hard enough to puncture the outer armor layer and dent the pod within, likely stunning the soldier inside it.

Roland pulled the armor off him and looked at the unit crest: Black Watch. Roland lifted his sword and chopped it down, severing the armor's waist. He cut off both arms with two more strokes, leaving the armor helpless…but alive.

The snap of gauss fire broke through the air and Roland went running toward it.

He turned a corner and almost ran into Morrigan as she came around. He held out a hand and she grabbed him by the forearm, using him to slow down. She activated her shield and took a knee, facing back the way she came. Roland followed suit.

The building corner broke apart under gauss fire and two more Black Watch ran into view. Roland and Morrigan fired. She hit one in the chest, Roland the other in the left knee, knocking the leg out from under the Union armor.

Roland charged forward, thrust the shield into the standing Black Watch's chest—lifting the armor off its feet—and slammed it into a building, cracking the damaged wall further.

"No one has to die here," Roland said.

"You do!" the woman inside the pinned armor shouted back. She hooked a blow against Roland's side, sending a ring through his womb. Two blows hammered his shield as she fired her gauss cannons into it at point-blank range.

Roland staggered back and the bottom half of his shield broke free and landed at his feet.

The Black Watch swapped a fist for a punch spike and thrust it at Roland's chest, a killing blow. Roland swiped his sword across his body and severed the spike from the Black Watch's arm.

Rounds cycled into the Union armor's cannons, readying for a second shot that wouldn't miss. Roland stabbed his blade tip into the other armor's chest, just barely piercing the breastplate.

"Don't," Roland said.

He heard the gauss capacitors' whine grow higher and lunged forward, running his blade through the Black Watch, embedding the hilt against her chest. She beat at Roland's shoulder for a moment, then the armor froze in place.

He stepped away and let the Black Watch slide off his weapon and onto the ground. Blood and amniosis fluid steamed off his sword.

Roland stared down at his weapon and the armor he'd just killed.

"It's not the same as with Kesaht," Morrigan said from behind. She stood over the other Black Watch, her sword pinning it to the ground. "Killing them feels good…this tastes like ashes."

Flaming debris streaked through the air overhead, tracing slow paths across the sky.

"The other drop pod," Morrigan said. "Bastards hit it before they could unload." She yanked her sword free and pointed it at the disabled Black Watch.

"You're too kind to them," she said.

"I thought…hoped…"

"Get that out of your skull. They're here to kill us and the Lady. Act accordingly," she said.

"Where's the colonel?"

"Dealt with the last Black Watch. He'll be here directly."

Roland looked from building to building and then to the iris behind him.

"Three of us," he said. "Giant Qa'Resh city and we don't know where Lady Ibarra is or how to find them."

The iris flared with light and Roland brought his sword up to strike.

Stacey Ibarra stepped through the gateway and caught herself as she saw Roland.

"My Lady?" Morrigan asked.

"My Black Knight's in sooty armor," Stacey said. "I saw you through the portals. How many ships did you bring? More armor? Wait…is that Morrigan in there?"

"Aye. We've one ship, one more armor," Morrigan

said.

"Then we best leave before the odds get worse. Who is this?" she looked up at Roland. "If that's Morrigan, who was in Union custody until now…then you must be…"

"Roland Shaw, My Lady." He raised the guard of his sword up to his helm in salute.

"Ah…then I have another mission for you, Roland. Nicodemus is in danger. Bring him back to me." She touched the iris frame and it lit up. "I can get you close to him. Hurry."

"Ferrum corde," Roland said and ran through the doorway.

"What?" Morrigan asked. "Nicodemus is my lance mate, Lady Ibarra, let me—"

"You're a better fighter, but Roland stands a better chance in that fight than you. His enemy's hate will make him sloppy. You…you he's used to wanting to kill."

"Gideon is here," Morrigan said flatly.

"Correct. I'm not entirely sure how many other Union armor are still lurking about, which is why I couldn't let you go with Roland. Now, there's our third coming around the corner. Let's bring in our ride home, shall we?"

Chapter 26

Gideon stepped through an iris and tapped his sword against the low tunnel's wall, but there was no trace of Stacey or her armor. He lowered the weapon to his side and stopped.

"These doors are connected somehow. Either I'm stepping across light-years or I haven't left the city yet." He reached up and touched the ceiling, then pulled a fist back and punched up. The ceiling sent out a wave of color from the impact. He hit it again and cracks spread from the impact, ruining the colors' symmetry like a broken slate screen.

White chalky material fell over his arm as he beat away at the ceiling. He rammed the blade into the damage and it broke through, revealing the overcast sky of the nebula over Nunavik. After clearing out an opening wide enough for his shoulders, he climbed out and found himself on a golden roof halfway between the central dome and the edge of the city.

Gideon jumped to the street below and took off running toward the center, his feet pounding against the ground, his armor never tiring. Through the corner of his vision, he saw a pair of armor legs jutting around a building. Terran armor.

He changed course and came around the corner, sword held high. The Black Watch lance lay strewn across the ground, their armor hacked apart, amniosis steaming from the torsos. All four dead were near an iris, and he could guess what had happened.

Ibarran armor had come out of the gateway and taken them by surprise.

Gideon stifled his rage, unsnapped a shield housing from a severed arm and attached it to his own. He was going for a gauss cannon on a dead suit when his acoustics picked up a thump in the air. Gideon stopped.

Thump. Even with the acoustics he could tell it was close.

He went around a building and there was Nicodemus, limping toward the Ibarran drop pod, a hip servo badly damaged.

Gideon brought his rotary cannon up and spun the barrels to life. Nicodemus whirled around, but not before a flurry of bullets tore across his armor, all bouncing off the plates but still severing the ammo belt feeding into his gauss cannons.

Nicodemus still had rounds in his chambers, and he fired them both at Gideon, who took the hits on his shield, cracking it down the center. He tossed it aside and advanced on his old friend.

"Nowhere to run," Gideon said.

"My duty here isn't to kill you." Nicodemus raised his sword over his head with both hands. "You never could see past yourself, could you?"

"If I am the last thing you ever see, it will be enough." Gideon reached for his sword behind him and charged forward, swinging a vicious strike across Nicodemus' breastplate.

The Ibarran braced the flat of his blade against an arm and absorbed Gideon's strike, then whacked the pommel of his sword into Gideon's optics, shattering a lens.

Gideon let go of his sword and grabbed Nicodemus by the shoulder and hip. He thrust the side of his waist into Nicodemus and used it as a fulcrum, slamming Nicodemus' shoulder into the ground. He kicked the Ibarran in the chest, sending him rolling away, his sword still in his grip.

Gideon picked his sword up by the blade, reached back and hurled it like a spear. The tip cut through

Nicodemus' chest just inside the shoulder.

Nicodemus cried out and fell to his side.

"Synaptic feedback is a liability, isn't it? You taught me that." Gideon kicked Nicodemus onto his back and planted a foot on the Ibarran's chest. He grabbed the impaled blade by the hilt and twisted it. There was a screech of metal and fluid bubbled out.

"I never bothered to learn your proper swordplay. Guess that caught you a little off guard, eh? The master must fear the amateur most of all—you can't predict those who don't know the rules. You didn't redline, did you? You should be stronger than that." Gideon wrenched his sword out.

"Gideon...my...my sons..." Nicodemus reached up with his other arm and Gideon slapped it away.

"Don't matter. You will die a traitor. Everything you were in life will be forgotten. Your name blotted out from the honor rolls. Your saint will be erased and only the Union, my Union will remain...and I'll tell Morrigan how I killed you." Gideon raised his foot off Nicodemus and his diamond-tipped anchor spike snapped from the housing in his heel.

Gideon lifted his leg up and the spike spun to life. He stomped down.

There was an electric snap and Gideon's leg was slapped to one side. The broken spike hit the ground and groaned to a stop.

Gideon looked up.

Roland, gauss cannon barrels smoking, advanced toward them.

"I'll make you a deal," Roland said. "Out of respect for you, for the Iron Dragoons…a life for a life. Back off and you'll live."

"Impossible." Gideon retracted the damaged spike and stepped between Roland and Nicodemus. "You should be in a cell, waiting for the noose."

"Yet here I am." Roland cycled fresh shells into his barrels.

"He's a traitor." Gideon waved the tip of his sword back at Nicodemus. "Why are you fighting for them? Them…against me?"

Roland touched the Templar cross on his black armor.

"I know who I am…and I don't need to be told what's right. It is us—all of us, Gideon—Union and Ibarran, against the galaxy. Earth was ready to murder innocents for no reason other than our enemies demanded it. If we let our enemies dictate what's right and wrong, what does that make us?"

"It makes you a traitor!" Gideon lunged forward, his sword aimed at the center of Roland's chest.

Roland snapped the hilt off his leg and activated the

blade. It shot out and the tip struck Gideon's weapon, pushing it to the side. Roland sidestepped Gideon and leveled his blade toward him at shoulder height.

"Last chance," Roland said.

Gideon whirled around, bent slightly at the waist, then yelled and struck a wild blow at Roland. Their blades crossed, and Roland jabbed his sword forward, destroying an optic cluster on the side of Gideon's helm.

Pressing off his back foot, Roland bashed his shoulder into Gideon's chest, rattling the soldier inside, then twisted and ducked beneath Gideon's return swing. He sliced his blade into Gideon's knee servo, embedding halfway through it. There was a high-pitched whine as Roland tried to twist it free.

Gideon smashed his arms against Roland's weapon and it shattered.

Roland grabbed Gideon by the wrist and stabbed what remained of his weapon into Gideon's chest. The jagged edge tore up the front of the armor, leaving a gash along its path.

As Gideon stumbled forward, his damaged knee gave out and he made a blind swipe at Roland. The blow knocked the broken sword out of Roland's grip and Gideon landed a punch that rattled Roland inside his womb.

Gideon thrust the side of the blade against Roland's

helm and ripped it down, cutting through the armor and destroying sensors.

"I am armor!" Gideon raised the sword high over his head. "I am fury!"

He chopped down, meaning to split Roland from helm to the base of his pod.

Roland crossed his arms over his head and the blade hacked into his armor. He twisted to one side, the blade came free, and he punched Gideon in the damaged knee. The leg collapsed. Roland grappled with his old lance commander and they went down in a roll.

Roland waited until he had the blade pinned between him and the ground, then pushed Gideon off him. Gideon rolled to a sudden stop, his hand still on the hilt.

Roland stomped a foot against Gideon's sword arm, then tore the hand and sword free from Gideon's body.

Gideon withdrew his other hand into the forearm and stabbed at Roland with the internal spike. Roland swiped his blade through Gideon's elbow and the spike clattered to the ground. Roland held the sword at his hip, the blade pointed away from Gideon.

"Do it," Gideon said, propping himself up on his remaining elbow. "No matter what happens from this moment, you will always be a traitor…and you will die a coward."

"You are fury," Roland said, his helm nodding. "Use it. Fight for Earth. Fight the real enemy."

"Do it. This will only ever end with one of us dead," Gideon said.

"Not today." Roland swiped the sword across Gideon's helm, slicing off the last functioning sensors.

Gideon's armor froze and a view port on the breastplate popped open.

"Stay here," Roland said. "Send for evac. You still have two armor in the dome. They'll find their way out…Lady Ibarra will see to it. Fight well, Gideon."

He turned his back on the armor and went to Nicodemus as Gideon's armor collapsed to the ground, his damaged limbs working hard to gain traction and stand up.

"Nicodemus?" Roland asked.

"I'm in bad shape," the Ibarran said. "Can't evac my pod without breaking the emergency seals keeping my fluid in place. Can you drag all of me?"

"I will." Roland locked the sword hilt to his thigh. In the distance, a corvette flew through a volcano plume toward the Qa'Resh city.

Chapter 27

Stacey Ibarra walked down the ramp of the *Ebaki*, her two bodyguards following behind her. The corvette fit with a few yards to spare on either side of the *Warsaw*'s flight deck. Demolished Destriers took up the back of the hangar. Admiral Makarov bowed slightly as Stacey stepped onto the deck.

Stacey looked back to the hangar opening as the front doors slid shut. Nunavik swept past them and the ship bore down on the Crucible.

"My Lady," Makarov said.

"I got what we came for," Stacey said. "Went down with three armor…came back with four. Well done."

"We have a number of Terran Armor Corps Templar aboard…as well as the crew of the *Narvik* and our sleeper agents," she said. "I wish there were more, but casualties were sustained. We'll be through the Crucible in minutes. The *Ardennes* is preoccupied with rescuing their armor from the city."

"We're not safe yet," Stacey said. "They're tracking us through the jump gates, and if we don't figure out how, we're in for a long trip home."

"My Lady," Tyrel said, stepping forward, "we have the answer. *I* am what they're tracking."

Stacey looked him over, her face a mask.

"The green blood cells we acquired from the Vishrakath," he said. "I received an immune-system booster shot before we searched the ruins in Renarra II."

"I remember," Stacey said.

"Gravitons from the jump gates activate the tracker." He touched his chest. "We detected it when the Union arrived. There is no way to remove it. It is…in my blood." He looked at Makarov. "Admiral. Open the hangar doors. I'll throw myself out. I cannot put this ship or our Lady at risk."

Makarov took a half step back. "There has to be another way. Send the *Ebaki* with him to another star after this jump—"

Stacey held up a hand. She motioned to the floor and Tyrel went to one knee, genuflecting.

"You are the best of us." She touched her guard's cheek. He didn't flinch as her icy touch froze his flesh. "What do you know of me?"

"You are the Lady, and you love us."

"I do." She kissed him on the forehead and took her hand away. "Makarov. Load him into an escape pod and jettison him before we enter a high-radiation zone."

"He's a procedural, my Lady. If the Union find him, they'll—"

"Some chance is better than none at all."

"As you will," Makarov said. "Tyrel, life pods." She pointed a hand to an exit.

Tyrel handed his rifle to his fellow body guard and took off at a run.

"See to your ship. Get us home." Stacey drew the data crystal out and rolled it between her fingers. She looked to the wrecked Union transports, then up into the corvette where armor technicians rushed up the ramp to tend to her damaged saviors.

"This is worth it," she said.

"You found the device?" Makarov asked.

"I found how to get to it…and once we have it, the galaxy will be ours forever."

****

"Make way!" a sailor called out as Admiral Lettow

pushed through a scrum of sailors on the *Ardennes* flight deck. A path opened and he hurried to a pair of armsmen pinning Tyrel to the deck. The Ibarran's open life pod was off to one side. Three armsmen lay on the ground, groaning and clutching broken arms.

"Someone want to explain this?" Lettow asked.

"Standard procedure with Ibarran prisoners, sir," said one of the armsmen with a knee to the back of Tyrel's neck. "Blood test. Check telomere levels to figure out if he's in violation of the Hale Treaty. He's been combative since we cracked his pod."

"*Izorra zaitez!*" Tyrel yelled.

"And we don't know what he's saying." A corpsman came over and swiped a reader against the armsman's bloody knuckles.

A hush fell over the crowd as the Vishrakath and Ruhaald delegation walked up to the admiral, Kutcher right behind them.

"This is all?" Horva asked. "All this effort and you recovered a single rebel?"

"You're here to observe," Lettow said, "not antagonize me into stuffing you into that pod and letting your bug buddies come find you."

Tyrel lifted his head, blood sputtering from his nose and mouth as he looked at the aliens and the admiral with undisguised hatred.

Kutcher went to the corpsman and read from her medical gauntlet.

"Well?" Horva asked. "Is this one illegal or not?"

The intelligence officer pushed the corpsman's gauntlet down and looked at the Ibarran.

"I do not understand human body language," Horva said. "Use your words to communicate with me. My superiors will know every detail as I experience it. Do you want my interpretation to be in the final report?"

"Let me up," Tyrel said. "Let me die on my feet like a man."

"He is in violation of the treaty," Kutcher said.

"Immediate destruction," Horva said. "Those are your orders, correct?"

Lettow drew his gauss pistol and a murmur rose through the sailors. Chief petty officers shouted down the dissent.

"Let go," the admiral said to the two armsmen holding Tyrel. They scrambled away and Tyrel used the side of his escape pod to right himself. He spat on the ground and wiped a sleeve across his bloody face.

Lettow kept the muzzle pointed to the deck.

"By general order ninety-eight, as signed by President Garret and ratified by our Congress," Lettow said as he half raised the pistol, "I hereby carry out my duties to…"

He lowered the gun to his side.

"No. No. I will kill Ibarrans in combat but I am not a—"

A single shot rang out.

Tyrel's head snapped back and blood splattered against the life pod. He fell back and slid to the ground.

Kutcher, a smoking pistol in hand, had his gaze locked on the man he just killed.

"Acceptable," Horva said. "We will return to our chamber."

Lettow stalked toward Kutcher and grabbed him by the front of his void suit. "Explain yourself," Lettow hissed.

"Orders," Kutcher said, "are orders. Especially in front of aliens looking to see if we follow those orders. You're welcome."

Lettow pulled a fist back to punch the intelligence officer, but Paxton caught him by the elbow.

"Admiral," she said, "you're no use to the fleet if you're in the brig. This fight's over. They won."

Lettow pushed the spy away. "Ready a void burial," Lettow said, looking at the dead Ibarran. "Full military honors. I will officiate."

Paxton was silent for a moment.

"Aye aye."

Chapter 28

Aignar walked down the barracks hallway, his left leg raw and sore from the repairs to his socket. He limped slightly, still not used to the new prosthetic.

The sound of slamming drawers came from a room at the far end. The closer Aignar got, the more certain he was that the noise came from his room.

He opened his door and Gideon was there, his uniform jacket off and Toth claw necklace swinging loose around his neck. Plastic boxes were strewn across Roland's bunk and the floor. Roland's dresser, desk and overhead space were all open. Personal items and clothing had been thrown into the boxes with little care.

"Sir," Aignar said.

Gideon nodded at him. Aignar watched as Gideon went back to packing away Roland's gear.

"Is he dead?" Aignar asked.

"Not yet," Gideon snapped.

"He's dead to me," Aignar said. "He's another Ibarran traitor now."

"Good," Gideon said. "Good. We'll catch up to him. End it."

"When?"

"Not soon enough."

****

Roland knelt in prayer, a Templar sword braced in both hands and the tip set in a small, purpose-built groove in the floor. The pure-white tabard was the same, but the black and red Ibarran uniform was different from the last time he put on his ceremonial attire.

"Rise," Martel commanded from the front of the auditorium.

Roland knew this room. He'd seen new Templar initiated into the order from the observation deck back…what felt like a lifetime ago. This was different. Only the Templar that survived the escape from Tholis were there.

General Hurson, the Ibarran armor commander,

came out onto the wooden stage.

"My brothers and sisters," he began, "the Templar Order is whole. Lady Ibarra does not demand our fealty. Lady Ibarra stands beside Saint Kallen as the protector of humanity, and we will fight beside Ibarra and her armies so long as she is true to that purpose. If the Ibarra Nation ever asks us to abandon the Saint, they will abandon us. No new oaths are required. You are all Templar. We are removed from Saint Kallen's tomb, but one day we will share her presence again."

"Amen," the Templar intoned.

"Report to your armor for lance assignment and training," Hurson said. "Dismissed."

Roland stood up, still feeling the aches and pains of the fight in the guard post. He felt so alone as the other Templar left the auditorium; most still had their old lance mates with them.

"Look at you," Morrigan said. "What an improvement." She wore the same uniform, her red hair in a tight bun.

"Bet you never thought you'd see me like this," Roland said, brushing a palm down a black sleeve.

"I thought you might come over after Balmaseda. You fight with the best, it's hard to go back to the rest. We both had to come home, but you took the low road and I took the high road and we both made it to Navarre at the same time. Fancy that." She smiled.

"I wonder which lance I'll be assigned to," Roland said.

"Why wonder? I know," she said.

"Well? You going to tell me?"

"Ask the lance commander that petitioned for ye—he's right there." Morrigan raised her chin.

Roland turned and faced Colonel Martel and Nicodemus.

"Roland," Martel said, "it's tradition that when a lance takes in two or more new members, it chooses a new name or one from the honor roll. As I carried Carius' legacy as the head of the Templar order, our…once-estranged brothers have allowed me to keep the name. The lance Templar lives on. Myself, Nicodemus, Morrigan…and you."

"I'm honored to serve under a more senior commander," Nicodemus said, "and one that's better in a fight than I."

Martel held out a hand to Roland, and the younger man gripped Martel's forearm. Nicodemus and Morrigan put their hands over the hold.

"For the Saint," Martel said. *"Ferrum Corde."*

"Ferrum corde," Roland said.

Iron heart.

****

Overlord Bale squirmed inside his holding tank as the Vishrakath fleet rounded a green and blue planet. The tendrils of the Toth's nervous system rubbed against the glass as the desire to feed gripped him. The temptation to summon a Sanheel officer or an Ixio was great, but eating the help had such a negative effect on command and control.

Besides, he had a snack waiting in his laboratory.

He waited in an immense cargo bay with Kesaht crescent fighters locked into launch claws around him. The setting for the meeting was a bit humble for his tastes, but the guests had been specific in their requests.

The alien fleet took up a battle formation against the lone Kesaht dreadnought hanging motionless in the void.

"They think they can beat us," Bale said to Tomenakai.

"Posturing nonsense," the Ixio said, gently waving fingers next to his large black eyes. "When will we bring them into the Kesaht fold, my lord?"

"When the time is right. They're more useful to us in other ways for now."

Soon, a Vishrakath shuttle landed in the bay and a trio of the aliens made their way to the Toth overlord. The

Vishrakath had thick collars around their necks, an accessory Bale had never seen before.

"Ambassador Wexil," Bale said, "it's been quite some time since we've seen each other."

"After what happened to the last envoy, you're fortunate to have this audience," Wexil said.

"A misunderstanding," Bale said.

"You ate them."

"They had information I needed to kill humans. Information they withheld. The nature of our agreement is quite clear on this." Bale's forelimb half reached toward Wexil, but he drew it back.

"That's why I have this." Wexil ran a claw against the collar. "If there are any further misunderstandings, the explosives within will make sure you never have another one."

"I'm hurt...and a little impressed. Enough of the pleasantries...what do you have to report?"

"New Bastion will not declare war against the humans, but they have expelled Earth from the mutual-defense treaty," Wexil said. "The humans' operation to capture Ibarra failed, but they showed enough adherence to the treaty to convince enough ambassadors to stop out-and-out sanctions. Unfortunate."

"You promised all-out war, Wexil! Not half

measures."

"The Vishrakath Imperium declared full-scale war against Earth and the Ibarrans this morning. We will launch a coordinated attack on their colonies in the coming days. The Naroosha are with us, as are Kroar mercenary armies. It should be enough."

"This is…acceptable," Bale said. "Earth is the ultimate prize. When can you attack?"

"Earth is a fortress," Wexil said. "The Vishrakath and our allies do not have the power to do that without massive casualties. I am here to coordinate the assault with the Kesaht."

"I want the humans," Bale said, his hunger growing stronger. "I want them all."

"That is our agreement. We want the Ibarrans' technology."

"Trinkets! You want toys when you could have worlds…but we don't know where to find the Ibarrans just yet."

"If we threaten Earth, the Ibarrans will come to their aid. You'll have enough prisoners to…examine," Wexil said.

"Tomenakai, summon the holy council," Bale said. "It is time the humans learned defeat…and sorrow."

Chapter 29

Stacey stood in front of a privacy screen, looking at her distorted reflection. She moved her fingers to signal the guards and the privacy screen fell.

Inside a cell, Marc Ibarra, his metal body a match for her own, looked up from a stack of data slates.

"Oh," he said, "I thought you'd forgot about me. Thanks for the reading material, sure beats practicing my show tunes."

"I found the ark," she said.

Marc set a slate aside. "And?"

"You were right. It isn't located anywhere within range of a Crucible gate…but I have a solution for that. Just waiting for the chance to…borrow it," she said.

"Not that I don't mind the company, but how does this involve me?"

"If we get to the ark, it does us no good if I can't use it...I need your help. I need someone that knows Qa'Resh technology better than both of us. If I had the time, I could figure it out for myself, but the Kesaht have accelerated things."

"And that someone is...her? You think she's still alive?" Ibarra asked.

"I'm counting on it. And I need you to convince her to help us."

"We didn't part on the best of terms."

"It'll get you out of this cell."

"I didn't say 'no.' Did you hear me say 'no'?" He looked up at the ceiling. "Play back the tape! No one said 'no'!"

"I know she escaped Bastion before the Xaros destroyed it. I just don't know if she wants to be found."

"I'll find Taria. I don't know exactly what she really looks like, but I'll find her."

"Open the cell." Stacey stepped aside and the bars rumbled to one side.

Marc Ibarra stepped one foot through the opening, then brought himself all the way out. "Thank you, honey." He reached to touch her face but she slapped his hand away with a *ting* of metal on metal.

"You'll have a bodyguard. If you try anything, you'll

wish you were back in here until the stars burned away."

"That's my girl."

THE END

The Series Continues with THE LAST AEON, coming summer 2018!

FROM THE AUTHOR

Richard Fox is the author of The Ember War Saga, and several other military history, thriller and space opera novels.

He lives in fabulous Las Vegas with his incredible wife and two boys, amazing children bent on anarchy.

He graduated from the United States Military Academy (West Point) much to his surprise and spent ten years on active duty in the United States Army. He deployed on two combat tours to Iraq and received the Combat Action Badge, Bronze Star and Presidential Unit Citation.

Sign up for his mailing list over at www.richardfoxauthor.com to stay up to date on new releases and get exclusive Ember War short stories. You can contact him at Richard@richardfoxauthor.com

The Ember War Saga:

1.) The Ember War
2.) The Ruins of Anthalas
3.) Blood of Heroes
4.) Earth Defiant
5.) The Gardens of Nibiru
6.) Battle of the Void
7.) The Siege of Earth
8.) The Crucible
9.) The Xaros Reckoning

Printed in Great Britain
by Amazon